GW00480571

Published in the UK in 2022 by Send The Word Publishing

Copyright © R. E. Bussell 2022

R. E. Bussell has asserted their right under
the Copyright, Designs and Patents Act, 1988,
to be identified as the author of this work.

All rights reserved. No part of this book may be reproduced,
stored in a retrieved system or transmitted, in any form or by
any means, electronic, mechanical, scanning, photocopying,
recording or otherwise, without the prior permission of the
author and publisher.

This book is a work of fiction, and except in the case of
historical or geographical fact, any resemblance to names,
place and characters, living or dead, is purely coincidental.

Paperback ISBN 978-1739631000
eBook ISBN 978-1739631017

Cover design and typeset by SpiffingCovers

THE OIL AND THE SWORD

R. E. BUSSELL

For my family:

Mum and Dad and all those now part of an
unseen dimension

And for Tim, Louise, and Faith

I love you

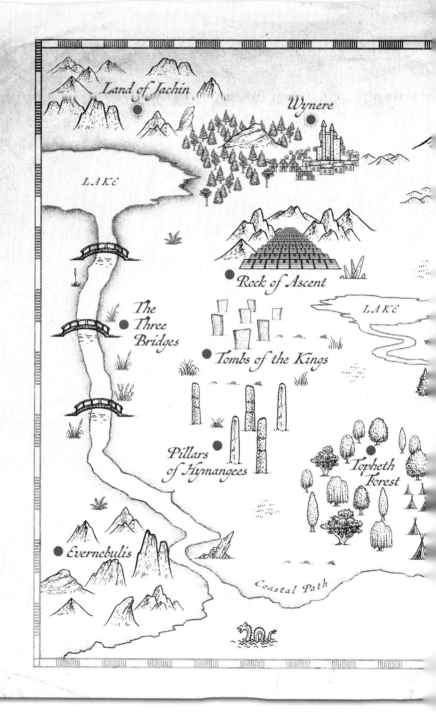

Cherith

Veiled Mountains

Heart of
a Man

Noah's
Peak

Tyron's
Farm

Twyndale

MOORS

River Tamore

East Gates

Tamore
Forest

Tunnels
of Tamore

Tents of Edom

Farmlands

Coastal Path

N
NW · NE
W · E
SW · SE
S

PROLOGUE

The robed figure waited a few more seconds before pushing the boat out into the waters of the lake. Jumping effortlessly into it he reached for the oars and began to row towards the land that lay ahead, his movements slow and powerful. It was hard to read the expression on this figure's face for his eyes stared straight ahead, cold and unblinking from the depths of the hood he wore.

As he reached the edges of the lake the air suddenly lay still. It was as though the whole of Cherith had held its breath and was watching with widened eyes filled with apprehension.

Glancing furtively around him he climbed out from the boat and began to drag it into a dense clump of reeds that lay in bedraggled masses at the edge of the water. As he did this, his left hand caught and tore on an old nail that jutted from the wood of the bow. Cursing, he reached for a rag that lay at the bottom of the craft, holding it tight against the wound to stem the drips of blood, before continuing to pull the boat out of sight. He was just in time. The moon had disentangled itself from the clouds and was now staring down at him.

As he climbed up the pine-covered slopes that lay in front of him, the length of his robe and the graceful strength of his movements made it appear that he was gliding over the pine needles. He had been taught well.

It was a while before the trees became more spread apart and the old, deserted farmhouse and disused well came into view. Walking towards the well, he swung himself over the side and, reaching for the rope that hung into its depths, he lowered himself down. The rope ended a way from the bottom, so he had to drop the last part, but he landed easily with a dull, soft thud. He paused in a crouched position, his fingers against the ground to hold his balance. Confident that he had not been followed, he felt for the opening that led to the tunnel entrance and, on finding it, began to crawl through. It was a narrow passage and he had to shuffle on his elbows and knees half dragging his body along. It seemed like forever in the dark with the damp smell of the earth around him but eventually the passage grew larger and wetter and rockier. He was now able to stand and, as his eyes became accustomed to the dim light, he could see the outline of the cave in which he now stood.

Purposefully, he drew his sword, listening intently but there was no sound. He exited the cave, his features transforming into a different image as he did so. So far all was going according to plan.

In the city of Wynere, the capital of Cherith, Nathan awoke suddenly. He felt afraid and couldn't think why. Sitting up, he drew his legs over the side of the bed and reached for his clothes, noticing as he did so that his wife was not there with him.

Standing on the landing he listened, but there was no sound. He frowned. Something wasn't right. It wasn't anything he could physically see; it was a feeling; a sense of loss; of dread. Instincts on high alert, he walked warily down the spiral staircase only to be met halfway by Naomi going up.

'Can you not sleep either?' she enquired. She paused as she saw the tension in her husband's face.

'Something's wrong!' she said it as a statement not a question, her eyes looking intently into his.

'It's just a feeling. I'm going to go and look around the city.'

'Shall I come with you?'

'No. Stay here. It may be nothing.'

As Nathan exited the house, his hand reached for his sword. It was as his fingers connected with the handle of the weapon that, a memory stirred in the back of his mind of an older man, charging him to keep the flame of Wynere burning. He remembered the gravity of the moment, the eyes of the man boring into his own as the Espionite sword was touched, first to one shoulder and then the other. As he had risen from his kneeling position, officially knighted as a Cherithite warrior, the older man had continued. 'Remember, were it to ever go out, it will signify the beginning of dark times for Cherith. Promise me, you will keep vigilant.'

Nathan had gripped the older man's forearm.

'I promise,' he had said.

The flame had been heavily guarded ever since, but still Nathan began to run, propelled by a growing feeling of unease. He crossed through the gardens and the courtyard cobbles of the city square and headed straight towards the Tower of the Lighted Flame. A sense of doom gripped his heart as he saw it lying in shadow. Two of the Keepers of the Flame were lying on the ground, blood seeping from sword wounds to the neck and heart. Kneeling beside each in turn, he felt for a pulse, but they were both dead, despite their bodies still being warm to the touch. One man appeared to be clutching something in his fist and upon prising back the fingers Nathan saw a small clasp lying in his palm. He frowned as he realised what it was and, picking it up, he quickly placed it into the pocket of his leather tunic before standing and turning towards the Tower. The door that led to its entrance stood slightly open, swaying gently on its hinges.

Resolutely, sword in hand, Nathan cautiously climbed the Tower steps, treading over two more dead bodies on the way. Reaching the top, he was greeted by a dense darkness. He already knew that he was too late, that the flame had been extinguished, but he had hoped for a remnant of a spark, something to reignite hope. There was nothing.

He walked towards the central pedestal and knelt on the floor, feeling for the outline of the slab of stone that lay next to it. The darkness in the tower hovered over him. It was like a great weight, a physical pressure that was squeezing the breath from his body. Using his sword, he prised the slab up and then leaned his weight against it to push it away. The sound of stone scraping against stone was loud in the silence and sent a shiver down Nathan's spine. Hastily, he felt into the hole that the stone had covered, but it was as he had feared. The Oil and the Sword, the two most treasured possessions of Wynere, were gone.

Somewhere, in a place outside of time, Melchi and Japhron looked on with troubled eyes. As the flame of Wynere had gone out they had sensed a rumble from the Underworld as though a great shout had gone up. It was a sound they had not heard in a long time.

CHAPTER ONE

THE ISLAND

An older man dimmed down the lamp and then, with his back tight against the wall, he slightly edged back a corner of the heavy black cloth that covered the window and peered out onto the street. He counted. Six.... Seven.... Ethan had only four more tolls before the city gates were shut and curfew began. The bell rang again, mournful, out of tune, sounding its warning into the night... Eight.... Nine ....

The steady tap of footsteps over the cobbles came as a huge relief to the watching man. He let the curtain drop back into place.... Ten .... The door opened and quietly clicked shut.... Eleven. The clanging ceased although its retreating echo could still be faintly heard reverberating against the city walls.

'Were you seen?'

'No,' Ethan panted, 'At least, I don't think so.'

'You're getting later each night.'

Ethan leaned back against the door, breathing hard and trembling. He was covered in fine sand and the damp night air surrounding him brought a chill into the room.

'There's no sign of him. Nothing! I waited and waited, but nothing.' The anxiety in his voice was clear.

'He will come.' The older man looked at Ethan and saw the doubt in his eyes. Walking over to him, he laid a hand on the boy's shoulder. 'He will come,' he reiterated as he looked him in the eye.

'How can you be so sure?'

The older man looked wistful for a moment as though

remembering a long-kept secret. 'Sometimes, when I shut out all the thoughts that say otherwise, my heart can sense he is not far away.'

Jed listened as the distorted echo of the last toll vanished into silence and was replaced with the barking and whining of dogs and the shouts of the night watchmen as they started their evening patrols. He heard the clanging and scraping of metal across gravel as the gatekeepers pulled back the huge wrought iron gates that separated the city from the sea beyond and the squeaking of the rusty hinges caused him to momentarily stop in his tracks. He was too late. All the inhabitants of the Island were well aware what happened to those who were found outside the city walls after curfew. Frustrated with himself for not having made it back in time, Jed turned and sprinted towards the dunes that were etched in shadows beside the shores.

The Island had once been uninhabited by man. The air had been clear and unpolluted; the fruit had been sweet, the crops bountiful and the flowers had exuded a gentle fragrance that had clung to the entire Island.

But, during the Barlkron Wars, hundreds of years before, it had become the place of exile for all foreigners, those sick or lame, the convicts and the homeless. Anyone weak in body and unable to defend themselves were captured as the Underworld forces attacked and ravaged city after city. Since then, it was as though the whole Island had been poisoned and weakened by the same historic diseases of mind or body that man had brought onto it, and now the land had to be coaxed into yielding anything wholesome. The sweet fragrance that had once permeated the air had been permanently replaced with a putrid smell of damp and rot. High grey walls hemmed them in and the gates leading down to the shores were always shut from midday until early evening and again from eleven at night until dawn.

The people lived by the laws enforced by whichever governor Barlkron inaugurated. On the surface, it appeared an ordered society, but the rules were rigid and controlled and the punishments were harsh. Strong emotions ran in a steady undercurrent, subtle and powerful like the ocean surrounding them.

Many people could no longer imagine what life was like beyond the shores they knew and no one, it seemed, entertained thoughts of escaping for those who had tried were always returned, washed up by the very ocean that they hoped would carry them to freedom.

But there were a few, a remnant of true Cherithite descent, who had been careful to pass on from generation to generation the truths of what had once been known. These few knew of the life that could be theirs; knew the name of the one who could make it possible; looked and waited for the day he would come; and remained in hope that they would be chosen when the time came.

From within his private chambers, Sharaaim, the current governor of the Island, extended his golden staff to the guard who had asked for an audience. The man entered, kissed the ornate wolf's head that crowned the staff and bowed low.

'Is the tower nearly finished?' the governor asked.

'It will be completed by the end of the week, my Lord.'

'And the census?'

The guard stretched out his hand and passed over a scroll of parchment.

'All recorded here, my Lord.'

Sharaaim unravelled the scroll and scanned his eyes down the list of names. He smiled – a distorted smile due to the slight scar that disfigured the left-hand side of his mouth.

'Keep a close watch on these people. If my sources are correct Asaph will be arriving any day. Ensure that not one Cherithite knows of his arrival or departure.'

The guard bowed his head, 'Yes, my Lord.'

Sharaaim dismissed everyone from his presence and sat with his hands curled around a silver goblet which held his favourite wine. He gazed into it and swirled the liquid around so that its crimson colour was caught by the firelight. Images suddenly attacked his mind, reminding him of a similar moment that had happened a long time ago; of another chamber belonging to a higher ruler; of a goblet, similar to this one, but this time filled with the thicker, stickier substance of human blood; The fresh cut on his lip, where he had been hit, had continued to drip as he had lifted the goblet to his mouth and drank. It had taken all his will power to prevent himself from vomiting.

Sharaaim squeezed his eyes shut and shook his head as if to dislodge the foul image from his mind, then, lifting his hand, he drank in one swallow before hurling the empty goblet across the room. It crashed, a heavy, metallic, clanging sound against the studs of the wooden door, assaulting the quietness of the night. Slumping back into his chair, he slowly drew his right thumb across the scar that lay imprinted upon his left palm. A constant reminder that his life was no longer his own.

Stirring from these dark thoughts, he reached towards the floor for a thick bound leather book that contained all the Island records. Turning to one of the more recent entries he began to look down the list of names, comparing it to what had been written on the census. On reaching one name, he stopped, confused. It can't be!

He looked again at what was written on the parchment he had been handed earlier and then turned back a few pages in the book he was holding, searching for more information on the family name that he had come across.

'How did this get missed?' he said out loud, his brow furrowed, but even as he asked himself the question, he knew the answer, for it was ancient law that some things must remain veiled until the appointed time for them to be revealed. Clearly, for some reason, this was one of them.

He smiled his crooked smile and, stretching his feet out towards the fire, he began to concoct a plan that could use what he had discovered to his advantage. 'Barlkron will be pleased,' he thought.

Ethan lay staring at the ceiling unable to sleep. Thoughts were swirling around his mind, each one taking centre stage before being pushed aside by the next, as though they were children vying for his attention.

"What are you doing wasting your time looking for a man you've only ever heard about," one voice announced to him.

"Asaph is on his way," another interrupted, its tone gentler than the first, although just as insistent.

"There is no way off this Island," a third voice roughly sent the previous one tumbling out of the spotlight. "Many have died trying."

"Even if Asaph does come, why would he choose you," yet another rudely barged in.

"You have been brought up believing these things. Do not doubt them now," another softer thought took its place on centre stage.

"How do you know if any of this is true?"

"My heart can sense he is not far away," his grandpa's statement came back to mind, temporarily silencing the other voices, but as hard as he tried, Ethan couldn't sense anything.

He turned over, thumping the cushion several times to try and get more comfortable before pulling his blanket close around his body. He eventually drifted off into a restless sleep.

Downstairs, Ethan's grandpa sat staring at the fading embers of the fire.

'He will come,' he had said, and he believed it, for there had been an increasing number of dreams among a few of the Cherithite people confirming that this was the case, and, despite the environment he now lived in, he still held great weight by these things. The reminder of his beliefs, instilled in him from another place, another time, tempted his mind to drift back several years, to a life that had been much easier than the one he faced here in this grey and harsh environment. He closed his eyes and indulged himself in remembering.

'It's a boy,' his son had shouted, causing excitement to reverberate throughout the castle. 'Father, come and see your grandson.'

He remembered being passed a small bundle and, pushing aside the blankets, he had seen a small, red-faced infant, its eyes screwed tightly shut as it cried with indignation at leaving the familiar and safe surroundings of the womb and being thrust into the bright light and unfamiliar sounds of the world.

'He looks like me does he not?' his son had said proudly. 'The future heir to the throne of Jachin.'

He had stared at this new arrival into their lives and smiled at him. The infant had, in that moment, stopped crying and stared straight at him and a sudden rush of love for this tiny being had flooded into the older man's heart, reminding him of the feeling he had had when his own son had been born. He held the baby tightly to his chest and kissed the silky down on the top of his head, overcome with a fierce sense of protection for this newest member of their household.

The land had celebrated the arrival of the young prince for many days, for a national holiday had been declared to mark this momentous occasion. The streets were filled with the joyful sound of music, which was accompanied by much storytelling, dancing and feasting, as was the tradition of this prosperous clan. The people were happy, reassured in the knowledge that there was now a future heir to rule this beloved place and that their way of life would be preserved for yet another generation.

However, those happy days did not last long for, a few weeks after the birth of the prince, tragedy fell. Just before dawn, one overcast morning, news went around from dwelling to dwelling that the Queen had died in the night, attacked by a sudden illness that the most skilled physicians had been unable to treat. After this, everything had changed. The King, overcome with grief, had withdrawn from both his family and his Kingdom, leaving the care of his son to his own Father and the rule of the land to stewards not old enough to govern wisely. The city had become hushed and subdued, limping along almost apologetically and, as the months had passed, the land had gradually fallen into disarray. The Underworld, realising this, had seized its opportunity and, while emotions were still running high, had incited the Edomites, who had long held a grudge against Jachin, to go into war against them. The King, on hearing they were about to be invaded by this vicious and lawless clan, had stirred himself from his anguish and made himself ready to lead his people into battle.

'You must take the prince and keep him safe,' the King had urgently said as he pressed the crying child into the arms of his Father. 'He is the future hope of our people. Now go. Quickly now. Find protection at the East Gate and I will find you when and if peace returns.'

It was the last time that the older man had seen his son. On his way to the East Gate with the child, he had been captured by a rogue band of thieves and sold to the Espionites, who in turn had sent both himself and the boy to the Island as a gift for Sharaaim. He had assumed that his son had died in battle for no-one ever came looking for them, and his hopes for ever leaving this forsaken place had slowly waned, until now.

The older man opened his eyes allowing his current surroundings to displace the old memories. He had never told Ethan the full story of how they had come to be here, although, through the years he had tried his best to impart the ancient teachings of their people. All that the boy knew was that his parents had died and that he was of Cherithite descent. Strangely, Ethan rarely asked questions about his past. The older man was glad about this, for he had wanted to spare his grandson the pain of knowing that he had been born to a life that he was unlikely to ever own. Now, sat here in this specific moment, on this particular night, he found himself questioning if he had done the right thing.

Hidden among the dunes, Jed shivered. The damp, sea breeze clung to his skin, and he ran his tongue over his lips tasting the saltiness of it.

'Asaph, how long will you be?' he thought to himself. He wished he dared raise his head above the grasses to see what was happening down on the beach below, but he was aware that the soldiers were still out patrolling the shores. He blew out his cheeks in boredom as he picked up a fistful of sand and let it drop between his fingers.

Maybe tomorrow he would come. Just maybe.

THE UNSEEN DIMENSION

Melchi and Japhron had been intently watching these scenarios, committing each detail to memory, when they were interrupted by the entrance of a young communicator, dressed in official clothing. The lion cub following at his feet was playfully tugging at the tassels on his slippers so that he nearly lost his balance.

'The Election Ceremony is underway,' he announced, trying to appear in control of the situation whilst gently shaking the young cub away. It pounced once more at his feet. Japhron turned to hide his amusement. 'I was sent to come and escort you for the assigning of your apprentice.' He gave up trying to get the young cub to behave and, bending down, he firmly picked it up and put it under his arm. It turned and, sticking out its fat tongue, casually licked him from chin to forehead. The communicator screwed up his face.

Melchi rose from his position, casting one last glance at Jed.

'Keep a close watch on them,' he said as he left with the communicator to take his place in the throng that had gathered in the election room. Japhron turned his attention back towards Jed as he lay hidden, Sharaaim as he plotted and Ethan as he slept, wondering how these scenes were going to unfold further.

Melchi had entered the vast space where thousands were watching the golden globe as it rolled and turned unaided above them. It bounced through the pillars of the hall, casting its golden hues around the room. In the atmosphere itself, tiny particles of golden dust shimmered and fell, delicately resting on all who were there until the whole room, and those within it, glistened. Eventually the globe lowered and drew still, and the master of proceedings reached their hand inside it and drew out a name.

'Felix of the house of Sion.'

Applause rang out, deafening and thunderous like the roar of the sea. Smiling, Felix stepped out from those stood on the podium and joined the others who had been elected to the office of Watchmen.

A hush of anticipation descended as the golden globe once more began its dance around the room.

'And now, to the Seer-ling who is to be assigned to the tutelage of Melchi.'

The globe hovered and, once again, the master of proceedings inserted their hand inside and withdrew a name. Slowly the paper was unfolded.

'And this great honour goes to…' The master of proceedings looked up, a twinkle in their eyes as they paused, keeping everyone in suspense.

'Mia of the house of Eli.'

Melchi watched as the young Seer-ling stepped out from among her classmates, her auburn pigtails bobbing and shimmering with the golden dust and her smile, wide, filling her freckled face. She stepped down from the podium and stumbled. A gasp went around the room, momentarily dulling the applause, but Mia, regaining her balance, grinned, waved and did a small bow to show all was well.

Melchi rolled his eyes.

She came and stood in front of him. 'Hello, Sir. I can't believe that it was me that got elected! I have dreamed of this for as long as I can remember. Which isn't that long I guess as I'm not really that old... Well, not in comparison to you, Sir.' Her words came out too fast, jumbling into each other so that when she suddenly stopped, Melchi felt like he had bumped into something.

'Sorry. That came out wrong. What I mean to say is that it's an honour to be your apprentice... I mean your mentee. Is that a word?'

Melchi took a deep breath. 'I believe the correct term is Seer-ling.'

'Oh, yes, I remember now. I'm Mia,' she said extending her hand.

Despite himself, Melchi smiled. 'Yes, I heard,' he said dryly as he bent down to grasp her palm in his own. 'Well, you had best follow me.'

Mia did just that, winding her way through the crowds and trying to keep Melchi in view, which was hard when one was so short, and his strides were so long. She wished she dared reach out and take hold of the end of his robe so that she would not lose him but knew this would be deemed as very irreverent. Thankfully, people parted to allow the revered Seer through, and she was able to follow in his wake.

Eventually, they reached the giant, mirrored doors that led into the jewelled corridor.

Mia found herself half skipping, half running trying to keep up. The light from rubies, emeralds, jasper and carnelian sparkled under and around her feet. It looked like she was walking on a rainbow of rich, undiluted colour.

'What's our first assignment? Is there one? Will I get to watch right now? And will we go to the Library? I'm just longing to see the Library.'

Melchi stopped suddenly, taking Mia by surprise, so that she stumbled into him. He reached out his hand to steady her. Keeping hold of her shoulder, he looked into her eyes.

'Now, what do you know of the Library?' he asked, not unkindly.

'Well, just that many answers to the realm of man lie in there and...' she faltered under Melchi's stare.

'The Library is not a frivolous outing. Only the most trusted can enter there and only then when they have the wisdom to not misinterpret what is revealed.'

'Of course, Sir, I mean Melchi, I mean Sir. I know that. It's just that it is my biggest dream ever to see inside the Library. I have ever so many questions you see.'

Melchi smiled and nodded. 'And I'm sure you will have many more in the days to come,' he said almost to himself as he walked back to his chambers, with his young apprentice in tow. His attention was already returning to the scenes he had left under Japhron's watchful eye and to the questions that he had himself.

CHAPTER TWO

BETRAYALS

⚓ CHERITH

Unable to sleep, Ephron sat around the oak table in the Council Hall, recalling the conversation that had taken place there two days ago.

'Two days!' he thought to himself. 'It has seemed like an eternity.'

He recalled the shocked faces of the elders, as they had sat in the early hours of that terrible morning, gazing at him in disbelief as he had told them what had happened.

'But how is this possible? Four guard's dead and not a sound, not a warning?' one of them had spoken.

'This is surely the work of more than one man,' someone else interrupted.

'You do know that with the flame extinguished, and the Oil and Sword gone, we are wide open to attack from the Underworld forces?'

'But why now, after all this time?'

The comments and questions, provoked by fear, had steadily risen in the room until they all began to overflow and spill into each other causing none to be distinguishable from the other.

One voice had shouted louder than the rest, 'You do realise that only a trained Cherithite has the power to touch the Oil or the Sword without being harmed?' The Council had gradually fallen into silence as this statement had cut through the air, piercing the hearts of everyone who heard it, for the idea that one of their own people had betrayed them was unimaginable.

'If it is one of our own people, then maybe the Oil and Sword are still here in the city,' someone suggested, hopefully.

'Possibly, but the power they hold protects us, so if the purpose is to attack us, it makes little sense that they would be kept here. But yes, a search must be made to ensure that this is the case. Nathan has taken some of our most trusted trackers to see what they can find out.'

As Ephron sat reliving what had been said, a sense of heaviness settled over his heart, for he knew that they had been in error by not keeping their watchmen in place on the city walls. They had been at peace for so long, it had no longer seemed necessary. Now, the land was disordered and unsettled. Houses had been searched and people questioned as to what they may have seen or heard, and a sense of fear had settled over the city like an invisible blanket, suffocating their peace.

Hearing footsteps, he looked up to see Nathan enter the hall, dirty and tired from the search of the last two days. He looked weary and defeated.

'We have found nothing,' he said with frustration in his voice, 'except for this bloodied rag down by the lake.' He threw the soiled cloth down on the table and Ephron picked it up to examine it before looking back at Nathan.

'As yet, there appears to be no enemy threat advancing against us. You should try and get some sleep while there are still a few hours before light. We can talk more tomorrow.'

Nathan nodded and took his leave, his mind whirring in different directions as he struggled to make sense of what had happened and the consequences that it could have upon them. He paused briefly at the Tower as he passed it, his mind reliving the terrible events of what he had seen two nights ago, before continuing to walk through the courtyard towards his house. As he passed one of the stone cottages, he became aware of someone watching him from a window but, seeing they had been noticed, the face had quickly withdrawn out of view. Nathan was too tired to give it any thought.

THE ISLAND

Jed peered furtively above the tall reeds that concealed him and held his breath. His ears strained to hear over the rise and fall of the distant waves and the whispers of the grasses as the breeze ruffled them. It had been a few minutes now since he had last heard any sound from the night watch and his restless nature was begging him to move. He slowly let out his breath before cautiously getting to his feet, all the while his eyes constantly darted about for any sign of a soldier, but all seemed quiet. He quickly slid his way down the dunes to the stretch of sand below.

Once on the flat strip of beach he headed to his left where a mound of boulders and rocks lay draped in haphazard formation, and it was over these that he started to scramble for he knew that beyond them there were caves where he might find better shelter while the tide was still out. As he climbed, his attention was caught by some movement beyond him. Straining his eyes, he began to make out the outline of a man dragging a boat ashore. He stared into the shadows. Yes, he was sure he was right, and there was only one person he could imagine that would be coming onto the Island, unseen, at this hour. Clambering faster over the rocks, cursing each time he slid on the slippery seaweed that covered them, he shouted,

'Asaph.'

The man continued walking backwards, dragging the boat further up the sand.

'Asaph,' he shouted again. A sound that was caught up by the wind and carried out of reach.

'Asaph.'

'Stay right where you are.'

The harsh voice came from behind him. Jed froze, hoping he hadn't been heard shouting out Asaph's name. Slowly, he turned back around trying to keep his balance as he did so, and realised that three, armed soldiers had crept up on him. Glancing furtively to his left he saw that both the man and the boat were now out of sight. He breathed a sigh of relief.

'I'll have to let myself be caught otherwise they may see Asaph and the boat,' Jed thought to himself.

He carefully climbed back down to where the soldiers stood and grinned at them nonchalantly.

'What took you so long? I'm freezing.'

'You'll be more than freezing if you don't wipe that smile off your face,' one of the men growled as he roughly handcuffed him and shoved him in the back to make him walk. 'You know the consequences of breaking curfew.'

'Well, that's one we can cross off the list,' Jed heard the other two talking from behind him. He jerked his head round questioningly, his eyes narrowing.

He was shoved in the back again, which caused him to slightly stumble on the damp, uneven sand. 'Keep walking.'

CHERITH

Nathan had hardly closed his eyes before there was a heavy hammering on the door. The sound in the silence of the early hours was intimidating.

'You go to sleep,' Naomi had stirred beside him. 'I will see who it is.' She hastily ran down the stone stairs and opened the door to find Ephron stood there, along with a soldier gripping a young woman's arm. She was clearly tense and upset.

'I'm sorry to disturb you Naomi, but can you fetch Nathan?'

Naomi looked at the scene in front of her and, whilst surprised by the agitation she saw on Ephron's face, she was desperate to protect her husband.

'Can it not wait a few hours? He has hardly had any sleep these last two days and is utterly exhausted.'

At that moment, Nathan appeared, curious as to what the urgent disruption was.

'That's him,' the woman cried, shaking free of the soldier's grasp. 'I saw him. He killed the guards almost in one movement. It was so fast. They didn't stand a chance.' Her voice grew louder and more hysterical as tears streamed down her face.

Ephron looked at the woman and followed the direction of her finger as she reiterated, 'It's him.'

'But this isn't true. How could it be? Search my quarters. Where would I have hidden the Oil and the Sword? And why?' Nathan shouted. 'Ephron, listen to me. This makes no sense. It isn't true!'

'I'm sorry Nathan,' Ephron replied, despondently. 'But you were seen. What can I do?' He turned to the soldier. 'Have this woman return home and put this man under house arrest.'

'Ephron, surely you know this is a mistake. No-one is as loyal to the ways of Cherith than Nathan. I would know if his heart had turned; if the enemy had overthrown him.'

'There was an eye-witness Naomi.' Ephron looked at her, his eyes pleading for her to understand. 'I can't believe it; my heart says it can't possibly be true... But he was seen.'

'Or someone who looked like him was seen,' Naomi retorted with a defiant toss of her head.

Ephron and Nathan's eyes quickly met as though the same horrifying thought had occurred to them both at the same time. Naomi looked at the expressions of the two men as they stood frozen in disbelief, confused by their reaction.

'A Masquerader?' Ephron whispered the word as though even uttering the name would attract the Underworlds unwanted attention.

'Well, that would make sense,' Nathan said slowly as he tried to come to terms with this thought.

'But Masqueraders only get their power to transform from Barlkron himself, and if only one of our own can touch the Oil and Sword without being consumed, are we saying that someone we know has made an alliance with the Underworld?' Naomi stared in horror at the two men.

'It would appear so, and if a pact has been made, it will have been recent, for eventually the contamination of the blood would make touching the sacred things impossible even for a Cherithite.'

'Well, there's a clue for us. What of the wound? There will be a scar on the palm from the pact ceremony. Maybe that could help identify him. If he is still among us that is,' Ephron pointed out.

'Our people work hard, and their tasks are tough. Many will have cuts purely from daily duties,' Nathan pointed out.

'You surely don't think they are still here among us?' Naomi asked, her eyes betraying her anxiety.

Nathan shook his head 'I don't believe so. On our own land, the Oil and Sword offer us protection. They would also, in time, expose the betrayer as we would begin to sense the evil in them. No, I fear whoever this is will have long left our borders by now.'

Ephron sighed again. 'We need to start gathering our men and preparing for battle for I am sure that the Underworld will not lose an opportunity to attack us while our defences are low.'

'It is good that we have reinstated the watchmen, but we should also send scouts to our outer borders,' Nathan added.

'Where is Asaph and Abbir-Qualal?' Ephron asked. 'We need to get word to them of what has happened. They will be needed to help lead us when the Underworld forces come against us. And Asaph may have some insight into what the enemy's plans actually are.'

'Abbir-Qualal went South a few days ago and Asaph is on route to the Island to fetch the chosen apprentices,' Nathan answered.

'Abbir-Qualal was to go to the East Gate before returning,' Ephron pondered. 'And Asaph will take the apprentices there for the first part of their training. Maybe we should send someone there to warn them of what is happening.'

'I will go,' Naomi declared resolutely.

Nathan started to object but Ephron was already nodding his approval. 'That is good but take extra precaution and try to not stop in open spaces,' he warned her.

Nathan looked worried as Naomi hurriedly kissed him and left the room. Ephron noticed his expression. 'I do not know who else we can trust for now,' he said, in defence of his actions. 'And we must get word to Asaph. Do not worry. I am sure she will be fine, and you are safer keeping under house arrest until I can convince the Council that it is a Masquerader that is at the root of all that has happened.'

Nathan nodded and said nothing. His mind was full of all that had taken place and there were still some questions that he needed to ask Naomi. He waited until Ephron had left the room before reaching into the pocket of his tunic and withdrawing the clasp he had found in the dead guard's fist. He sat staring at it for a long time, turning it around in his fingers, wondering how it could have possibly got there and why.

THE UNSEEN DIMENSION

Melchi and Japhron watched as these events unfolded before them. Mia glanced at them.

'Don't just stand there,' Japhron addressed her, smiling. 'Pull up a chair.'

Mia reached out into the empty void next to them and, as she did so, a chair formed under her fingers. It was small, intricate in design and had upon it a soft, fluffy, pink cushion.

Japhron looked at Melchi and grinned. He knew the older Seer would find Mia's creation garish.

'I wonder if any of them realise how cleverly woven together everything actually is,' Melchi commented, appearing not to have noticed what was going on next to him.

Japhron returned his focus to Nathan and the talk of the Masquerader. 'I am troubled to be unable to see the face of the betrayer.'

Melchi was silent for a moment. His features gave nothing away. He too was puzzled as to why this had been withheld from their sight.

'There will be a reason,' was all he ventured.

Japhron smiled fondly at him. 'Oh, ye wise one of few words and many thoughts.'

Melchi took the good-natured teasing in his stride and rolled his eyes at the younger Seer, only then noticing Mia's chair.

'Do you like it?' Mia asked as she fingered the softness of the cushion she sat on.

'Hmph,' was the gruff response.

Japhron laughed. 'Shall I take Mia with me to the realm of the Guardian's? We need to find the chosen two for this next assignment.'

Mia looked at him, hopefully.

'That is an excellent idea,' Melchi answered, nodding his head, and trying not to appear rude in his eagerness for them to go. The idea of having his space to himself for a few moments was a welcome prospect.

'Come on then, young Mia.'

The Seer-ling bounced to her feet, her hair still glistening with the golden dusting from the Election Ceremony and her face lit with the joy of anticipation.

'Are we really going to the realm of the Guardian's? Will I get to meet some of them? Will I get to choose who will go on assignment? I am just so excited. It's been one of my biggest dreams ever...'

Her chatter grew fainter, and Melchi sat back in his chair, relishing the peace.

'I will be glad to have the Guardians chosen, commissioned, and ready to be discharged the moment we have word,' he thought to himself as he cast his attention back to the two boys. 'They are going to need all the protection we can offer them.'

CHAPTER THREE

WORLDS APART

❦ THE ISLAND

The holding cells where Jed had been imprisoned were part of a maze of cellars that had been built under the governor's quarters. The floors were of cobbled brick and thankfully dry although still very cold. Jed hadn't been able to sleep, not so much because of the discomfort of his cell but because his curiosity was still burning in him by seeing Asaph arrive on the island just before dawn, and by what he had overheard the soldiers saying down on the beach.

Pretending to sleep, he had kept his ears open, hoping that the night guards would enlighten him further, but he was out of luck as they hadn't said anything of interest so far.

Bored, he had eventually pulled the thin, itchy blanket they had thrown at him more tightly around his body. 'I wonder if Asaph will find me down here,' was his last thought before he drifted off into a light sleep.

Ethan was awoken by a heavy banging on the door of the cottage in which he and his grandpa lived. Grabbing his clothes, he hastily pulled them on and ran down the stairs just in time to see two soldiers push open the door that his grandpa had begun to open. The force of their movements caused the older man to stumble, and Ethan ran forward to help steady him, but he was dragged back by one of the soldiers.

'By order of the governor, you are to accompany us.'

'But why?' Ethan started to question but he was just grabbed by the shoulders and made to walk towards the door.

'Grandpa…' Ethan shouted, panic in his voice as he tried to twist out of the soldier's grasp.

'Don't worry,' the older man shouted back, 'I will go for help.'

What Ethan didn't see as he left the cottage was the second soldier striking his grandpa, knocking him to the floor. As he fell, he hit his head on the corner of a table. Blood began to slowly seep from the cut the table had made and it steadily trickled down the side of the older man's face and onto the floor. The last thing he remembered before losing consciousness was seeing the red, sticky puddle that was forming next to his head. He wondered if it would leave a permanent stain.

Ethan was escorted through the streets and towards the square amidst the stares of the towns people. The atmosphere around him was tense and fraught. In the marketplace, traders were setting up their stalls as usual, but in hushed tones and with furtive looks, as though desperately trying to not draw attention to themselves. Ethan became aware of soldiers standing outside many of the cottages inhabited by people of Cherithite descent and he also noticed that the gates leading down to the beach had not yet been opened.

A young girl ran up to Ethan, skipping alongside as the soldiers kept up their brisk walk with him in between them. 'If you see Jed, tell him that I found him,' she said.

'Found who?'

'Amos.'

'Who's Jed?'

'My friend, but I think he is in the cells. I can't find him.'

'Get going little girl,' the soldier on Ethan's left glared at her.

'Sianna, come here,' another girl's voice shouted sternly from behind them. 'Don't go bothering people.'

Ethan turned back to look and saw someone, who was probably the girl's sister, grab her by the shoulders, turn her around and march her back through the marketplace. The image of the girl's black braids tied together with a dirty pink bow disappeared into the crowd of market sellers and out of sight. The soldiers continued to march him forward and he had no choice but to focus on where he was going and not on what was happening behind him.

Beyond the town square was the tower that Sharaaim had ordered to be built. It had been the topic of many a conversation since work on it had begun as no one was quite sure of its purpose yet. It rose higher than the city walls – each grey brick placed with extreme precision, creating a smooth exterior that was only broken by the door at the bottom and the large opening at the top. It had been the design of the most skilful Cherithite craftsmen. As Ethan was escorted by it, he noted that even there it was silent. There was no sound of tools and no worker in sight. His mind was whirling in a million directions as his heart hammered in his chest. 'What on earth is going on?' he thought to himself.

Once past the tower, Ethan was taken up a tree lined road that wound along the side of a hill which led up to the governor's Castle. This imposing structure overlooked the city, as if it had been deliberately designed to keep a watchful eye on all the activity going on below. Not only this, but, for the inhabitants of the Island, it was a constant reminder of their own insignificance.

Ethan was led through the forecourt, where a huge fountain gushed a towering spurt of water over a sculpture of a wolf's head. The fierce expression of the wolf appeared almost mocking to Ethan and he hastily averted his gaze away from it. The soldiers continued to march him around the side of the Castle and then down stone steps that led into the cells. Ethan thought that he was going to be locked up and so was surprised that he was pushed forward through the centre of them. As he passed each cell, he tried to not look at who was behind the prison doors, but he couldn't help his eyes from flitting to the gaunt, dirty faces as they stared out at him. One face in particular, of a boy who looked about fourteen, the same age as himself, caught his attention. Ethan had often seen him down on the shores, gazing out to sea, and had wondered if he too had been watching and waiting for Asaph. They seemed to have nothing else in common though, as the imprisoned boy was brown skinned and stockier in build than Ethan and his head was a mass of dark, curly tangles unlike Ethan's straighter, cropped, blonde hair.

'Welcome! Are you to be a guest too?' the boy shouted out sarcastically as he looked out, his fingers gripping the bars.

Ethan quickly turned away in the hope of not drawing any

more attention to himself.

'Don't trust a word they say,' the boy shouted. There was a clanging sound of iron against iron and a yell. Clearly a guard had done something to make it known that shouting was not allowed. Ethan flinched.

At the far end of the cells was a spiral staircase built inside a tower, and it was up these that the soldiers took him. It wound round and round, higher and higher, until it eventually ended at an archway that opened out into a small room where two guards stood stationed in front of a large oak door. One of them produced a huge, iron key from the pocket of his leather tunic, opened the door and gestured for the soldiers and Ethan to go through it.

They walked down endless corridors, the walls of which were covered with thick tapestries or the heads of wild boar, stag, and bear. Ethan wondered where they had come from as none of these animals inhabited the Island he had grown up on. The longer he spent walking alongside them, the more he sensed that he had entered a completely different world to the one he knew. Wide eyed and cautious, his heart pounding and his hands clammy, he took in everything he saw, wondering why it was that he had not been locked up in the cells.

Up more steps and through yet more rooms they went until, at last, they entered a larger, open space. Archways flanked the sides of this Great Hall and a huge fire blazed at the far end of it. Tall-backed chairs were drawn up to face the fire and from one of these a man purposefully rose and turned, the floor length, fur robe that he wore rippled as he moved. He had long, dark hair that was tied back with golden thread which interwove through fine, plaited braids. Dark eyes stared at Ethan from a face that remained deathly pale despite the heat of the fire. The man smiled, a twisted smile that only lifted one side of his mouth.

Ethan noticed he had been holding his breath for, as the man had turned, he had realised that he was standing in the presence of Sharaaim himself.

'Come,' the governor of the Island said as he gestured to the second chair, 'sit.'

Jed watched as the soldiers and the boy with them walked past.

The face was familiar to him as, for several days now, Jed had noticed him sitting on the dunes gazing out to sea. He had never approached him though, for Jed was not one for making friends or trusting people, but he had wondered if the boy had also been looking out for Asaph.

His knuckles stung from where the guard had just hit against them with an iron bar, the pain worsened because his hands were so numb with cold. He rubbed them hard, and they started to tingle and burn as the circulation began to return.

'I wonder what's going on,' he thought to himself for what seemed like the thousandth time. 'Whatever is Sharaaim up to?'

Ethan was wondering the same thing.

Sat in front of the roaring fire, Sharaaim had not done or said anything to cause him any alarm. In fact, he had done the very opposite. Before Ethan had even sat down, a servant had approached bearing a tray on which sat a silver goblet filled with a warm, spiced beverage and a basket of bread that had been baked with currants, cinnamon, and sugar. All of this was a luxury to Ethan, and he gratefully accepted them. As he sat before the warmth of the fire, enjoying the hospitality of the Castle, he found himself feeling almost grateful to the governor for showing him kindness and, bit by bit, he had felt less nervous and started to relax.

Sharaaim noticed that the boy was not as tense as he had been at first and smiled. Leaning back in his own chair, he stretched his feet out in front of him and then turned to face Ethan.

'You probably noticed, as you passed through, that there was a lot going on in the town today,' the governor talked in a confiding tone.

Ethan didn't reply. He just nodded and took another sip from the goblet he held.

Sharaaim paused. 'Sometimes, I get to hear about things that may cause trouble or unsettle our ways of doing life here and then I have to make decisions as to how to protect people. Sometimes even from themselves.'

Ethan again made no comment but continued to stare at Sharaaim, trying to understand why it was that Sharaaim was telling him these things.

The governor carefully placed his goblet on the small table next to him, his fingers gripping the rim as he carefully turned it around in a circle a couple of times as he continued to speak. 'I have heard that a number of your people have been plotting to usurp my authority here.'

'My people?' Ethan questioned nervously.

'Come now Ethan,' Sharaaim's voice held a hint of amusement as he turned his attention away from the goblet and shifted his focus once more on the boy. 'I know of everyone's descent here on the Island. I know of the Cherithites and their supposed beliefs of a saviour. I know you think that Asaph is on his way here to what? Rescue you?'

Ethan started to feel sick. He thought that the news of Asaph coming had been kept quiet. The soldiers standing outside Cherithite houses and the closed city gates now began to make more sense. They were all being imprisoned so that they couldn't leave with Asaph. The wisp of hope he had been holding onto seemed to vaporise and, despite the heat of the fire, he shivered.

The governor continued to talk in low tones. 'I wish I could offer you some hope that this is true, but I have been here for many years now and there has never been any sign of this… Asaph.'

'But what do you mean about people trying to usurp your authority?' Ethan bravely spoke up. 'I have heard nothing of this. If that is the reason you have brought me here, then I am of no use to you.' He paused, letting his words hang in the air, hoping they would detract the conversation away from Asaph as Sharaaim's statement had poked at the nerve of doubt already rooted in his heart and he couldn't bear how empty this made him feel.

Sharaaim smiled his twisted smile. 'I am glad to hear that you are not involved in this treachery. But no, that is not the reason I have wanted to talk with you.' Sharaaim paused for effect before leaning forward conspiratorially. 'Tell me Ethan, have you ever been told the whole truth of your lineage other than that you are of Cherithite descent?'

Ethan stared into the pale features of Sharaaim. 'What do you mean?' he whispered, frowning.

Sharaaim told him.

Around the edges of the hall, unseen by human eye, strange creatures looked on. They were toad like in appearance but black in colour and with legs resembling those of a rat.

They had retreated when Ethan had first entered, skuttling about in chaotic frenzy, but now they lay huddled together in a slimy mass under one of the archways. As Sharaaim had talked and Ethan had listened, they began to move in closer around them and were now sat ugly, watchful, menacing at their feet.

THE UNSEEN DIMENSION

Melchi watched as this scene played out in front of him, very aware of the subtlety of Sharaaim's tactics and wondering what his intentions were in trying to beguile this young Cherithite. His thoughts and peace were momentarily shattered as Mia came bounding back into his space, followed closely by Japhron.

'Melchi, Sir, I mean Melchi, the realm of the Guardians is one of the most exciting places I have ever been to. Thousands upon thousands were there, all lined up looking so regal and strong and dazzling with light. Actually, blinding light. Like it was glowing from within them. And some actually swooped off to a battle while we were there, faster than a blink and then they were gone, leaving a trail of fire and silvery smoke behind them. I have never known anything so exciting. And Nehari and Oho.. erm…'

'Oholiab,' Japhron helped her out.

'Yes, Oholiab, who is really, really tall, have been assigned to us.'

Melchi felt almost windswept by this tirade of excitement. 'Nehari and Oholiab then!' He turned away, nodding his approval. 'Yes. That is very, very good.'

From behind them came the sound of excited chatter and a group of Young-lings from across the dimension entered. They were each dressed in bright colours and carried a small satchel indicating they had come from the Chambers of Learning. One was also holding a large, clear bag of some cloud like confectionary.

The one carrying the bag approached the three Seers. Their eyes were vibrant green, reminding Mia of the emeralds from the jewelled corridor.

'We have been making something new in class and our advisor told us to share it with as many people as possible,' they said as they extended the bag for Melchi to extract some of the substance within it.

Another small being spoke up from the crowd. 'The only thing is, we only have the one bag, so we don't think that many people will be able to be included.'

'Is that so,' Mechi said with a smile as he pulled a large amount of the soft, sugary, cloud from the bag and handed a portion to both Japhron and Mia.

Mia popped some straight into her mouth and her eyes widened with joy at the taste of it. It melted into nothing almost immediately, but she was left with the taste of the fruits from the orchards of the scented gardens. It reminded her of a summer's day.

'Oh!' She exclaimed, 'It is the most amazing thing I have ever tasted.'

However, the small crowd of Young-lings were not listening to her. They were staring at the bag that the green-eyed being carried, which had somehow expanded in size.

Japhron watched in amusement. Melchi was enjoying himself.

'How has that happened when he took so much?' Mia heard one Young-ling whisper to the friend next to them.

'It must be magic.'

Melchi turned and beckoned them all closer until they were stood or sat around his feet. Taking the bag off the green-eyed being, he took handfuls of the concoction and handed it around to all of them. The bag continued to grow back in size.

'There is no magic in our dimension,' he patiently explained. 'But there are great mysteries. When you choose to share what you have, you will find there is always more than enough. What you give away will always grow into more. It is the great mystery of generosity. And no doubt, this is what your advisor wished you to experience.'

He handed the bag back. 'Now then, off you go. Keep sharing your creation. It will not run out. And you can tell your advisor what you have discovered.'

The Young-lings exited the space with a great amount of

giggles and chatter. Melchi chuckled.

'So, what did we miss while we were in the realm of the Guardians?' Japhron enquired as he pulled up his chair next to the older Seer and gazed at Ethan and Sharaaim.

As Melchi summarised what had been going on, Mia peered in to have a closer look. Her eyes grew wide in astonishment when she noticed the strange creatures sitting around the feet of Ethan and Sharaaim. She had only ever heard stories about the Underworld and so found herself fascinated and repulsed in equal measure.

'Will that boy be alright?' she asked, grimacing at the ugliness of the creatures.

'It depends somewhat on the choices that he makes,' Melchi replied without taking his eyes off what was going on.

'But what of the prophecies?' Japhron questioned.

'What has been written will come to pass one way or another but, whether Ethan finds his path within it all, is down to the decisions he makes in the end.'

Japhron turned back to watch, not comforted in any way by this reply.

Mia's curiosity was piqued by the reference to the prophecies but could see that this was not the time to ask questions.

'I wonder how I can find out without bothering Melchi?' she wondered.

CHAPTER FOUR

REVELATIONS

CHERITH

Nathan sat in his chair, feeling restless and uptight. It was nearly midday, and Naomi had been gone for several hours now, far too early to be sent word of her safe arrival at the East Gates. But waiting was not one of his greatest strengths. His fingers drummed impatiently against the cushioned arms. Agitated, he rose to his feet, and went to stand at the window but watching the commonplace activities of the townsfolk irritated him. He went and sat back down. His foot tapped on the stone floor. Hearing footsteps, and the steady click of a walking stick, he hastily rose to his feet and turned towards the door. He was hoping that there would be some news from the continued search within the city and that the elders were going to allow him to be released from house arrest so he could continue his own investigations. Ephron entered the room and the two men approached one another and clasped the other's forearm, as was the Cherithite way of greeting. Not for the first time, Nathan marvelled at the strength of the older man for there was no frailty in his grip and he still held himself tall and straight despite the old injury to his left hip.

Nathan screwed up his nose.

'What is that foul smell you have brought in here with you?' he asked the older man as a stagnant, acrid odour invaded his nostrils.

Ephron grimaced. 'Isn't it utterly pungent!' He drew a rag from the pocket of his tunic and flung it at Nathan. 'It's what you found down by the lake, but the blood on it has begun to emit a very nasty smell.'

'This pollution of the blood confirms our suspicions then,' Nathan said, frowning.

'There is also something else of possible interest,' Ephron continued, 'A group of children were exploring the deserted farmyard that used to be Old Tyron's property. I don't know if you remember there's an old well there?'

Nathan nodded.

'One of the boys climbed up onto the well and in his silliness lost his balance and tumbled down into it.'

'I gather he survived, given the nonchalance in which you tell the tale?'

Ephron rolled his eyes. 'Oh yes. The boy survived with nothing amiss other than a broken leg and wounded pride. Apparently, he had been dared to climb onto it by some young lass.'

Nathan stared at the older man wishing he would get to the point. 'So, you tell me this because…?'

Ephron paused, 'The elder Silas was one of the men who went to help pull the young lad out and he noticed that there was a rope hanging down into the depths of the well.'

'Nothing surprising about that is there?' Nathan's frustration was causing him to be curt.

'Not on its own no. But with recent events Silas was curious and spent some time exploring the bottom of the well. The rope itself had traces of blood on it which was also beginning to emit the same smell as on the rag that you found. He discovered an opening that led into a narrow tunnel and on shuffling along it he found the tunnel went right under Tyron's property and the city walls where it ended in the cave at Noah's peak.'

Nathan raised his eyebrows, 'That is interesting.'

Ephron nodded in agreement, 'Yes. At least we know how someone could have gotten into the city after dark, for anyone wishing to enter or exit unseen could have done so using this route. It looks like they would have come or gone by way of the lake if the bloodied rag is anything to go by.'

'Knowing how they entered or exited does not really help us to find them though or understand the reasons as to why all of this is happening,' Nathan pointed out.

'That's true,' Ephron sighed as he heaved himself back up onto his feet and reached for his staff. 'The elders have agreed to you being released from house arrest as long as you do not leave the city. They want it to appear to the townsfolk that we have the situation under some control, so will be stationing a soldier outside your house at night still.'

'Since when have the elders been more concerned about appearances over the truth?' he commented wryly.

Ephron pursed his lips, 'These are not easy times, and it is important that the city has faith in its leaders,' he said defensively. He blew out his cheeks, 'The sooner that we have news from Asaph the better. I just hope that Naomi is not too far from the East Gate and that Asaph has not been delayed in any way from his mission.'

The land that lay between Wynere and the East of Cherith was largely farming country and so was accentuated by many fields that were woven together with winding roads which were hemmed in by tall, dense, green hedges. However, there was one stretch that was more like open moor land. Masses of gorse and heather grew over much of this and small, round ponies with shaggy manes covering their eyes, grazed upon it. It was a halfway mark between the Capital and the East Gate, and it was here that Naomi took rest. She had been travelling since the early hours of the morning and it was now noon. She had made good time.

Tethering her horse, she sat on one of the boulders that lay scattered around, removed her boots and began to massage her feet. Although the events of the night had deeply troubled her, she was excited to be returning to her homeland. She had been brought up at the East Gate, her family still lived in and around Twyndale and it was where she had met and married Nathan.

She smiled as she recalled Shakirah first introducing her to the handsome Cherithite warrior.

'How alike you women of the East Gate are,' he had said, a little in awe at being surrounded by the beauty of these women.

'So people say,' Shakirah had commented. 'I however am left-handed, while Naomi is right, so if you should ever be confused as to who is who, look out for that.'

Although Shakirah had smiled as she said this, Naomi had sensed a sharpness in her tone as she had spoken and had wondered if her cousin had set her own hopes on this young man who stood before them in his warrior clothing. The moment however had passed, and nothing had ever been said again to suggest that this was the case. In fact, she was sure that Shakirah had set her heart on Abbir-Qualal, which was of great relief to Naomi as she had once suspected that this young man was maybe growing fond of herself. Nathan had put a stop to all that though. She smiled at her reminiscences realising that it had been a long time since she had thought about these things. But soon her mind had returned to Wynere and the night the flame had been extinguished. She was troubled that she had not had a chance to talk to Nathan privately before she left. 'I hope you will understand,' she said out loud.

In that moment, her attention was diverted by a sense of anxiety that suddenly prodded at her. She paused for a moment to try and ascertain why, but all she could sense was that she was in some kind of danger. Hastily, she bent down for her boots, but, before she could put them on, she was interrupted by a strange sound. Looking up, she saw in the distance, that a dark mass was advancing towards her and at an alarming speed. With it came a sound like the rumbling of thunder and the amplified buzzing of a swarm of wasps. Without hesitation, she ran over to the gorse and laid down flat, pushing herself as deep as she could into the coarse bushes. She covered her body and head, as much as was possible, with her cloak, chiding herself for having not heeded Ephron's advice when he had said to avoid stopping in an open space. At least she had dressed in her Cherithite cloak which, being made from a special cloth, had the added benefit of acting as armour. It was not easily penetrable.

The sound overhead grew overwhelmingly louder and more chaotic. Whatever it was now hovered directly above her. She braced herself as she began to feel the sinister weight of it pressing down against her body as thousands of large, wasp-like creatures were stabbing, retreating, and then stabbing at her again and again. They swarmed around her, persistent in their attack as they looked for an opening of exposed skin in which to insert their poison. Naomi felt a sharp stab of pain in her right foot and cried out. She had momentarily forgotten her feet had been uncovered and she immediately began to feel suffocated and sick.

Through the riot of noise, she detected another sound - the clamour of hooves and a loud shout. Immediately, the weight began to lessen and the noise retreat. The heavy, cloying atmosphere that had formed around her also began to dissipate.

Slowly, Naomi sat up feeling dizzy and disorientated. Her vision was blurred but she could vaguely make out the outline of a figure coming towards her.

'I'm so glad to see you,' she said faintly as the figure bent down to lift her up. With that, she lost consciousness and knew nothing of being put onto her horse and swiftly taken away.

THE UNSEEN DIMENSION

Melchi glanced at Mia as she watched the events surrounding Naomi. Her brow was furrowed in concentration.

'What is it you see?' he asked her.

She looked at him, confused. 'What do you mean? We have just seen the same thing. That woman has been attacked by those evil things and someone has rescued her?'

'But let us look a little deeper. What happened just before she detected the Scorpion Wasps? Look carefully now.'

Mia went back over Naomi's movements, drawing on every detail from her memory. 'Hmmm,' she said, her eyes brightening with revelation. 'It looks like she was aware that something was about to happen.'

'Very good,' Melchi praised her. 'Naomi is a descendant of the women of the East Gate and is gifted with a level of insight into the unseen dimensions. She was maybe sensing that all was not well.'

'But then why has this happened? Could she not have avoided it?'

'Ah. Their insight is not like ours, Mia. It is limited. They also have the Underworld trying to confuse and distract.'

'So, she may have realised that all was not well but not known what it was?'

'That is right.'

'How can they live so small?'

'They do not realise that they are. And the women of the East

Gate live more expansive than most for they have understood some of the principles that sustain life. Whenever someone starts to understand this and pursue it, their lives become a great adventure of discovery and insight.'

Mia smiled. 'And we get to help with that?'

Melchi smiled back at her. 'Yes. We get to help with that. But remember, we cannot ever interfere with someone's choices. Our insight is so that we can protect and only then within permission.'

Mia sighed. There seemed such a lot to learn and the more she was taught, the more questions she had.

'Who was her rescuer?'

Melchi paused. 'For some reason, their face was veiled.'

'But they are good? Naomi will be safe?'

Melchi did not answer. His heart was troubled by some of what was happening, and he questioned if Naomi had been rescued as it seemingly appeared. But the old Seer also knew that certain things had to play out for now without any interference from them.

🐺 THE ISLAND

Following his talk with Sharaaim, Ethan had been escorted to the West Wing of the Castle and shown into a suite of rooms where he had been told to make himself comfortable. The bedroom alone was larger than the entire cottage in which he and his grandpa lived, and Ethan found himself gazing in awe at the four-poster bed, covered with its plump cushions and silken sheets, the roaring fire, the thick luxurious sheep skins on the floor, the heavy velvet curtains at the latticed windows and he couldn't help but grin with delight at it all. Someone had laid fresh clothes out for him and, stripping off what he was wearing, he dressed himself in the beige linen trousers, dark leather boots, a white shirt, a tan leather tunic and an ornate belt which held an engraving of a wolf's head on the buckle. As he pulled each garment on, he felt something in him change as though they were not just clothing his body but also cloaking him with a newfound confidence. Ethan decided he liked the way that they made him feel and, picking up his old clothes, he threw them down into a crumpled heap in a corner of the room where they couldn't be seen.

Walking out of the bedroom, he found himself in a smaller

room where one wall was covered from floor to ceiling with shelves and shelves of books. A table was laid out in here hosting bread, cheese, meat, and fruit and soft, inviting chairs were strewn about entreating any visitor to want to stay for longer than they had been invited. Ethan sat down at the table and picked mindlessly at a cluster of grapes that draped gracefully over the edge of a bowl. He was struggling to process the events and revelations of the morning for it had all been so confusing and unnerving. But he had to admit it had also been a little bit exciting and so he was glad to have some time to himself to reflect on it all. Ethan recalled what he had read in the Island records, which had confirmed what the governor had revealed to him. Apparently, he, Ethan, was not just a Cherithite, but was of royal lineage. He was born to be wealthy and influential. He was born to be a King.

'Of course,' Sharaaim had told him in his low, confidential tones, 'If Asaph were real then it would only be right that you go with him to the land of your father, and of course, I would never hold you back. But as I fear that he is just a myth, I would like to invite you to rule here with me. I will train and teach you all the royal ways of governing which by right you deserve. You will in time be my heir and the new governor of the Island.'

As the governor had spoken, Ethan had found himself enticed by the invitation. After all, if he was of royal descent then, of course, he should live in the Castle and have the privileges that royalty brings. It made perfect sense especially if Asaph was not coming, or worse, was not even real.

Now, as he sat dressed in his new clothes, surrounded by opulence and ease, Ethan found his heart desiring to stay. A wisp of a thought drifted across his mind, subtly pricking at his conscience, reminding him that Sharaaim's rule was not of Cherithite origin, but Ethan batted the thought away and it disintegrated without argument.

'After all,' he reasoned to himself, 'this is a way I can help bring change to the Island and make a difference to the way of life here. And grandpa will be able to live at the Castle with me and help me to govern the Cherithite way.'

The thought of his grandpa caused him to frown. "I will go for help," the older man had shouted as Ethan was dragged away by the soldiers. But no help had come.

A knock on the door interrupted these thoughts and quickly brought him to his feet. A young servant boy entered the room to clear away the remains of his meal.

'You may tell Sharaaim that I am ready to speak with him,' Ethan addressed the servant in what he hoped was an authoritative tone. 'Inform him that I have made my decision.'

'Yes sir,' the boy answered without looking up. Ethan noticed that the boy's hands were shaking as he collected the platters and reflected how nice it was to be the one that others were afraid of for a change. He smiled. A smile that only lifted one corner of his mouth.

Down in the cells, more people had been imprisoned. Jed found himself sharing his space with five others and from them had discovered what was happening in the city. It appeared that anyone of Cherithite descent was either under house arrest or confined here in the cells of the Castle. What was confusing was that this was supposedly happening because of a discovered plot to overthrow Sharaaim's rule – a rumour that was taking each Cherithite by surprise. Jed dared not mention that he had seen Asaph arrive on the Island, or air his suspicions that this was the real reason for what was happening.

'Asaph, where are you?' Jed questioned again privately to himself. 'Why are you taking so long to get me out of here?'

There was no answer.

⬥ CHERITH

Nathan could not settle. As night had fallen, his strategic mind had kept him awake as he tried to work out how someone could have possibly come into Wynere, extinguished the flame, taken the Oil and Sword, and gotten away with little trace. There was also a more disturbing thought that was nagging at him whenever he recalled the absence of Naomi on the night that all of this had happened. 'Where had she been,' Nathan kept asking himself. 'And why was our family clasp in the clenched fist of the dead guard?'

In the end, the pressure that these unanswered questions gave him, forced him into action. He hastily rose from his bed, grabbed his cloak, lifted the hood over his head, placed his sword in its sheath around his waist and, collecting a few other items, he quietly left his room. Creeping to the back of the house, so that he could avoid the soldier stationed outside the front door, Nathan carefully climbed out of a window. No one, it seemed, had any suspicion that he would not follow orders, and Ephron had unwittingly told him how to exit the city unseen. It made an escape far too easy. Furtively, he headed straight for Noah's peak.

From deep in the Underworld, Barlkron sat staring at the robed figure as he updated him on all that was happening.

'So, the two boys are confined?'

'One is. The other, being of royal blood, can be used to our advantage when the time comes.'

'And the others?'

'In utter confusion.'

Barlkron smirked. Confusion was one of his favourite ploys for it interfered with wise decisions and caused people to be easily suspicious of one another.

'That is good,' he commented. 'Keep it that way.' He waved his hand in the air, dismissing everyone from his presence, pleased with how things were working out.

The robed figure left the throne room, relieved that the news he had brought had allowed him to leave unscathed. Although the plan was going in their favour so far, he was under no illusion that any error on his part would result in dire consequences, for, in the end, everyone was indispensable to the Lord of the Underworld, whatever their alliance might be.

THE UNSEEN DIMENSION

Japhron looked at Melchi as he watched Ethan talk with Sharaaim and then at Jed as lay in the damp confines of his cell, increasingly frustrated that Asaph had not yet rescued him. The quietness from the Underworld was also menacing in its silence, like a pot sitting on fire, slowly coming to a simmer before reaching boiling point.

'Is there still no word from Asaph? Can we discharge the Guardians to help the boys?' He spoke quietly, so as not to awaken Mia, who had gone to sleep, curled up like a kitten on her pink, fluffy cushion.

Melchi shook his head. 'Not yet.'

Japhron sighed. 'I know there is always a purpose in seeming delays, but it doesn't make it very easy to observe.'

Melchi agreed. Experience had taught him that delays were always so that everything important had time to get into its correct position but, none-the-less, it never made it any less tense to watch.

CHAPTER FIVE

FIGHTS AND FLIGHTS

🐺 THE ISLAND

Ethan faced his opponent, feet apart, body centred as he had been shown. Jed held his position and stared back quizzically. He had been surprised and slightly amused to be escorted from the cells to be this boy's combat partner. Jed surmised that he had needed someone who was roughly his own age and height to practise with, but he didn't mind as he was only too pleased to leave the dark, cold, confines of the cells. He was also a little intrigued by the figure that stood before him in royal clothes, for the talk of the cells had been rife about the young Cherithite who Sharaaim was apparently making his heir. Jed noted the white pale skin and the blue eyes which bore a harder, more defiant expression from when he had last seen him. But he was slender and looked physically weak. This was not going to be a fair fight.

Ethan saw the nonchalance in Jed's face and felt angry. He remembered Sharaaim laughing at him the first time he had been frustrated in a lesson.

'Good. Use that anger to fuel your strength,' the governor had shouted to him from the gallery where he was observing the boy's tuition. Ethan tried to do this now, moving quickly towards Jed, fists raised, before aiming a punch in his opponents' direction. But Jed pulled his torso in and away from the advance, twisting to the side as he did, so that Ethan's punch barely grazed his shoulder. Jed used the flat of his hand to block a further move, and in a swift manoeuvre wrenched Ethan's arm behind his back and brought him kneeling to the floor. Ethan furiously shook him away and jumped to his feet. He ran at Jed for the second time but was easily tripped up and pushed face down onto the ground again with his arm held behind him and Jed's knee pressed on his back pinning him to the floor. Jed released him and Ethan stood up, his face red with anger. He clenched his fists and for the third time lunged at Jed. Everything in him wanted to hurt this arrogant prisoner as much as possible. He threw a punch towards Jed's face and, yet again, found he was blocked. His fist was caught and twisted behind his body so that he was forced in front of Jed with his arm trapped firmly behind him.

Jed let him go. He was not even breathing hard. Ethan turned and kicked him in the shin before storming out of the room.

Sharaaim laughed. 'Take this boy back to the cells,' he ordered. Jed scowled as he rubbed his leg and shrugged off the grip of the guard. He had hoped to at least have been released for his complaisance.

Back in his room Ethan was half crying with fury and humiliation. He swiped his hand over the earthenware platters that had been laid out for him on the table, causing each to crash to the floor, spilling food everywhere. He didn't care. In that moment he wanted Jed to be punished for making him look so foolish. He stood still as an idea formulated in his mind, and once formed, he strode out of the room, through the Castle and towards the cells.

Around his feet, unbidden and unseen, the toad like creatures skuttled. They were very much at home around bitter, angry thoughts and the more that Ethan indulged in them, the closer they kept to him, scampering over him in their desire to keep as close as possible.

⚓ CHERITH

Nathan, on leaving his house, had managed to reach Noah's Peak unseen. From there he entered the cave and shuffled along the tunnel until he reached the bottom of the well. Using the hammers and hooks he had brought with him, he managed to climb up to the top and then swing himself over the side before quickly making his way to one of the neighbouring farms. Finding the stables, he had saddled one of the horses and then ridden straight to the East

Gates without stopping. He knew that his actions would no doubt add to the accusations already stacked against him, but, at this point in time, his priority was to find Naomi and put his mind at rest about her whereabouts on the night the flame had gone out.

The scenery had been a blur as he rode, obscured by the speed of his horse and the scattered thoughts of his mind as he kept reliving the events of the last few days. The fields gave way to moorland and then to wooded areas, but none of them caught his attention as they normally would. Time passed by, out of its usual pattern and when, many hours later, he reached the East Gates, he was almost surprised to have arrived. He dismounted his horse and waited in front of the immense iron structures. His heart was beating hard within his chest, for he anticipated that there may be answers awaiting him that would test his loyalty. Hearing voices approach, he quickly straightened his posture, and waited for the gates to swing open and for the women of the East Gate to grant him access. As it happened, only Reniah stood there to welcome him, accompanied by two watchmen. On seeing Nathan, she quickly moved forward, pressing first one cheek to his and then the other in greeting. Her waist length, silken, black hair was soft and cool against his skin and reminded him of his wife.

'I am so glad to see you. We have sensed a dark shadow over Wynere for a few days now and have been anxious to find out if all is well,' Reniah said, her low voice almost musical in its dialect. She looked behind him. 'Is Naomi not with you?'

'Is she not here? She left in the early hours of yesterday morning in the hope of intercepting Abbir-Qualal or Asaph.'

'No, she never arrived. And neither Abbir-Qualal or Asaph have yet passed through here, though we do expect them in the next few days.' Reniah's face was troubled.

Nathan drew in his breath, deeply disturbed and anxious.

'Come,' she said, sensing more than she had been told. 'You are tired and fraught and have much on your heart to unburden. Shakirah is away at present but should return shortly.'

Nathan nodded as he followed Reniah through the gates and into the land of Twyndale. For once, he was completely oblivious to the beauty of his surroundings for he was deeply worried as to what had happened to his wife. Or indeed, what she may have gotten herself involved in.

Reniah walked next to him in silence, lost in her own troubled thoughts for, try as she might, the whereabouts of Naomi was veiled even to her.

Naomi stirred. Her head was still foggy and sitting up took some effort. Holding a hand to her forehead she tried to focus, blinking hard, but her vision remained blurred.

'Ssshhhh,' a familiar voice urged her, 'lie still and rest. Your body is still fighting the poison.'

Naomi laid back down and closed her eyes. She couldn't place whose voice it was that she heard, as everything sounded like it was under water, all distant and echoey. She was vaguely aware that she felt disquieted but frustratingly found that she hadn't the energy to discern why this was. Unable to help herself, she drifted off into a troubled sleep.

The person with her looked on with an impassive face before kneeling next to her and examining both hands and feet for the stinger from the Scorpion Wasp. They eventually discovered it embedded in Naomi's right foot. Putting their finger on it, they traced the shape of the thorny sting that lay resting just underneath the skin and wondered what to do for the best. Eventually, they reached for their knife, lay the blade into the flame of a lamp for a few seconds and then cut straight into the skin. Naomi moaned and grew restless but did not regain consciousness. Carefully, Naomi's rescuer extracted the poisoned dart and, using a piece of cloth, held it up to the light of the lamp to examine it further. They had never seen the sting of a Scorpion Wasp up close before and its sharp, needle like point held a certain fascination to them. Turning back, they stared at the unconscious form of Naomi, their expression remaining neutral as they considered what to do next.

🐺 THE ISLAND

Ethan had ordered the guards to put Jed in 'The Pit.' This was actually less of a pit and more of a hole that had been dug into the earth. It lay on the far side of the Island next to what must have once been woodland but was now marked by blackened trees which stood lifeless and foreboding in the shadows. Those placed in the hole had to sit with knees bent against their chest as there was no room to sit with their legs in front. Heavy iron bars covered the top of it which meant the rain, rats, dirt, and wind could get at whoever was imprisoned there. It was a foul, cruel punishment thought up by Sharaaim himself.

Ethan peered down at Jed through the bars and smiled. Now who was the victor!

'You may leave us,' he addressed the guards. They nodded and left, perspiration dripping off them from the exertion of moving the grate.

'What have I done to deserve this, apart from beat you in a fight,' Jed shouted angrily.

Ethan shrugged and smirked.

'If you are of true Cherithite blood, you have been corrupted. This is not our way.'

Ethan looked at him disdainfully. 'I am of true Cherithite blood and royal descent so you should be careful how you talk to me,' he called down arrogantly. Standing above the trapped boy, Ethan felt powerful. The sting of his earlier defeat began to abate a little.

'I don't think that Asaph…'

'There is no Asaph!' Ethan interrupted bitterly.

'There is. He's here. I saw him.' Jed cried out in defence of his beliefs and hopes. He quickly stopped himself from saying anything more as he realised he didn't know if Ethan could be trusted to keep this piece of information from Sharaaim.

'You've never met him, so how do you know it was Asaph you saw?' Ethan retorted.

Jed was momentarily silenced. This was true. It also occurred to him that he had spent three nights in prison since his arrest, so if it had been Asaph who he had seen then where was he? Had Jed been left behind?

Frustrated, he threw one last verbal stone in the hope that it would smash through the lies that Ethan was believing. Something he had been told in the cells.

'Did Sharaaim tell you that your grandpa is really sick from the attack by the soldiers?'

Ethan looked at Jed in confusion. 'That's not true! He told me that…'

'And you trust what Sharaaim says?' Jed flung back at him, disdain in his words.

The old fear closed in around Ethan's heart, causing it to beat painfully within his chest. 'You know nothing,' he shouted and ran off into the night leaving Jed imprisoned in the confines of the earth.

For all his strong will and survival instinct, Jed was scared. Closing his eyes, his heart whispered, 'Asaph, where are you?'

Not too far away, a man was stealthily making his way up the cliff face that lay on the other side of the Island. He was dressed in black with a blue tunic bearing the symbol of a flame. Around his waist was a belt through which a sword was sheathed.

Melchi and Japhron saw him, and their hearts lifted. At last, it was time to send the Guardians.

Ethan having left Jed, ran straight into the hall where Sharaaim sat reclining. As he entered, he thought he saw the outline of someone retreating into the shadows behind the arches, but he was so angry and scared that he paid no attention to this.

'Is it true?' he cried out.

Sharaaim narrowed his eyes, 'Is what true exactly?'

'Your soldiers attacked my grandpa?'

Sharaaim shifted position in his chair, calculating his next move. 'Ethan, I had not wanted to tell you for fear you would be upset but...'

'So, it is true!' the boy interrupted.

'It is true that our soldiers restrained your grandpa, but it is for very good reasons. Reasons that I am not sure you will either understand or be able to handle.'

'I think you should tell me,' Ethan glared at him.

Sharaaim sighed deeply as though the answer was going to cost him a great deal of emotion to say. The robed figure laughed quietly to himself as he looked on, amused by Sharaaim's actions.

'As you wish!' he said eventually. 'It transpires that it was your grandpa who was at the heart of the plot to usurp me, my authority, and your position here. Did you not ever wonder why he never told you the truth of your lineage! Clearly, he has been keeping secrets from you for some time. Have you not wondered why this was?'

In that moment, Ethan had a momentary flash of clarity. Although he was confused as to why he had not been told the whole truth about his family line, he also knew that his grandpa was completely incapable of what Sharaaim was accusing him of. What Jed had said also explained why his grandpa had not come to the Castle to help him as he had promised. Pretending to believe what he had been told, Ethan nodded. 'I'm sorry you felt that you couldn't tell me,' he said, forcing himself to smile.

'I am glad that you know. I did not like having secrets from you, as I hope you will never keep secrets from me!'

Ethan promised, but his heart did not agree. The toad like creatures withdrew from him slightly, although their yellow cat like eyes continued to stare at him, much like creatures who, with their prey in sight, lie waiting for an opportune moment to pounce and devour.

As he left the hall his mind was racing with thoughts of what to do next. He knew that if he escaped the Castle, and Sharaaim's guardianship, he could be in great danger. He also realised that there was nowhere he could go to on the Island where he wouldn't eventually be found. There was only one person who could maybe help him, but he wasn't sure if they would be willing to.

Sharaaim watched him go, suspicion in his eyes and distrust in his heart. The frog like creatures on noticing this gathered around him, nestling up close.

'Do you think he believed you?'

'I believe he has been enticed enough by the thought of wealth and power to want to believe me,' was the reply.

The robed figure looked away, unconvinced that this would be enough. He knew that family ties could be much stronger than Sharaaim seemed to believe.

Jed had used all his will power to keep calm, but as the hours had passed and the night had fallen, he was feeling a sense of panic. His knees ached with cramp, and he longed to be able to stand to his feet and stretch but the iron grid was too low and far too heavy for him to move. His mind wandered again to the mystery figure he had seen arrive on the Island the night he had been captured. If it hadn't been Asaph, then who had it been? He recalled Ethan's words, bitterly hurled at him a few hours earlier, 'There is no Asaph!' Jed's heart sank at the memory of this but even as it drifted into his mind, he disregarded it. 'I don't believe it!' he said out loud, 'I refuse to give up hope of getting away from here. And there have been too many dreams lately telling us that Asaph is on his way. It must be true.'

As he said this, seemingly from out of nowhere, a sense of deep peace settled in, over and around the imprisoned boy and, despite the circumstances he found himself in, Jed felt strangely comforted.

The reason for this was that a tall being had arrived and was standing next to the pit. He was dark skinned, clean shaven and held himself with a noble lift of the head. Above his black trousers was a golden sash in which a sword was sheathed, and a shield was set upon his back bearing the emblem of a flame. In his hand he held a tall spear on which many intricate drawings were carved and all around him, a halo of silvery light glowed.

As Jed had spoken out his beliefs that Asaph was real, this unseen Guardian had smiled.

'He is on his way, dear one,' he had uttered in a deep, clipped accent. 'Do not fret.'

Ethan had gone to bed fully clothed and waited. At some point, long after the last toll of the curfew bell, he had heard the door of his room open, and someone enter. He tried to keep his breathing low and steady so that whoever it was would think he was asleep. It felt like an eternity before they had left, shutting the door quietly behind them. Ethan settled down to wait for the first glimpse of light as he had noted that most residents of the Castle tended to be asleep then.

Sharaaim left Ethan's room and strode back down the corridors of the Castle. His robe billowed out behind him and under it the creatures kept shelter, skuttling beside him in their haste to keep up. Arriving back at the Great Hall, he poured himself a goblet of wine, and then seated himself by the fire, where the robed figure stood.

'Is the boy alright?'

'Yes. Asleep in bed. I told you all would be well.'

The robed figure did not comment. He did not want to incite the governor's wrath by appearing to doubt him further. 'I think I will check on the boy myself when all is quiet,' he thought to himself.

'And all is well with what was entrusted to you?' the governor broke into his thoughts.

'Yes. And they will benefit you greatly now that you have obtained the services of one who can both handle and use them to your advantage.'

Sharaaim smiled his cold, twisted smile. Things were going better than he could have hoped for. A few more days and all will be ready.

The robed figure turned and spoke again, 'Asaph is nearly here. I can sense him.'

'Then do all you need to do to keep him from gaining access to what he has come for,' Sharaaim snapped, unnerved by the mere mention of Asaph's name.

The early morning light had just broken through when Ethan carefully eased back the covers and got to his feet. He listened intently at the door for any sound and then, hearing nothing, he cautiously opened it, looking intently into the shadows to check that no-one was there. Seeing the empty corridor, he quickly made his way out of his quarters and down to one of the lower parts of the Castle where he hoped he could exit without being seen. He didn't look back, but if he had, and had been able to see into the unseen realm, he would have noticed that a shorter, broader shouldered warrior was following him. He was brown skinned with long, dark, curly hair and embedded into his skin were black markings depicting battles, swords, fire and water. This warrior wore dark trousers and had a sword strapped to his waist and a shield upon his back. His presence was the reason that Ethan managed to remain unseen as he exited the Castle.

Jed had tried to watch for the elusive transition between dark and dawn but had fallen into a light, fitful slumber. He was awoken by the soft thud of running footsteps, and the forced whisper of a voice telling him to wake up. Coming round he was surprised to see Ethan's face staring down at him. He glared.

'I'm going to try and move this covering.'

'You may need a better plan than just you!' Jed said sarcastically, remembering how the two guards had both struggled with its immense weight. But, as Ethan placed his hand over the iron bars and pulled, the whole structure lifted easily away. The shorter Guardian, who had followed behind Ethan, laughed as he helped to lay the heavy iron grate onto the ground. The taller Guardian grinned at him.

'It is a good job that you have been exercising my friend,' he joked. 'I wondered if you would struggle. It looked very heavy, and you have been very lazy of late.'

Nehari laughed. 'If you can call the battle we have just won in the middle realm being lazy then I misunderstand what you would call work,' he retorted playfully.

THE UNSEEN DIMENSION

Melchi and Japhron looked on with great delight. They enjoyed watching these two warriors spar against each other and they were more than a little relieved that they had at last arrived to help the boys.

Mia stirred from her restful state, immediately awake.

'You're just in time,' Japhron said to her, nodding his head towards what was happening. 'Look.'

She peered in and immediately her face lit up with her enormous smile. 'It's Nehari and Oho... Oho...'

'Oholiab.' Melchi reminded her, rolling his eyes.

'Oholiab...The battle they went to fight can't have taken that long then. Japhron said they had to go and stop the Invaders from the Underworld from attacking a village in the Southwest where the people from Wynere were headed and ...' Mia's flow of chatter was interrupted by the approach of another figure. She gasped in delight. 'Is that who I think it is? Really?' She almost whispered, clasping her hand over her mouth. 'Oh, this is the most exciting day ever.' She beamed at the older Seers before turning her attention back to the scene in front of her.

'Yes,' Melchi nodded, smiling at her. 'He has arrived at last.'

🐺 THE ISLAND

Ethan knelt and stretched out his hand to help Jed out of the pit, when, out of the corner of his eye, from the charred trees beyond, he saw someone coming towards them. Ethan froze.

'What is it?' Jed hissed at him. 'Help me up!'

'Sssshhhh,' Ethan whispered back. 'Someone's coming.'

'Who is it?'

'I don't know. He's coming from beyond the Forbidden Cove, I think. I'm not sure. He's not from around here.'

As the man drew closer, he raised his hand in a wave. He was white skinned, though tanned, with dark hair brushing to his shoulders and a beard that indicated he had probably been travelling rough for a while. Approaching Ethan with a smile, he extended his arm to help pull Jed out of the hole. As the man's hand gripped his own, Jed felt strength returning to his body and, despite having been in such a cramped position for many hours, he found he was able to stand without pain or stiffness.

'Well,' the man said with a laugh, 'I thought I may have to break both of you out of your relative prisons! You've made my life much easier by being in the same place at the same time.' Despite their caution, the sound of his voice stirred both the boy's hearts. Something about this man brought not just hope but a longing for adventure and the courage to face it. Even the foul smell that usually permeated the air around the Island seemed to evaporate in his presence and they could suddenly smell the saltiness of the ocean carried over to them on the breeze.

'Asaph?' Jed uttered the name with hesitancy.

The man grinned, his eyes twinkling in the early morning light.

At that moment, seemingly, from out of nowhere, another man's voice called out to them. 'Ethan, Jeduthun, I've been looking for you.' Startled, the boys turned around to see yet another figure approaching, striding from the opposite direction from where the first man had come from. He was dressed all in black, unlike the first man who wore a blue tunic. The boys looked from one to the other completely confused for, apart from their clothing, the two men looked completely identical.

Oholiab, the taller Guardian, growled deep in his throat. 'Masquerader!' he uttered with contempt. Nehari had his hand on his sword ready to draw it if asked.

The first man was looking intently at the second figure, a slight frown furrowing his brow.

THE UNSEEN DIMENSION

Melchi and Japhron looked closely but try as they might, they were still unable to discern the true identity of this cloaked figure.

Mia looked at them and then back at the man and the second robed figure. She had always loved a mystery, but this was a very puzzling one. She found within herself a great desire to solve it.

CHAPTER SIX

UNSEEN DANGERS

 **THE ISLAND**

The first man was staring intently at the second figure. It was startling to see his own face reflected back at him. The eyes in front held his stare with cold, unblinking eyes, before turning away and holding out his hands towards the boys. The first man frowned at the gesture, momentarily distracted. 'Is that something I do myself?' he was thinking before being brought back to the moment by the sound of his own voice speaking from the other person's mouth.

'Come,' the second figure was saying, 'It is time to leave. You have waited for me long enough and we have a long journey ahead.'

'Asaph?' This time it was Ethan that uttered the name with hesitancy.

'Yes,' the figure answered without smiling. 'It is I. Come, Ethan. It is time to go. Do not hesitate. I will take you to see your grandpa before we leave.'

On hearing the mention of his grandpa, Ethan moved towards him. The man held out his arm, beckoning him closer.

"He's not Asaph,' Jed called out. 'Ethan, can you not sense it? Ethan,' he shouted in frustration.

'Stand behind me,' the man in the blue tunic whispered to Jed. The boy immediately ran and positioned himself behind the man's back. Peering out, he watched Ethan as he continued to cautiously walk towards the figure beyond. 'I think he has been hypnotised or something,' he whispered.

'Come, let's go see your grandpa,' the other voice cut in louder and a little harsher as Ethan hesitated.

The first man then called out, 'Ethan, look at me,' Ethan continued to stare at the second figure as though transfixed. 'Ethan! Look at me.'

The boy stopped and slowly turned back around.

'I know your mind is confused as to the truth right now but try to shut out the thoughts that are conflicting within you and listen with your heart. Who do you sense is real?'

Something of a fogginess began to lift off Ethan's mind as the man spoke, for what he said was so like the words his grandpa would use when speaking of Asaph or Cherith. He stopped and turned looking from one man to the other.

'What does your heart sense, Ethan?' the man gently asked again.

'Come now, Ethan. We must go,' the other voice coaxed.

Ethan glanced at the figure in black one last time before making his decision, but as he turned towards the first man and Jed, he suddenly found that his legs felt pinned down to the ground.

'I can't move,' he cried out in dismay. 'Something is holding my feet down. Asaph, help me. I can't move,' he said again, panic in his voice as the unseen weight he felt lying on his legs was unnerving.

Asaph imperceptibly nodded his head and Nehari immediately drew his sword and slashed at the creatures that were sat interlinked on Ethan's feet preventing him from being able to lift them. The black toads, on seeing that they had no power against this armed warrior, ran off with high pitched squeals. Ohaliab grimaced. The sound was foul to his highly tuned hearing.

Ethan, finding that the restriction had lifted, ran, stumbling towards the first man and Jed. It was in that moment that the sound of horns blasted through the silence and the air was filled with men's shouts and the barking of dogs. His disappearance must have been discovered he thought. The figure all in black immediately retreated, seemingly melting away into the shadows and out of sight.

'Quickly now,' Asaph said to the boys, tearing his eyes away from the retreating image of himself, 'we must go. Keep as near to me as you possibly can. No-one will be able to see you as long as you stay close.' The boys increased their pace, with the Guardians protecting from behind.

 THE UNSEEN DIMENSION

Melchi and Japhron smiled at each other. They had waited a long time for this. Certain prophetic events, spoken of from many ages' past, were beginning to unfold before their very eyes and for them it was a privilege to see.

Mia, seeing that the older Seers were engrossed in what was going on, quietly rose to her feet and with one last glance to check she had not been noticed, turned and tiptoed out of the room.

Melchi waited a few seconds before turning towards where she had been standing.

'Hmmm,' he said, lifting his finger thoughtfully against his lip. 'I believe I will let her try.'

THE ISLAND

Asaph led the way through the damaged, ravaged trees. It looked like there had once been a fire here for scorched stumps lay stubbornly embedded into the ground and huge rotted branches were strewn haphazardly in their way. It was a section of the Island that had been forbidden to the inhabitants, but Ethan found himself wondering why, as it was not somewhere he could imagine anyone wishing to go to. Eventually, the trees, such as they were, began to grow increasingly spaced apart and they now stood at a cliff edge which held a set of very precarious, uneven steps leading down to the cove below.

The sound of the soldier's shouts and the whining of the dogs was growing louder from behind them. Asaph began to climb down the steps.

'Have you brought the boat around?' Jed called out as he balanced himself on the stony ledge behind him.

'No,' came the reply.

Jed frowned as he threw glances at the enclosed cove that they were heading towards. The tide was out and an exceedingly long line of rocks heading towards the sea hemmed them in on both sides.

'I think we will be trapped going this way.'

Asaph continued climbing down. 'I have a plan. Don't worry,' he called out.

Ethan was worried. He too couldn't see a way out or around the cove. He was also anxious that he hadn't said goodbye to his grandpa or told him where he was going. The old, familiar sense of panic began to rise causing his heart to beat faster. 'What if this wasn't Asaph,' he began to question, 'And what if they were caught? What if he couldn't keep up and got left behind? What if his grandpa died before he saw him again?'

They had now reached the bottom few steps. Asaph turned around to help the boys as they jumped down beside him. As he reached for Ethan's arm to help steady him, Asaph whispered, 'Ethan, all is prepared. Do not be anxious about your grandpa. I went to his house first and all is well. He knows you are with me, and you will see him again.'

Ethan was so emotional he found he couldn't speak so just nodded. He felt like Asaph had known exactly what he had been thinking and found this thought both comforting and a little disturbing at the same time.

Asaph smiled at him. 'Now, we must keep moving.'

Jed had run on ahead trying to find a hiding place. He shrugged his shoulders and raised his arms in a questioning gesture. Asaph laughed at him. 'Come on. Keep close.' He began walking towards the sea.

'I can't swim,' Ethan called out from behind him, 'at least not very well.'

'No swimming required,' Asaph replied cheerfully as he continued walking. It wasn't until they had caught up with the shallow waves of the sea that the boys saw they were on a strip of sand which stretched in a shimmering pathway to the shadow of land ahead.

Walking either side of Asaph, the boys kept staring first ahead and then back at the place they had felt imprisoned on their whole lives. No wonder this side of the Island had been forbidden and the gates had always been locked at low tide.

Asaph looked at them and smiled. 'There was always a way out,' he said.

Before either boy could comment further, something swished by Jed's ear and landed a little way ahead of them. He ran to pick it up.

'It's an arrow,' he exclaimed holding it up for the others to see. 'They're actually shooting arrows at us!' he said in disbelief.

'They're shooting arrows at me. Just keep walking,' Asaph directed. 'Remember they can't see you if you stay close.'

'Can they hit us though?' Jed queried.

'Very doubtful,' came Asaph's reply, a mischievous look on his face.

Behind them, Oholiab and Nehari were fending off the arrows with their shields. The sand was now littered with hundreds of the lethal darts.

'You missed one,' Nehari chided as the arrow that had whizzed past Jed's ear flew by them.

'It will not happen again,' Oholiab said with a glint in his eye.

Ethan looked back. 'Jeduthun, turn round and see!' he said.

'My names Jed,' the boy corrected with a scowl. He wasn't ready to make friends with Ethan just yet. He glanced around anyway and saw the arrows piling up behind them as if they were being blocked by an invisible shield. He also noted that, as they walked, his and Ethan's footsteps did not show in the sand.

'Asaph, look!' he said.

Asaph obligingly did so. 'Their aim needs some attention,' was all he said but he caught the eyes of the two Guardians and winked.

'Why don't they chase after us?' Ethan asked.

'Because they can't see that you are with me, and their attack is to drive me away from the Island. They imagine that they have succeeded. It is just an added benefit to them if they actually manage to hit me.'

The boys could hear that the arrows were being fired less frequently now and on turning round again, saw that the soldiers were beginning to turn away and head back to the city.

Sharaaim looked on from the tallest tower where he could easily see the land linking this Island with the next. He continued to watch the distant outline of a solitary man walking away.

'And so, you failed, Asaph,' he spoke out loud to himself.

The movement behind him made him jump. He had not heard anyone enter the room.

'You think he's failed?' the voice was almost sneering.

'Yes,' he snapped, 'The boys are not with him, and it will not be long until they are found. There are few places here in which to hide.'

'You have been deceived then. Of course, the boys are with him. Just because you cannot see them does not mean that they are not there. Asaph can shield anyone from view if they are close enough to him.'

'What?' Sharaaim roared. 'It was your role to ensure that this did not happen.'

'I had to withdraw or even more of our plans would have gone awry,' the figure in black replied, not in the least bit ruffled by Sharaaims outburst.

'Barlkron will hear of this,' Sharaaims voice held contained anger and his dark eyes glittered with rage.

'Do not concern yourself, governor,' the figure said with a slow smile. 'There is a long way to go before they reach Wynere and there is more than one way to prevent them from getting there.'

'I'm listening,' Sharaaim said, his voice calm again.

THE UNSEEN DIMENSION

Mia stared at the massive doors that lay between her and the Library. She hesitated for a moment, remembering Melchi's words, but her desire to discover answers overcame the warning in her head. Using both hands, she pushed with all her strength against the left hand side door until there was just enough of a gap for her to slip around it.

Once inside, she turned. The place was flooded with beautiful light, but it wasn't just this that caused her to be stunned into stillness. What she saw was vaster and more incomprehensible than she could have possibly imagined. She was reminded of a small spider she had seen scuttling around the election room the day before the ceremony. Her imagination had wondered what it must have felt like being so small, in such a huge space. Now she knew. The shelves of books were stacked from the floor, high up into an open topped ceiling, where they continued to tower into the sky, beyond her view. She went and stood in-between two of the aisles and realised that the Library also stretched far and long in front of her. She wandered down one of them, her hand trailing against the books she could reach. If she had turned to see behind her, she would have noticed that as her fingers touched the books, the names written on them shimmered and jumped out from the spines. The individual letters jostled into position before standing to attention in mid-air, seemingly awaiting a command. But when no such command was given, they slowly fluttered back into place.

Mia felt she was in a village, with each street revealing yet more books of all shapes and sizes, thickness, and colour. She was more than overwhelmed.

'Where do I even start?' she said out loud.

'At the beginning,' a female voice answered in a singsong, story-telling tone. 'A story always starts at the beginning.'

Mia tried to see where the voice was coming from. She couldn't see anyone.

'Hello,' she called out. Her voice was small and there was no answer.

Sighing, she took a deep breath and straightened her shoulders.

'If I only knew whose beginning to start with?' she whispered. She sat down on the floor and crossed her legs. Putting her hands over her mouth to remind herself to concentrate, she turned her attention to the events that she had seen from the Seer's vantage point.

One face in particular came to her memory.

'Yes.' She said confidently, getting to her feet. 'I believe I will start with you.'

CHERITH

Wynere was getting ready to defend itself from attack; Watchmen now lined the city walls ready to sound the alarm as soon as there was any sign of the enemy; The women, children, the elderly and the vulnerable had been sent to the West County to seek refuge in a neighbouring city and scouts were on the high lands positioned to see the first sign of invaders and be ready to sound the battle horns when they did.

The city was tense with waiting for imminent attack but were not being overly alert to the darkness that had already permeated among them. The flame, kept alight by the sacred oil, was not just symbolic. It held an immense power that meant while it burned the city came under its protection and peace. Without it, the very nature of some of the Cherithite people began to corrupt. Suspicion, anger, resentment, and disputes were breaking out everywhere. Some knew enough to understand what was happening and were practised enough in Cherithite ways to combat it. Others were not. Many younger people were falling into deceptions that caused them to question their identity and the authority around them. Everywhere, unseen, invisible creatures from the Underworld already operated, winding their threads of strife, envy, and rebellion wherever they were given permission.

Ephron stood waiting for the Silversmith to sharpen his sword and daggers. He wished he knew where Nathan, Asaph and Abbir-Qualal were but he had been sent no word. News of Nathan's escape had put himself under suspicion among the other elders and he was aware that there had been a few secret meetings held in which the focus was, no doubt, about whether his authority should be dismantled. He sighed to himself. Leadership was a lonely road at times, and he felt too old to be facing yet another battle.

SOMEWHERE BETWEEN THE ISLAND AND CHERITH
Asaph and the boys were not too far from the neighbouring Island. The early morning sun now shimmered over the rippled sand, bouncing off the sheen of water that sat in shallow puddles and the sound of gulls screeched above them. The air was fresh on their faces, the salty tang of the ocean on their lips. At first there had been much to talk about as both boys had questions about Cherith and their training.

'I have been brought up to be a Cherithite though,' Ethan had said at one point. 'Will there be much more for me to learn?'

Asaph looked at him, kindness in his expression along with some amusement. 'Being brought up a Cherithite doesn't always make you one,' he answered gently, 'and no doubt there will be some things to unlearn because of the environment you have been in, and the experiences you have faced.'

'We will learn to fight though?' Jed interjected.

Asaph laughed. 'A little. Maybe not always in the way you imagine though, Jed. Some of the greatest battles we war against are those that rage within us and the initial training you receive will probably surprise and perplex you. It is important to remember that everything you have the opportunity to learn will have a purpose.'

'Asaph, who was the other man, the one who looked like you?' Ethan interrupted, changing the direction of dialogue. Jed scowled at him.

Asaph went quiet for a moment. 'I am not sure.'

Jed frowned. 'What do you mean you're not sure. He must be your twin or something? He looked just like you.'

A look of sadness momentarily clouded Asaph's features before he answered. 'Come,' he said, 'let us not give our attention to the things of the dark on such a beautiful morning.' He turned and smiled at the boys. 'Look, we are not far away now.'

As the boys turned their attention to the land ahead, there came a sudden, violent tremor beneath them. The sand underneath their feet shifted causing Ethan to lose his balance and fall to his knees. Jed managed to steady himself and now stood with feet apart and arms extended. From his knelt position, Ethan could feel the ground fiercely vibrating underneath him.

'Is it an earthquake?' he called out to Asaph. There was no reply. Asaph had drawn his sword and was now circling, watchful, staring at the ground beneath them.

From below where they stood, the shape of something began to be made visible, a long, thick, serpent like creature, winding and swirling in a circle under them. The imprint of itself was clear against the sand.

'This is no earthquake,' Asaph at last replied. 'This is an ancient Sand Serpent that has been roused from the depths of the ocean floor.'

Oholiab and Nehari, swords also drawn, were following the line of movement, trying to detect where the head was, whilst also shielding the boys. Without warning, the creature reared up, still cloaked behind the heavy weight of sand. The ground trembled as it arched and dove back down into the depths, toppling both boys to the floor. It writhed between them in a figure of eight before rearing up and crashing violently down again, causing a wave of wet sand to hit against the boys. As they clawed their way out, Asaph and the two guardians were back-to-back, in a circle, poised ready to strike.

'Jed, catch this,' Asaph ordered and tossed a leather bag across to him. Jed deftly caught it by the handle and then strapped it across his body.

The Serpent was moving again. Its slithering shape easily defined under the surface of the sand. It snaked between them so that Asaph and the boys were separated. Its body rose in an arch and Asaph thrust his sword deep into the middle of it. The creature withdrew in a slippery, frenzied retreat.

'Boys, listen to me. Take that bag and head to land. Everything you need is in there including a map. Go to the East Gate and I will catch up with you there.'

The land began to forcefully quake. The creature had burrowed deep down. Asaph realised it was going to tunnel up with all the strength it had to unleash its fury upon them.

'Quickly, go,' Asaph shouted. 'It will take a while for the dark forces to realise you are not with me. I will divert their attention and meet you as soon as I can.'

The Serpent began to spiral its way out of the ground like a tornado. The boys could make out the shape of its jagged head and open jowls. Higher and higher it rose, towering over them.

'Go,' Asaph shouted, urgency in his voice.

'But…' Ethan started to say. Jed pulled forcefully at his arm.

'Come on,' he ordered fiercely.

The boys turned and ran, leaving Asaph to battle the Sand Serpent alone. The tide was coming in and their steps were now splashing in shallow water. They didn't dare turn around to see what was happening behind them. The Guardians followed, while Asaph continued to hold the vile creature off until the boys had neared shore. The Serpent slithered its tail under him, and then lifted him up high, coiling its body around itself until its tail was level with its head. Asaph balanced himself, put both hands on the handle of his sword and brought it straight down through the top of its head and between the creature's eyes.

It froze for a second, the Serpent's shape held in suspense against the blue sky before plummeting down. Asaph managed to jump off it just before it crashed and sank into the depths of the sandy bed.

Asaph didn't pause to watch further but turned and sprinted towards the shore, splashing through the deepening waves. He needed to keep the eyes of the Underworld away from the boys and on himself for as long as possible.

The robed figure frowned as he watched from his vantage point on the Island. He had intended the Sand Serpent to defeat Asaph. 'At least the boys are now separated from him,' he thought to himself, hoping that the Underworld would quickly know this and act.

THE UNSEEN DIMENSION

Melchi and Japhron watched the various scenes unfolding before them. Wynere preparing for battle, seemingly unaware of the war that already waged among themselves; the Masquerader, using the power of the Underworld to awaken the ancient Sand Serpent; the flight of the boys to the East Gate accompanied by the two Guardians, Asaph acting as decoy to give them some time; And Naomi, for some reason, out of their view.

There was a lot happening, but if this was a prophecy unfolding, then all of this would be significant, Melchi thought to himself, wondering at the same time what Mia was up to.

Japhron looked over at him, 'Shall I go and get her?' he said in response to the unspoken thought from the ancient Seer.

'Not yet. Let her learn,' was the reply. 'She is in safe hands.'

CHAPTER SEVEN

CHERITH

 **THE UNSEEN DIMENSION**

Mia stood, unsure of how to go about her quest.

'What is it you are thinking?' the voice she had heard earlier spoke again.

Mia turned and looked but still could not see anyone.

'I am thinking about the women of the East Gate,' she answered. 'I was wondering if...' Suddenly, from all around, books began to leap off the shelves and line themselves up in front of her. Mia jumped back, startled.

'Oh,' she exclaimed. The fact that the books had found her was really, really helpful but, there were masses of them. They continued to fly from all over the Library, each flapping into place until there was a long, sweeping line of them that stretched far, far away.

'I only wanted to know about the ones who live there now,' she spoke out loud, hoping that the unseen voice would give her some help. As it happened, it was unnecessary, as the majority of books, on hearing what she said, all fluttered back up into the air and returned to wherever they had come from. Mia had to duck. It was like a swarm of butterflies were flying over her head.

When all was quiet, she stood up to find just one book hovering in front of her. It was large, blue in colour, with gold, embossed writing. Excited, Mia drew her finger over the title, enjoying the feeling of the bumpy words under her skin. Then, carefully, she turned the front cover.

The words inside jumped off the pages and separated into individual letters which danced about before her, causing her to step quickly back. Faster and faster, they swirled until all Mia could see was a kaleidoscope of colours that eventually materialised into an image. It was blurry at first. But the more she watched, the more in focus it became.

'This is the most exciting thing ever,' she breathed out in wonder.

She sat down on the floor, wrapped her hands around her knees, rested her chin upon them and watched with rapturous attention.

In front of her, the image of the East Gates was in view. She saw the waterfall and rivers that surrounded and ran through it and the mountains and meadows that overshadowed and dressed it. It was a beautiful place as far as the realm of man was concerned.

Two women stood within the grounds, dressed in flowing, purple garments that shimmered as they moved. Both were tall and regal in appearance. They were also remarkably similar in features.

'They look so very like Naomi,' she was thinking to herself when the unseen voice spoke.

'Remember, they are of the same house. They have much similarity both in gifting and in genealogy.'

'What are their names?'

'Reniah.' The face of this woman zoomed in close. Mia felt like the lady was actually watching her rather than the other way round. She noticed great wisdom in her features.

'And Shakirah,' the voice continued. Shakirah's face now gazed into Mia's own. There was a sense of grace and stoicism that ran through her being like a thread of silver.

'I wonder what their weaknesses are?' Mia thought.

The books pages rustled and yet more words bounced off from it and transformed into a visible image. This time, it wasn't of one scene but many involving, not just the two women just seen, but also Naomi, Nathan, Asaph, and another man whose name she did not yet know. Mia sat and watched the story of their lives unfold in picture form before her. Now and then she noticed that amidst the vibrant colours surrounding the women of the East

Gate, there was sometimes a splash of grey that appeared like a small bruise on their bodies or their heads.

'What is that?' she asked, hoping that the voice would answer, but this time, no one spoke.

'Show me where the grey marks come from,' Mia commanded the book.

The images reversed and re-ran themselves, this time much slower.

Mia saw the three women as children throwing a ball to each other. One was arguing about who was in charge and the older woman with them had to intervene. The pout on the child's face indicated that they were not happy with the outcome.

Time and time again, Mia saw this trait between two of the three young girls. A jostle for the lead and a jealous reaction. Sometimes it was friendly competition. Sometimes it was not. And when this happened, the grey mark appeared. Sometimes it was on their head as a thought was not resolved kindly. Sometimes it settled on their heart as a negative emotion became embedded there. The children grew into young women and those moments came into view less. However, the grey bruises remained.

Mia watched scene after scene and saw the personalities of each woman unfold. Reniah, the eldest held great wisdom and kindness and insight. She often withdrew from crowds though and could be seen, a solitary figure, roaming the hills or standing near the waterfalls surrounding the city.

Shakirah, the homemaker, never seemed to wander far from the grounds of the house. She was often looking for approval from the other two and glowed with happiness when she was surrounded by family and friends. Mia noticed that she appeared sad when everyone was absent from home, wandering about aimlessly looking for something to do or someone to talk to. Mia found herself feeling slightly sorry for her and then felt bad for this. Shakirah was, after all, a woman of the East Gate. Beautiful and noble and filled with insight.

Naomi was the warrior. All through her life she had shown an adventurous spirit. It was she that attracted men's attention. And it was she that was the most confident. Athletic, quick witted and with the beauty marking all three women, she was indeed blessed. Mia watched all these things enact before her eyes and then blinked hard as the features of Naomi looked straight at her. Perfect, apart from a grey mark upon her forehead.

Hearing footsteps, Mia jumped to her feet. 'Enough for today I think,' she said to herself and faster than a wink, the images returned into letters and then into words. The book opened its pages to them, and they fluttered back to their home. The book itself then closed around them and flapped back to its place in the Library until all was still.

'There you are,' Japhron looked at her, and noticed her head was full of new memories and information. 'Melchi sent me to look for you.'

'I guess he will admonish me as he did imply that I was too young and inexperienced to be here, but I just didn't want to disturb you and I have found out such mysteries that I think will help us unravel who the betrayer is and…'

Japhron interrupted her. 'You must be careful young Mia. It takes great wisdom to look upon the past and view it correctly in the present.'

They left through the giant doors. From within the Library, another door closed as someone left from a different exit. The light in the Library immediately dimmed.

⚔ CHERITH

Melchi was watching Ethan and Jed as they scrambled over the rocky, pebbled beach to the cliff face that towered in front of them.

'Over here,' Jed called out once he had discovered the clumsy, stone ledges that had been dug into the rock to form an uneven set of steps leading to the top. Ethan ran over, pausing when he saw what he had to climb. He looked at them dubiously.

'Come on,' Jed ordered, irritated by Ethan's hesitancy. He started to ascend, using the overhanging boulders and tufts of grasses to pull himself up. Ethan followed slowly behind, checking each step gingerly before committing to placing his full weight on them.

Oholiab went in front and Nehari behind to ensure all was well and to catch the boys should they stumble. It was in this way that they eventually reached the green, mossy cliff top.

The air here was fragrant, still the tangy, salty ocean breeze but also the smell of earth and grass. Both boys, bent over from the exertion of the climb, breathed in deeply as if their bodies instinctively knew that they needed the good, clean, fresh air to flush out the toxicity of where they had come from.

Jed looked back down to the cove below. The tide was fully in now and there was no trace of the sandy pathway or the Serpent or Asaph.

'I hope he got to land alright!' he thought to himself uneasily before kneeling down and emptying the contents of the bag onto the grass. Ethan came over to look.

It was a random selection of objects. A map, an ornate vial holding some kind of liquid, a net that appeared immensely strong despite being finely woven, a dagger and an elaborately decorated key. It also contained two leather water pouches and both boys grabbed one and drank thirstily of its contents before spreading out the map to examine it.

The East Gate and their current position were clearly marked and appeared to almost be in a straight line from each other. Jed folded the parchment back up and placed everything back into the bag.

'Right, let's go. I think we need to head in this direction,' he instructed, already striding over the grassy space to the road ahead.

Ethan was so tired that he was quite happy for Jed to take charge. He was beginning to feel light-headed from a lack of sleep and the adventures of the day so far.

The cliff top met a dusty, gravelly road that led them further inland. The boys found themselves walking with steep rock on their left and stone walls, edging against rolling, green hills on their right. Trees grew from behind the wall, arching over the road and creating intricate, lacy, shadowy patterns around them.

Ethan was getting slower and slower. 'I think we should stop for a bit,' he called out to Jed.

Jed didn't like to admit it to Ethan but was also feeling very tired. 'Alright, if you need to rest, we can try to find somewhere away from the road,' he said as he continued to stride on ahead.

A little further on he came to a stile which led over the rocky wall and into dense, green woodland. All around was quiet. The leafy trees within extended their branches in interlocking archways offering both shade and refuge. A gentle breeze blew around Jed's curls and he lifted his hand to swipe them out of his eyes. He called out to Ethan who was lagging some way behind.

'Let's see where this leads,' he called out. Without waiting for Ethan to catch up, Jed climbed up and over the stile and then jumped down, not noticing a mound of rock that lay half hidden under the mossy earth. As he landed, the rock caused him to lose his balance and he fell, twisting his knee. A jolt of pain caused the colour to drain from his face and a feeling of nausea rose in his throat.

'Are you alright?' Ethan questioned as he carefully climbed down from the stile.

'Yes, I'm fine,' Jed replied curtly. He stood up cautiously and tried putting his weight down onto his injured leg. He gasped as another current of pain shocked his body. 'I'll be alright in a minute,' he said shrugging away Ethan's offer of support. 'You go ahead and see if there's anywhere where we can rest.'

Ethan hesitated before running off, leaving Jed to slowly limp down the dry, dirt path that lay in front of him, trying to be careful to not jolt his knee over any exposed tree root that poked up from beneath the ground. 'How am I going to make it to the East Gate?' he questioned, frustrated at having hurt himself and sweating with the effort of walking.

'Jed, I've found somewhere,' he heard Ethan call out, thankfully from not too far away. The boy came back into view. 'There's a shed, just around this bend. It's not far.' Ethan waited for Jed to catch him up and then led the way down a short dirt path to a wooden hut. No one appeared to be about, although a fire had not long gone out. The grey ash within was still warm.

'Hello,' Ethan called out.

'Ssshhhh,' Jed glared at him as he cautiously pushed open the door and tentatively peered in.

'It's empty,' he whispered to Ethan. 'Come on.'

Once inside, they found themselves in what appeared to be a tool shed, but there was a bed in it and a low wooden chair. A work bench lay against one wall on which various carvings that had been chiselled out of wood were laid. The smell of the wood was comforting. As was the quiet.

'Do you think it's alright for us to be in here?' Ethan asked picking up one of the wooden sculptures of a woman holding hands with a small boy. The image made him sad for some reason and he quickly put it back down.

Jed shrugged, 'I don't know, but I'm not going anywhere,' he replied as he gently lowered himself onto the bed and propped up his knee with a rolled-up blanket. 'We won't stay long.'

Ethan sank into the chair and closed his eyes. He could hear the chirruping and whistling of the birds from outside and a sense of peace enveloped him. After a few minutes, despite everything, both boys had fallen into a deep sleep.

Oholiab stood at the door while Nehari kept watch at the window. They sensed that the Underworld was still unaware that the boys were not in the company of Asaph and so were happy for them to waste a little time resting.

Nathan stood holding Naomi's boots in his hands. He and three others, who were skilled in the art of tracking, had painstakingly searched the route that Naomi should have taken, and this was the first piece of evidence they had found of her having been there. He looked at the boots wondering why she had taken them off.

'What were you doing?' he whispered out loud. He turned as one of the trackers approached him.

'Nathan, it looks like she may have laid here in the gorse.' Abigail beckoned him to follow her so that she could show him the flattened imprint. 'These indentations show she would have been lying face down. Can you see?' She knelt into the flattened areas of gorse to indicate how Naomi would have lain.

'There are hoof prints leading down towards the river,' someone else called out from beyond. 'It looks like two beasts.'

Nathan frowned. 'So, something caused her to hide and then she and her horse were either taken or willingly led away? Is that what we are saying?'

Abigail had continued to search the gorse and now saw a glint of something embedded deep down in the bush. Using a piece of cloth, she carefully picked it up and held it to the light.

'Nathan, look at this!' she called to him. 'This looks like a stinger from a Scorpion Wasp.' She held it out for Nathan to look at.

As he examined it, the third tracker came running up from the direction of the river.

'There are two sets of hoof prints on the other side of the river heading towards Hymangees,' he informed them.

Nathan mounted his horse. 'Send word to Reniah and Shakirah. They may have some more insight into all of this. I will ride to Hymangees to see if there is any sign of Naomi there. I will meet you back at the East Gate.'

Reniah had spent the morning travelling to the veiled mountains. She now stood on a ledge behind the great waterfall, gazing at the rush of water that fell in relentless torrent into the river beneath it. The whereabouts of Naomi and the news of what had happened over in Wynere had deeply troubled her and she found the thunderous noise was a balm to her ruffled spirit. As she stared, the noise retreated, and the rushing water hung still, as though suspended in time. Within the centre of it, an image began to come into focus, and as it became clearer, she saw it was of Naomi's face. She could see the outline of her brow, the high cheekbones and defined jaw. She saw the almond shaped, green eyes, the olive skin, and the long, dark, silky hair, parted in the middle. Her mouth was curled in a smile, and she brought up her hand as though to wave. So real was this that Reniah found herself raising her own hand to wave back. Suddenly, into the scene, out of nowhere, a great flame appeared, and the image became distorted in its fierce blaze. Naomi's face wavered in it for a second longer before disintegrating and, without any warning, the flame was suddenly snuffed out leaving a cold chill in the air. Reniah shivered and not just with the cold.

Naomi stirred. She had no idea of the day or the time or of what had happened to her. Tentatively, she sat up. Her vision was clear again and, from the light of burning candles, she saw that she had been moved and was now in a cave, lying on a handful of blankets and cushions. The cave itself was dry and smelt of earth and dusty rock and she could see from the flickering shadows that the walls were covered with what looked like childish drawings. She stared at them. The story they told seemed vaguely familiar to her but, try as she might, it was all out of focus and blurred around the edges. She felt her brain was searching hard for some clarity, but it was as though it was a futile hunt for a memory that was not her own.

Someone had placed some water in an earthenware bowl next to her. Picking it up, she sniffed at it cautiously and then drank thirstily before falling back down on the cushions and closing her eyes, exhausted with the effort.

Immediately, images assaulted her of dark, foreboding creatures, of fire, blood dripping into a goblet, a twisted smile in a pale face, the swish of a cloak as someone turned away from her view, a flame burning – its colour vibrant. She saw her own face, suspended in the wavering flame and then, suddenly, the light went out.

Ethan was stirred from sleep by the sound of scuffling. He opened his eyes and the first thing he saw was a brown and white dog with long, silky ears sitting, staring at him. Seeing Ethan was awake, the dog's tail began to thump against the floor, and he gave a small bark. Ethan leaned forward to stroke him, and the dog flopped to the floor before rolling onto his back for Ethan to rub his tummy.

'Ee's taken a liking to thee,' a voice came from behind Ethan's chair. Startled, he jumped to his feet.

'Don't ye go a gettin' all afraid like.'

'I'm s-sorry…,' Ethan stammered. 'We needed somewhere to rest. Jed hurt his knee and couldn't walk very far.' His voice faltered, not knowing what else was safe to say.

The elderly man glanced over at Jed who was still fast asleep on the bed. 'Aye, I can see t' lad is int' pain. Let 'im be.' Jed was evidently restless and even in his sleep he let out a small groan.

'Now, 'ow about ye tell me yer name and yer story and how ye came to be 'iding out in my shed? It wouldn't 'ave anything to do with Asaph now would it?'

'Do you know Asaph?' Ethan asked, relieved.

The man laughed a deep laugh that caused his periwinkle blue eyes to light up in his tanned, weathered face. 'Aye. I know Asaph. Him and I go way, way back,' the man answered. 'My family 'ave been gardeners on these lands for many a generation. Amos is my name, and I can recognise new apprentices when I see 'em.'

Any reservation Ethan had evaporated with that laugh. It was as though the sun had suddenly shone through the window, casting out any shadow of fear that lurked around Ethan's heart.

Jed stirred. The sound of friendly chatter reached his ears. Sitting up, he looked around, but the shed was empty. The smell of a fire wafted through the open door though and he could hear Ethan's voice coming from beyond it. He tried moving his leg, but the swelling on his knee caused him to flinch.

'Let me 'ave a look at that there leg of yours young 'un,' a deep voice said.

Looking up, Jed saw an elderly man, dressed for outdoor work, standing in the doorway. He had thick, grey bushy eyebrows that hung over startling blue eyes and smelt of freshly mown grass and earth. A dog was stood at his side, wagging his tail.

'Where's Ethan?' was all he managed to say.

'Out there, stirrin' a pot of stew. Right then, roll up yer trouser leg and let's see what damage yer done to yersen.'

Jed struggled to understand what the man was saying. His way of talking was broad and of an accent he didn't recognise.

'Aye, you'se right twisted that. Is there anythin' in yer bag that may 'elp?' the old man said.

For reasons Jed didn't understand, as it went against his very nature, he found himself both liking and trusting this man. He reached for the bag and emptied the contents out beside him.

'That'll do,' the man exclaimed, picking up the small vial. He pulled out the stopper and sniffed at it before letting a few drops of the contents fall onto the wounded knee. The liquid bubbled and foamed and then there was the sound of a slight click. Immediately the swelling went down, and the pain completely subsided. Jed tentatively bent his knee and sighed with relief.

'I can't believe it!' he said, wonder in his voice.

'Well, that's Asaph for yer. Ee will always make sure you'se got what yer need to do whatever ee 'as asked yer to do.' the man said with a smile. Now 'ow bout some food?'

Jed didn't need to be asked a second time. 'Yes please,' he said with a grin as he jumped to his feet.

That hour spent in the company of Amos was one that left an impression on the boys for years to come. The old gardener had regaled them with stories of the land and the earth as though they were age old friends.

'I were taught to speak t'earth an' t'flowers an' t'shrubs like they can 'ear me like. An', I am t'sure that be true. Time agin, I 'ave talked to an ailing snip of a thing that 'as then bloomed and blossomed.'

He spoke of the battles fought and the Cherithite ways, some that he had been told and others that he had lived through.

'Did you fight in the Barlkron wars?' Ethan asked without thinking, and been answered by a long, hearty laugh. The old man's face had wrinkled with mirth until tears had run down his cheeks, causing both boys to laugh with him.

'Nay lad. I were nowt but a mere twinkle in my Mam's eyes and she in her Mam's eyes and I can keep sayin' that for generation to generation. Aye. T'last battle I fought was over in't Southwest when the Edomites went t'war against the King of Jachin. Sad tale that be. T'land there now be desolate and t'King never found.'

'Tell us more about Asaph,' Jed asked as he helped himself to the last scrape of stew.

'Asaph now. Well, he be full of strength and truth and nobility that be for sure. But, far be it me to tell yer. You will see for yoursen as yer training continues. He is best known by actually knowing him like. Not just from me passin' on me own tale.'

Throughout the conversation, the boys began to feel the connection to their own culture and heritage. This was their land and history that he talked of. Ethan felt his world expand beyond him and his grandpa. Jed felt as though he were no longer an orphan and had a link to something far greater than he had ever understood.

Oholiab watched on. He was enjoying getting to know his young charge and liked the adventurous, warrior spirit he sensed in Jed.

Nehari laughed at him. 'You are growing fond of him already I see!'

'As are you!' Oholiab said, nodding in Ethan's direction.

'He is a noble one, full of compassion and with a strong heart,' Nehari agreed.

 ## THE UNSEEN DIMENSION

From beyond time, Melchi and Japhron also looked on. The Guardians had a great ability in being able to see the boys as they would be and not as they currently were. It was a vital gift in the role that they had to play. Mia watched but her attention was not as it should have been. She was still trying to make sense of what she had seen in the Library with what she was seeing in front of her.

Melchi glanced at his young charge. 'I must keep a check on her insights,' he thought to himself.

CHERITH

Amos had sent the boys to wash in the small stream that lay just beyond the shed.

'Yer don't want to arrive at t' East Gate smellin' of t' Island now,' he said. 'You'se be wantin' to make a good impression.'

The stream was crystal clear and freezing cold, happily gurgling over pebbles and rocks and between boulders. The view beyond it was of gentle, rolling, green hills, home to woolly sheep who were tame enough to come near to the water's edge, bleating indignantly at the sight of two humans splashing about in their territory. The quiet of the countryside caused different reactions in the boys. To Ethan it was soothing and restorative. To Jed it was unsettling. He was so used to being alert to danger or threat that even in quietness he found it hard to fully relax.

While they were gone, Amos spread out the parchment map over his knees and studied it, tracing various routes with his finger, his brow furrowed in concentration as he tried to envisage the best route that the boys should take.

'It looks like yer best 'eading for t' Tunnels of Tamore,' he said to them when they returned, still damp from their wash in the stream, their hair glistening. I can take yer there on my cart and then all yer need to do is 'ead straight through t' tunnels in a straight line like. It will bring yer out at t'East Gate.'

'That would be amazing,' Ethan said, greatly relieved. He

had thought they would be walking for hours in country that was unfamiliar to them and was also aware that, by stopping to rest, they were probably way behind Asaph by now. This was going so much better than he could have hoped for.

'Now then, gather yer things,' Amos instructed as he lit two lamps from the embers of the fire before spreading earth over it, putting it out. He handed one to each of the boys. 'Try keep em lit. You'se'll need 'em in't tunnels for there be no light inside there.'

From the Underworld Barlkron looked on. 'I see you,' he said out loud to himself. He quickly turned causing the dark creatures sitting around him to scatter out of his way to avoid being trodden on. One didn't move quick enough and was now a squelchy, inky, stagnant puddle on the floor. The others shrieked and withdrew even further from the Lord of the Underworld.

The boys sat among sacks of potatoes in the back of the cart, carefully holding the lamps that Amos had given them. They had ridden down winding roads and across fields with the sun casting its friendly warmth down upon them. Amos, his dog beside him, whistled as they went, lilting melodies that neither of the boys had heard before.

'Have you ever seen the lighted flame, Amos,' Ethan had shouted once there was a lull in the music.

'Aye, that I have, and it were the most terrifyin' and bootiful thing I ever beheld,'

'How did it come to be in the first place?' Jed asked. Not having been brought up in a family environment, Jed was not so aware of his heritage as Ethan. Much of what he knew had been passed on in dribs and drabs or learnt from books.

'Well then. There were a time long ago when t' ways of Cherith were well known among all mankind and t'world that yer know. People were governed by one King. T'King of Cherith,' Amos said this proudly, as though he was actually announcing the entrance of the King to them. 'In them days, life were lived to a diff'rent pattern to t' one we use now. T'ground were fruitful like, and there were none that were poor.

'Barlkron, though ee were na called that then, once served t'

King but his heart were proud and t' shadow of conceit began to eat away at 'im till he were consumed. Taking wit 'im sum of t'King's men he rose against Cherith, and, for a long time, war waged.

'The rift between Cherith and t' rest of t' world grew larger as t' years passed, for Barlkron were determined to erase all memory of it and of t' King. Things that were grown for their healing properties now began to poison and corrupt instead.'

'So that was the time of the Barlkron wars?' Jed interrupted.

'Aye. That they were and they were indeed dark times. T'King of Cherith fashioned two weapons to bring light, guidance and protection to his people. T'Oil and t'Sword. While these have remained among t' Cherithite people, Barlkron canna destroy em. It's these emblems that light the flame.'

'And the flame is in Wynere?'

'Aye. That be right. While it burns, there is peace on these 'ere lands for all who will accept it and live by t'Cherithite ways.'

'What if it ever went out?' Jed asked.

'That not be worth thinking 'bout young un. Right,' he said finishing the conversation, 'We be not far away now.'

'I'm so glad we found Amos,' Ethan whispered to Jed. He then tutted. 'I've just remembered something.'

'What?' Jed said only half listening.

'The day I was taken to the Castle a small girl asked me to give you a message, only I didn't know who you were at the time.'

Jed looked at him, 'Well?' he prompted Ethan to continue.

'It was just to tell you that she had found Amos. Does that mean anything?'

Jed nodded with a glimmer of a smile. 'That will have been Sianna. Amos is her pet monkey.'

'Is Sianna your sister?'

Jed scowled. He wasn't comfortable being asked personal questions. 'No. I don't have family. Sianna's mum would give me food sometimes.' He turned away from Ethan and gazed at the rocky incline on his side of the road hoping Ethan would stop talking to him.

Ethan took the hint. He sensed Jed didn't like him very much and who could blame him after everything he had done to him. 'Jed, I'm…' he started to say but was interrupted by Amos shouting down to them.

'We're in Tamore and are nearly at t' tunnels. I hope yer lamps are still burnin',' he said.

The Guardians looked at each other. They knew that while Jed continued to hold a grudge towards Ethan, and if Ethan allowed guilt to keep weighing him down, they would both attract dark forces towards them. Already these two warriors had sensed some movement from the Underworld. It had become known that the boys were not currently in the company of Asaph.

'I'm glad that we are not far from the East Gate,' Nehari said.

'Let us hope that there is nothing awaiting them in the tunnels,' was the grim response.

'Right en, young 'uns,' the gardener called to them. 'This is where yer need to be off. The tunnel yer need is right there on yer left.'

The boys looked at the gaping entrance which was easily accessible from the road.

'Remember, ter go straight ahead like. No turnin' off or you'se'll be lost,' the gardener warned them.

'Amos, thank you,' Jed called as he jumped down off the cart.

Ethan looked over at the elderly man. 'Go on wit yer now,' the gardener said gruffly acknowledging the unspoken thanks. 'Give me best t' Asaph when you see 'im.' Ethan nodded and smiled before jumping off the cart to join Jed. They both watched until the horse and cart had turned round the bend and disappeared from view before turning to face the mouth of the tunnel that lay waiting for them.

Jed didn't hesitate and went straight in holding his lamp up high. 'Come on,' he called to Ethan, 'let's get to the East Gate.'

Ethan glanced behind him briefly before setting his foot inside the tunnel and following Jed into its depths.

THE UNSEEN DIMENSION

Melchi and Japhron watched. They had sensed the movement from the Underworld. Barlkron would certainly not want Ethan or Jed to reach the protection of the East Gate, but as long as the boys did not stray from the path they had been shown, and used what they had been given, the Guardians would be able to protect them from any scheme the Underworld had to harm them.

Mia was fidgeting in her chair. She desperately wanted to see behind the East Gates but, for some reason, it seemed that she would have to wait for the boys to get there first.

CHAPTER EIGHT

THE TUNNELS OF TAMORE

◆ CHERITH

The tunnel was wide and high and stretched out straight in front of the boys. Jed shouted and heard his voice echo back at him. He shouted again, 'Woohoo…'

'Woo woo woo,' the echo bounced back.

Ethan joined in. 'We are Cherithite warriors,' the sound came back but it was confused and distorted.

'You're saying too much,' Jed told him.

Ethan was quiet. He did not want to tempt the echo or Jed to mock him again.

Nehari glanced at him and then at Oholiab. 'There is much to undo in them,' he commented.

'True. But that is the same for everyone. They will learn,' was the reply.

The deeper they journeyed into the dark, the more the boys realised that the tunnel they were in was merely one of a group of underground passages, the others of which branched out either side of them.

'I'm glad we are going straight,' Ethan remarked. 'We could easily get lost otherwise.'

'Stay here a minute,' Jed said. 'I just want to see what is down one of them.'

'Don't Jed. We should keep together.'

'I won't be long. Just stay here and wait for me,' was the response. 'Here, catch this,' he threw the bag at Ethan who caught it and strapped it across his shoulder as Jed ran off down the tunnel on his left. Ethan sighed with frustration.

The passageway that Jed had taken wound in a twist of bends. He lifted his lamp high above his head to project a longer beam of light out in front of him and immediately his attention was caught by the sight of strange drawings on the cave walls.

'Ethan, come and take a look at this,' he shouted back towards the way he had just come.

He was met with silence. 'Fine. Stay where you are then,' he tutted as he continued to follow the direction of the pictures. They were crudely drawn, almost childlike in their appearance, and reminded him of the pictures that Sianna would sometimes draw.

As he continued to walk, examining the walls, he felt his right foot step on something hard. Lifting his boot, he bent down to see what it was. It looked like an old metal clasp, the sort that would hold the top of a cloak together. Jed picked it up to examine it more closely and it was then that he heard footsteps coming from beyond him. Looking up, he thought he saw the outline of someone disappearing out of view. In that moment a waft of stagnant air, seemingly from out of nowhere blew around him. And then his lamp went out.

Ethan stood in the tunnel, nervously waiting for Jed to return. It felt like he had been gone for ages although in truth it had only been a few minutes. His lamp flickered.

'Jed, hurry up,' he shouted into the tunnel entrance. He was greeted with silence, not even a strain of an echo.

Ethan wondered what to do. He was torn between staying on the route that Amos had instructed and following Jed, but he decided to wait where he was as the gardener had been so insistent that the boys should not stray off the straight path and had pointed out how easy it would be to get lost.

'Jed,' he called out again, impatiently.

Jed was trying to get his bearings. He knew that the tunnel he was in had twisted around but there had been no others leading off from it so he was confident that he could find his way back. He edged to the left-hand side, feeling for the rough rock and then slowly followed its outline. Something flapped past him. 'A bat!' he thought to himself and gave an involuntary shudder. He could hear the flapping of more wings from behind him. Jed went a little faster.

Oholiab followed. He was unable to do much at this moment as Jed had strayed off the instructed path. The boy would have to realise this for the Guardian to be released to help. He glanced behind him. His highly tuned hearing could hear a multitude of leathery wings.

'Come on, young warrior. Call for help,' he said out loud.

'Ethan,' Jed shouted. He was met with silence. The turns of the tunnel were blocking his voice from carrying very far.

The sound of flapping wings was growing louder. A couple of creatures flew past and one landed on his shoulder gripping its sharp talons into him. He shook it off and started to run.

'Ethan,' he shouted as loud as he could.

Ethan had grown restless with waiting and had sat down on the tunnel floor, placed the lamp on the ground beside him, and was examining the small dagger which Asaph had given to them. He fingered the pattern which had been intricately carved into the handle wondering, as he did so, who had made it and what battles it may have known. Lost in his imagination, he didn't see the bat that came flying out of the tunnel, until he felt it close to his face. Ethan jumped to his feet, resisting the urge to scream, and flattened himself against the rocky wall. The creature was followed by a few others. He glanced at them as they flew off down the tunnel but as he watched, one stopped, turned slowly back around, looked him right in the eye and flew straight at him. Ethan swiped up the lamp and swung it at the creature. The flame within it illuminated the bats face and this time Ethan did let out a yell for the bat had fangs and red eyes. It hissed in his face, a loud, vicious, gravelly sound from the back of its throat. Ethan slashed frantically at the air around it with the dagger and the creature flew away, leaving a nasty smell behind.

'Jed,' he shouted as loud as he could before quickly turning back to see where these evil things had gone. They had, thankfully, disappeared out of view.

'I'm coming,' came Jed's voice.

Ethan was so relieved that he stepped into the opening of the tunnel. Lifting his lamp, he stared intently into the dark, hoping for a glimpse of Jed.

'Ethan, get ready to run,' Jed's voice came over urgently. 'There's something coming behind me.'

Ethan could hear it. It wasn't a sound that he recognised. It was like a thousand trees rustling in a breeze but with a steady flapping beat to it. It wasn't just the sinister sound that made his heart beat harder in fear, it was also the smell. There was a foul, rotten stench that was permeating the air. It made his stomach retch. It was worse than anything he had ever known, even from on the Island.

At last, he saw Jed pelting towards him, his eyes wide.

'Where's your lamp?' Ethan yelled.

'Went out,' Jed panted. 'Come on, we need to go.'

He had hardly finished speaking before the creatures began surging out of the tunnel behind him. Both boys instinctively dropped to the floor.

Ethan hurriedly reached into the bag and pulled out the net.

'Quick,' he ordered, 'get under this.'

With fumbling fingers they unravelled the net, hastily pulling it over themselves, as best they could, kicking against it as it tangled around them. There they lay, huddled, clutching the net tightly over their heads as what seemed like hundreds of the bat like creatures flew over them.

Oholiab and Nehari drew their shields and covered the boys so that none of the evil things could land on them.

From the depths of the Underworld, Barlkron growled and, further down the tunnel, the bats stopped in their tracks. In the dark they began to transform, their bodies separating into hundreds of thousands of large flies. They made no noise but hovered in the air waiting silently for the next command.

'Did you see them up close,' Ethan said to Jed as the last of the creatures had disappeared down the tunnel, leaving nothing but a foul stench behind them. The boys were still trying to disentangle themselves from the net.

'No, but did you smell them. It was foul.' Jed stomped on the net with his right foot so that he could pull his left away, but it caught again on his boot causing him to bend down and forcibly pull it off. He angrily cast it aside.

'I know. I thought I was going to retch. One hissed in my face. It had fangs and its eyes were red.' Ethan spoke whilst bending down to retrieve the discarded net. Bundling it up he shoved it back into the bag.

'I'm glad my lamp went out then,' Jed replied and pulled a face.

Relief made the boys talk fast, reliving the experience as people often do when, having faced the same danger, they have come out of it unscathed.

'I told you not to go in there,' Ethan chided him.

Jed tutted. 'I think someone was down there. I found this,' he said by way of changing the subject. He handed Ethan the clasp.

'I think Asaph had one like this,' Ethan remarked after examining it under the light of the one lamp. 'I'll put it in the bag with everything else and then let's get out of here. We are hopefully not far from the East Gate now.'

Nathan had, at last, reached Hymangees. There was little to look at here. Old, crumbling, stone pillars stood in a vast open space; the only remains of what had once been a small castle. The wasteland on which he stood was yellow and aged with a few dried-out bushes scattered around which rolled about aimlessly in the humid breeze. A large bird screeched overhead and swooped, lifted a small hare in its talons, and bore it away. Nathan watched as it soared out of sight. There was no sign that anyone or anything else had been here, no remnant of a fire, no hoof or footprint in the dusty ground. It was what he had always known it to be. An empty, desolate wilderness.

'This is a typical ploy of the enemy to have me wasting so much time. I should have known better,' he chided himself as he swung himself back onto his horse.

Barlkron smiled. His plan to keep Nathan out of the way was working well. 'I will wear you all down with suspicion and distrust if you keep playing into my hands like this,' he muttered to himself.

The boys had walked further into the depths of the tunnel by the light of the one lamp.

'Why didn't you bring yours with you? We could have relit it.' Ethan commented.

'I didn't think of it.' Jed replied, annoyed with himself but not wanting Ethan to know that. 'We can't be too far away though.'

The tunnel curved round in a bend and the boys followed its direction before stopping. In front of them was nothing but rock. There was a tunnel leading from the right and one to their left but there was no route straight ahead.

Ethan frowned. 'What do we do?' he asked Jed. 'Amos said to keep on the straight path.'

'Well, there isn't one,' Jed replied sharply. 'Maybe there's been an earthquake or something that has brought these rocks down.'

'It doesn't look like it,' Ethan said peering at the wall in front of them. This looks like it has been built.'

'Maybe he got it wrong. It's probably been years since he was last here. Let's try one of these other passageways.'

'I don't think that's a good idea. Look at what happened last time you disturbed what was hidden in a tunnel you weren't supposed to be in.'

Jed scowled. 'Have you got a better idea?'

Ethan hadn't.

'Show me the map,' Jed demanded. Let's see if there's anything on it that will help us.

'I'll hold the lamp. You look inside the bag,' Ethan suggested, turning round so that Jed could get at it.

The boy rummaged in the bag for the parchment map, his hand brushing against the small vial as he did so.

'Come on now. Think!' Oholiab said.

Jed paused. 'Amos said to me that Asaph would have given us everything we need for whatever he has asked us to do,' he said to Ethan. 'There must be something in here that will help us.'

He fingered the net, the clasp. 'Is there something that this would fit into?' he asked, lifting up the ornate, iron key.

Improbable as it seemed, hope rose in the boys. They carefully searched the rocky impasse before them for any sign of a keyhole.

It was tedious work with the light of only one lamp.

'Nothing!' Ethan sighed, ages later.

'That only leaves the dagger,' Jed commented as he picked it up and stared at it.

'I can't see that doing much,' Ethan said glumly.

'Me neither,' Jed agreed as he jabbed feebly at the wall with the small blade.

Ethan looked up quickly. 'Do that again, Jed,' he said, holding the lamp up higher and peering more intently at the rocks.

Jed jabbed at the wall again.

'Did you see that?' Ethan said excitedly.

'See what?'

'Give me the dagger and you stand and hold the lamp. I'll show you.'

Jed held the lamp up as high as he could while Ethan jabbed at the wall with the dagger. The blade hit what felt like rock but the whole wall quivered as though it was just a painting on a sheet of cloth.

'Do that again,' Jed demanded, peering closer.

Ethan stabbed harder, a few jabs this time. The rocks shimmered and wavered again.

'Do you see it?' Ethan demanded.

'I do. It looks like the whole wall is a mirage,' Jed said with confusion in his voice as he peered closely at the rock. He paused. 'Maybe that's what it is,' he said excitedly. 'Maybe it's just a test and none of this is actually real.'

Oholiab laughed, a deep, sound that resonated around the space they were in.

'He's on the right track,' Nehari said. 'But I'm not sure this is part of Asaph's plan. The air still stinks.'

Both Guardians drew their swords.

'What should we do?' Ethan asked.

'I don't know,' Jed replied. 'But maybe if what is in front of us is not actually there, we should just run at it? You go first with the dagger in front of you and I will follow on behind.'

Ethan looked uncertain. 'It feels real though,' he said hesitantly as he poked the dagger at the wall and felt the resistance of its rocky exterior.

'Have you a better idea?' Jed asked impatiently.

'Maybe you go first?'

Jed tutted with impatience. 'Give me the dagger.'

The boys stood behind each other. Ethan carried the lamp and the bag and Jed the small knife.

'I think we should just run at it really hard.'

'At least we have the magic healing potion if we should knock ourselves out,' Ethan said.

'We won't be able to use it, if we are knocked out,' came Jed's sarcastic reply. 'Come on. On the count of three.'

He counted. 'One, two, three.'

They ran towards the wall, Jed with the dagger stretched out in front of him. As he reached the impasse, his arm and hand, which was holding the blade, disappeared straight through the rocky image and as this happened the whole wall disintegrated into a monstrous swarm of large flies. They rose into the air, with a crack like thunder.

'Run,' Jed shouted.

Ethan did not hesitate. They pelted through the cloud of winged creatures with an arm held over their mouths because of the smell that was attacking their nostrils.

The two Guardians held up their swords and flashes of blinding light emanated from them causing the flies to panic. They swarmed up into the air above the boy's heads.

'I can see light,' Jed's muffled voice shouted at Ethan through the protection of his sleeve.

The darkness of the tunnel began to dissipate as the exit came into view and the boys, with great relief, spilled out of it. The flies came after them, surging high into the air and evaporating out of sight.

From the Island, the robed figure heard the rumble of anger from the Underworld and flinched.

The boys stood side by side looking around them. The tunnel had brought them out onto a mountainside where a dirt path wound gracefully to the bottom of it. From their vantage point, through the tall trees, they could see the ornate iron structures of what had to be the East Gates.

'We made it,' Ethan smiled.

Jed grinned. 'Come on,' he shouted as he ran down the path towards them.

Oholiab and Nehari ran gently behind.

'They did well back there,'Nehari shouted in triumph.

'They did indeed,' Oholiab agreed, smiling.

THE UNSEEN DIMENSION

Melchi and Japhron applauded.

Mia's attention was still fixed on the sight of the East Gates and the land that lay behind them.

'I wonder if I'm right?' she was thinking to herself, impatient to see what was beyond them.

CHAPTER NINE

THE EAST GATE

CHERITH

The East Gates were steeped in history. They had withstood the Barlkron wars, the battle of the Seven Moons, fire and flood and yet, to look at them, you would never know. They towered high between the walls that surrounded the land of Twyndale, proud, beautiful and yet also formidable in their appearance.

'My grandpa told me that these were built by the Espionites,' Ethan said, as he gazed up at them, impressed by the architecture.

'I've heard of the Espionites,' Jed remarked. 'Didn't they use their knowledge of battles and skill in weaponry to make an alliance with the Underworld?'

Ethan nodded. 'My grandpa said that they have kept themselves to themselves since the battle of the Seven Moons when they were defeated by Wynere.'

'Well, that's probably a good thing,' Jed said as he examined the gates. 'How do you think we are supposed to get in?'

As he said this, the gates began to open away from them and they could see, standing in the middle of the gap, two women, each dressed in dark blue flowing trousers and long tunics. Both were olive skinned with green eyes and dark hair that shimmered like a sheet of silk down to their waists. They moved with great dignity and elegance which caused both boys to suddenly feel unkempt and clumsy.

'Welcome to Twyndale,' one said with a smile that somehow gave the impression that their arrival had been greatly longed for.

'We are the women of the East Gate,' the other said, also with a large smile that banished all nervousness from the boys. 'I am Reniah, and this is Shakira, and you are both most welcome. We have been expecting you.'

Shakira beckoned the boys forward with a graceful movement of her hand. 'Now, have you the key that allows you access?'

Ethan rummaged in the bag for the final item that Asaph had packed for them. He grasped the ornate key and handed it over.

'Is this it?' he asked uncertainly.

'It is. The key to the city. All who enter must have one.' She handed the key back to Ethan who looked puzzled by this. 'Whoever enters here must feel that they can come and go as they choose.' Shakira explained, smiling all the while.

The boys stared around them as they entered, a little overwhelmed by their surroundings for Twyndale was the most beautiful place they had ever imagined. Ahead of them, in the far distance, lay the realms of the veiled mountains, which were shrouded in mist so that they were but a blurred image, glowing in hazy pastel colours. A waterfall cascaded through the haze, flowing in turn into a river that eventually landed in a crystal-clear pool in the grounds of Twyndale. Reniah and Shakira went and filled a golden bowl with water from its depths and held one out to each boy.

'Please,' they encouraged them, 'wash your hands and face and be refreshed.'

Obediently, although feeling incredibly self-conscious, both boys splashed the water on their hands and faces and dried them with a soft white cloth. The water was icy cold and, as it touched their skin, it seemed to rejuvenate them as well as wipe off all traces of dirt and grime.

'The water comes from the veiled mountains and is pure. It needs no cleansing properties,' Shakira spoke.

Both women reached into the pockets of their trousers and brought out a pair of supple leather slippers.

'Please, remove your boots and put these on,' Reniah spoke. 'They will soothe and comfort your feet after the long journey you have both made.'

The boys hadn't realised, until that moment, how much their

feet ached. As they removed their boots, they saw that they had blisters on their heels. The slippers were each a perfect fit and were soft against their skin giving the impression of walking on very springy moss. The effect was incredibly soothing. The moment the slippers touched their feet, the blisters immediately disappeared leaving renewed skin. Both boys looked up, puzzled, but the women of the East Gate merely smiled and offered no explanation.

'Is Asaph here?' Ethan asked as Jed examined his heel again, unable to believe what had just happened. This was twice in one day that he had experienced miraculous healing properties and he couldn't get his head around how it had happened.

'He too has just arrived. Your timing has been perfect.' Reniah answered as though the boys had been incredibly clever to have achieved this.

'Now, Jeduthun, take my arm,' Shakirah moved forward and interlinked his arm through her own as though they had known each other for years. Ethan wondered how they knew who each of them were as the women hadn't asked their names. Reniah smiled at him, her eyes twinkling as though sharing a joke. She linked his arm though hers and they began to walk down the white brick road towards a large white house that stood facing them. Ethan smiled back at her, finding himself surprisingly relaxed and comforted in her presence. As he walked, he often looked around him, soothed by the pristine grassland and large overhanging trees that lined the path, its leaves shimmering and dancing in the breeze. In front of him, Jed was torn between feeling very awkward and yet gratified by the attention of such beautiful women. Their dignified way of speaking and of moving made both boys stand up straighter and walk with their heads held a little bit higher.

From behind them the Guardians watched, enjoying the spectacle immensely. It was not long since they had left the Island but already there were some imperceptible changes in their charges.

Reniah surreptitiously glanced over her shoulder and smiled at them. The Guardians inclined their heads in a bow. Not many knew of their presence but her gift of seeing into the unseen realms meant she could sometimes glimpse them, and they always felt incredibly honoured when she did. They glanced at each other. It was time to take their leave. They would not be needed while the boys were under the protection of the East Gate.

Asaph was standing in front of a statue in the garden. It was a sculpture of two hands reaching out towards one another and whether it was seen as a gesture of friendship or combat depended on the imagination or maybe the circumstances of the onlooker. As this seasoned warrior stared at it on this particular evening, he felt a sudden wave of sadness wash over him. The feeling caught him by surprise but, before he could think about why this was, he was interrupted by Ethan and Jed approaching him, accompanied by Reniah. The boys had changed out of their Island clothes and were now dressed in the attire of a Cherithite apprentice. Linen trousers and shirt with a leather belt and leather tunic with the crest of a flame upon it.

He smiled at them. 'Well, you look more like a Cherithite and less like an Islander now,' he laughed.

Ethan was more at home in his clothing, largely because of what he had been given to wear at the Castle. But Jed fidgeted under Asaph's gaze, pulling at the neckline of his shirt.

'I don't see why I can't wear what I usually do,' he complained.

'Ah, it's important to dress according to where we are going and that may mean changing out of that which marks where we have come from,' Asaph answered cryptically with a grin. 'You look like a young warrior, Jed.'

'I'd feel that more if I had a sword,' Jed replied, his eyes lighting up with hope.

Reniah and Asaph laughed.

'In good time,' Asaph said to him. 'For now, let us get used to new clothes. How was your journey here?'

The boys looked at each other. Jed pulled a face. 'Well, we met Amos and that was good.'

'And he took us to the Tunnels of Tamore, and that was also good,' Ethan added.

They paused.

Asaph chuckled. 'I understand you had an adventure within the tunnels.'

Jed jerked his head round to look Asaph in the eye. 'How do you… I mean… What?' he stumbled, confused that Asaph seemed to know of things he hadn't yet been told. The contents of the bag came back to mind; just two water bottles, the dagger, the net, the vial, the key. Everything pointing towards the fact that Asaph seemed to have known what was going to happen to them.

No more was said for a gong sounded from within the white, stone house behind them.

'Come,' Reniah gestured for them to follow her. 'There is a special celebration tonight in your honour, but it is also the feast of the Seven Moons where we remember and are thankful for the victory that was won. It is one of the most important events in our year.'

She turned and led the way inside. Jed paused briefly before following the others. His mind was heavy with the unanswered questions that were building up inside his head and he didn't like where they were leading him.

The hall where the feast was taking place was already brimming to capacity with laughter and chatter and music. Guests stood around in colourful evening attire, goblets in hand, clearly excited to be together. Down the centre of the room was the longest table that either boy had ever seen, and the fullest. Tall candles lit what was laid upon it adding festive sparkle to the vast platters and gigantic bowls. In the centre, taking pride of place, were two glistening, suckling pigs, surrounded by figs, whole onions and potatoes. The aroma that filled the room made Jed's stomach rumble and Ethan's mouth water. It seemed a long time since they had been sat around the campfire with Amos, eating bowls of stew.

Musicians were playing native melodies from the top gallery, which looked down onto the hall below. Ethan recognised some of the music as what Amos had been whistling when he drove them to the Tunnels of Tamore. Somehow, this tiny sense of familiarity helped him to feel like less of a stranger, for he had found, that despite his desire to be here, he felt insecure being away from what he knew and understood. He wondered how his grandpa was.

Reniah raised her hand and the music immediately dipped in volume enabling her voice to be heard across the room. Ethan turned.

'Dear friends,' she said with a smile. 'Welcome to the feast of the Seven Moons.' She was interrupted by a splattering of applause as guests clapped hands against wrists to avoid spiling any wine.

'This evening is a particularly special one as we have Asaph and two new apprentices among us.' The boys both felt self-conscious as the eyes of the room turned to stare in their direction and, once more, polite clapping filled the air. Asaph turned and raised his goblet to them, grinning as he did so.

'Now, please, if you can all find a seat, let us enjoy the company, the food,'

'And the wine,' some red-faced man interrupted. The room laughed and the music swelled and intertwined with the increased volume of chatter creating a crescendo of happy sound.

Asaph sat at the head of the table with the boys either side of him. Reniah was placed next to Ethan but the seat to Jed's left was empty.

'Is Shakira not joining us?' Asaph asked.

'She has had to leave on an errand but will return tomorrow or possibly the day after that. She sent her apologies for missing your first evening here,' she addressed this last part to the boys. 'Now, can I pass you some meat, Jed?'

Much later, as plates were cleared and fruit and cheese were brought to the table, a bell was rung from the upper gallery and a man dressed in some ancient costume, with a strange hat upon his head, moved forward, to the laughter of the people below.

'It is tradition on feast night to enact the battle of the Seven Moons,' Asaph explained in a whisper. 'Although, I must warn you, the facts usually become blurred by both comedy and good wine!'

Ethan found himself looking forward to what was about to happen. He enjoyed stories and history and drama. When he was little, his grandpa often used to enact scenes from books they were reading. Again, his mind drifted to the Island and his grandpa. Jed was unsettled and felt trapped and bored. He was not one to sit around and would have much preferred to go and explore Twyndale. Reniah watched them, observing the different characters of the two boys. It never failed to amaze her how diverse people were.

The sound of a horn brought the company to a general hush, although there were still whispers and stifled giggles.

The man in the hat dramatically unravelled a very long scroll. It dropped over the parapet and down to the floor below.

'I hope that's not the length of the script,' someone from around the table quipped and the guests laughed.

The man cleared his throat dramatically and wiggled his eyebrows.

'Many, many years ago, deep in the mountains of Evernebulis, lived the tribe of the Espionites.' As he said this, a group of people came into view carrying various weapons which they held up for the audience to see.

'Boooooo,' came the sound from around the room.

These people were highly skilled in fashioning all manner of weapons and other items made from iron, silver and gold.'

'Oooooh,' the audience cried in mock appreciation.

'For many, many years they had supplied the Cherithites with all manner of weapons as well as helping to design and build great fortified structures to keep them protected.'

'Hurrah,' someone prematurely called out and was laughed at for their solitary participation.

'The chief of this particular tribe enjoyed the prosperity and fame that the skill of his people brought him, and, in time, they extended their services far and wide throughout Cherith. They became famous in the land, not just for what they made, but also for their inventive minds which progressed our way of life for the better.'

A man stepped forward, dressed like a King, and waved his hand at the audience as though bestowing a blessing.

'But the heart of the Chief became corrupted with pride and with greed,'

'Boooooo,' the audience cried. The musicians began to play a sombre, thumping beat and the chief pulled a menacing expression.

'Desiring to rule the whole of Cherith, the chief went into the deep dark of the Underworld to meet with Barlkron himself.'

A couple of actors ran around with cloths of red before another tossed blazing torches so that fire lit up the gallery.

'Careful,' one of the musicians cried out as a spark landed near to him. He jumped up from his seat, taking his wooden, stringed instrument with him. The audience laughed in delight at the averted threat of danger.

Two more figures, with hideous masks on, came stomping into view followed by a tall person, robed in red, wearing an evil looking mask. The chief bowed before the Lord of the Underworld.

The narrator continued. 'Barlkron made an agreement with the chief. He would bestow wealth and power on him if he managed to execute the King of Cherith and extinguish the flame. The chief agreed, believing that he would be able to do just that. As he left Barlkron's presence, the land went dark and a moon, the colour of blood, rose from the lake.'

'That isn't what history says,' someone shouted out.

'It is what my script says,' the man in the hat quipped back.

'Oh well, it must be fact then,' a woman laughed, joined by a few others sat near to her.

'As I was saying,' the man in the hat continued with mock gravity, 'A moon, the colour of blood, rose from the depths of the lake and staggered its way up to the sky where it hung, suspended in time.'

'Ooh, highly poetical,' another woman heckled as the narrator paused for dramatic effect - his hand stretched towards the ceiling.

The music became more sinister, and someone stepped forward holding up a prop representing the moon.

'The King called his army to battle.'

The actors stepped forward with their weapons, brandishing them high in the air with loud, threatening cries.

'And for seven nights, the battle waged.'

The fake moon dipped behind the parapet and then rose again six times.

'And all the while, the flame of Wynere burned brighter and brighter not allowing any of the enemy anywhere near it, for whoever tried was consumed and turned into ash. In his arrogance, the chief had underestimated the power of the lighted flame. As the seventh moon rose, the King called out to the chief, imploring him to turn from his alliance with Barlkron.'

The actor depicting the chief stepped forward. 'If you will bow down and serve me, then you have my word that I will break my alliance,' the chief shouted.

An actor with a crown upon his head came to stand opposite

the chief.

'The sword that lights the flame will decide who should rule,' he said, holding up a sword in front of his face. It began to glow.

'How have they done that?' Jed whispered to Asaph, drawn into the story despite his intention not to be.

'It's a trick done with light and glass,' he answered, leaving Jed none-the-wiser.

The chief covered his eyes. 'Noooooooo,' he said with a dramatic cry.

'Yesssss,' the delighted audience cried out.

The chief began to crumble towards the floor and the music started to swell. The moon began to dip.

'The Espionites, seeing that their chief had been defeated by the power of the flame, which burned from within the sword, ran away, defeated. And the battle was won.' The enactment came to a rather abrupt end, and the musicians sounded a final dramatic cadence of one short and then one long burst of a chord.

The audience stamped their feet and cheered as the actors came and took mock bows to the applause of the guests below.

'Is that really what happened?' Ethan turned to Reniah.

She laughed. 'It was much more complex than just denoted, but the chief was overcome by the power of the sword, yes.'

'And by the lighted flame,' Jed added.

'True,' Asaph agreed. Ethan noticed a strange look suddenly pass over the warrior's features. It was as if he had just recognised someone he hadn't expected or wished to see.

'Boys, if you will excuse me for a moment,' he said as he pushed back his chair from the table and left the room, nimbly winding his way through the mingling guests.

Ethan and Jed looked at Reniah.

'Is he alright?' Ethan asked.

Reniah's eyes had followed Asaph as he left but she now focussed on the two apprentices who were staring at her in concern.

'Yes. I am sure he is fine,' she said brightly with a smile. 'No doubt he has remembered something that he was supposed to have done. He has many responsibilities both here as well as in the Capital and has been away from them for a few days. Now, you have both had a long day and tomorrow will hold new adventures.

I think it time you perhaps got some sleep. Do you agree?'

As both boys chose that moment to yawn widely, they couldn't really argue with the suggestion and nodded their heads.

THE UNSEEN DIMENSION

Mia had watched the feast with great interest.

'Why do they all eat and drink so much?' she had enquired of Japhron as she had seen the piles of food upon each plate.

'In the realms of men, people get hungry,' he had replied.

'What does it feel like?'

'To be hungry?'

Mia nodded.

'Hmph. I'm not sure,' the Seer had answered. 'But I believe that their stomach makes strange noises, like a small internal rumbling.'

Mia pulled a face. 'That sounds horrible.'

'And then they have an overwhelming desire to eat. Also, remember, in their realm, they must eat to stay alive.'

Mia sighed. The realm of men seemed a very complicated place to live in. Here, in her own dimension, people ate purely for the joy of taste and for celebration, and in the same way, slept to be rested not because one was tired.

Japhron laughed. 'You are learning many new things young Mia, are you not?"

She put clenched hands to her head and then pulled them away, opening her fingers whilst making an explosive sound with her mouth.

'Mind blowing,' she answered unaware that she had made Melchi jump with her dramatic gesture.

CHERITH

The last of the guests had finally gone, leaving the house in welcome quietness. It felt very still after the activity and noise of the celebrations and Reniah relished the sense of peace that this brought. Walking out of the Great Hall, she gracefully wound her way down the stone steps that led out into the gardens. Standing for a moment, she breathed deeply of the still, fragrant, air, before removing her shoes so that she could walk barefoot over the grass.

It was cool and soft against the soles of her feet, and she scrunched up her toes against it, relishing the sensation it gave her. Crossing the front lawns, she spied Asaph, standing once more by the statue, his hand resting against it. Quietly, she went and stood next to him. He turned to her.

'You have sensed the flame has been extinguished,' she said without preamble, looking into his troubled eyes.

Asaph looked at her. 'I was aware of increased activity from the Underworld but had not seen this was the reason. When did it happen?'

Reniah took a deep breath. 'There are a few things to tell you. There just has not been a moment of privacy since you arrived.'

Asaph listened as Reniah told him of Nathan's arrival, Naomi's disappearance and what had happened in Wynere.

'Some things are veiled to me,' she confided. 'I have no insight as to where Naomi is, except I do have a sense that all is not well with her. Nathan has gone to Hymangees as the trail pointed there.'

'Things remain veiled either for a purpose or because the Underworld is weaving a web of deception,' Asaph reminded her. 'It would appear though, especially with the arrival of the two boys, that this is possibly an ancient prophecy unfolding before our very eyes. So let us take some comfort in that.'

'That is true,' Reniah smiled. 'How exciting that we should get to see it. What will you do about Ethan and Jed?'

'For now, we continue with their training. Hopefully, Nathan will soon return with news of Naomi.'

'And Abbir-Qualal?'

'He should not be too far away. His mission was only to have lasted a week. Maybe when we are all together, we will have more of an understanding as to what to do next.'

'Wynere are preparing for war.'

'We need to wait and see if it is war that Barlkron is wanting or whether there is another plot afoot. My sense is that there is something that we do not yet understand and until we know more, we need to hold our position here, uncomfortable as it is. If the prophecies are unfolding, as it would seem, then our greatest role is to protect the boys.'

Reniah nodded in agreement as she stared out over the gardens.

She realised that the peace she knew was about to be shaken and she shivered.

'Come, you are cold.'

'It is not the cold that chills me,' she said as they walked back towards the house, both lost in thought.

◢▨◣ THE UNSEEN DIMESNION

Melchi and Japhron looked at each other.

'They are sensing the same as us,' Japhron commented.

'Yes. Asaph is right to not rush back to Wynere.'

'I wish we had more insight into the plans of the enemy.'

'It will be revealed soon enough,' Melchi reassured the younger Seer. 'It's all a question of timing. But for now, we watch, and we wait.'

'Why can we not see where Naomi is?' Mia asked as she searched for a glimpse of her. 'And Shakirah? Where has she gone?'

Japhron glanced at Melchi. This was the first thing that Mia had said to indicate anything of what she may have seen in the Library.

'Sometimes things are veiled when it is not time for us to see.' Melchi replied. 'There are lessons and discoveries that the boys must find out for themselves without us interfering. We must stick within the boundaries of our given assignment.'

'Why do you ask about those two women in particular?' Japhron pressed.

'I was just wondering.' Mia answered.

CHAPTER TEN

ROOTS

CHERITH

It was nearly midday before Ethan awoke. Realising how late it was, he had quickly risen and dressed and gone in search of the others. The thought that they might already be up and about caused him to feel anxious and displaced. He hurried down the spiral staircase and pushed open a few doors that led off from it, but the rooms they led into were all empty which made him feel even more nervous and disorientated.

'Can I help you with anything?' a voice spoke from behind him, and Ethan turned round to see a pleasant faced man standing there with a cloth draped over his arm.

'Do you know where everyone is?'

'Most are still sleeping. If you go into the dining hall, I am sure they will join you shortly.'

The doors to the Great Hall were already open and Ethan saw that lunch had been laid out in there, the leftovers from the previous night's feasting. He wandered in, feeling small in the emptiness of the space which felt especially vast after the activity of the night before. The atmosphere was so quiet it was as though the room itself was still in slumber and not wishing to be disturbed. He found himself responding to this by treading around quietly and not touching anything.

'Where is everyone?' Jed's voice came loudly from behind him making him jump.

'I don't know. I looked around, but no-one seems to be about.'

Jed stretched, interlocking his hands behind his head and yawning. His hair was wild and tousled from sleep and he scratched his scalp, running his fingers through the unruly curls before heading straight to the table to see what food was there.

'Ahhh, you are both awake.' Reniah entered, bearing a jug, which she set down before reaching for three goblets and proceeding to pour the contents from the jug into them.

'I'm sorry I was not here to greet you when you first came down, but I had taken a walk down by the lower pools. How did you both sleep?' she asked as she handed a goblet to each boy.

Ethan relaxed as he realised that he had not missed out on anything after all. The feeling gave him a sudden sense of happiness and well-being.

'Good,' Jed said before gulping noisily and then added, 'thanks,' as he wiped a hand over his mouth.

Ethan nodded and smiled. 'Me too,' he said, slowly sipping at his drink, savouring the taste of berries and mint.

'Please, help yourselves to food,' Reniah urged them as she passed around platters of fruit and bread, honey and dates. I am sure Asaph will not be too much longer. I am yet to have seen him today.'

They had just started eating when the sound of footsteps came thudding down the stairs and Asaph's cheerful voice called out.

'I thought you two might sleep all day!' he said as he bounded into the room freshly shaved and exuding energy.

'Hardly surprising after the travels of yesterday,' Reniah remarked as she helped herself to some fruit. 'I'm surprised that you did not sleep longer.'

'Me, I was up and about with the dawn,' he said with a comical grin at the boys, implying that he had done no such thing. He reached for some bread and honey.

'Can you pass me a drink, Jed,' he asked.

Nathan arrived back at the East Gate, deeply frustrated and anxious. He strode into the grand entrance of the house, his heart sinking when he heard the sound of chatter coming from the dining hall. He handed his cloak to the servant who had opened the door and enquired as to who the visitors were.

'It is Asaph, my Lord and the young trainee Cherithites,' was the answer. 'Will you be joining them?'

Nathan frowned as he nodded. He washed his hands in the bowl of water that the servant held out for him and dried them on his shirt. He felt uneasy, dirty, and weary, and was not in the mood to be civil to strangers. He took a deep breath before straightening his shoulders back and pushing open the doors that led into the hall.

Asaph on seeing him, immediately rose from his place at the table and went to greet him with a smile. The men clasped the others forearm and Asaph placed his other hand on Nathan's shoulder.

'Naomi?' he mouthed his question by just uttering her name.

Nathan gave one small shake of his head in response.

'It is so good to see you, my friend,' Asaph said, his voice louder, before whispering, 'I know we have much to speak of, but let us wait until later,' he urged as he glanced slightly over his shoulder towards the boys. Nathan nodded slightly. 'Come boys, let me introduce you,' Asaph said, raising his voice again as he led Nathan to the table and handed him a plate.

'This is my friend and my brother, Nathan. He will no doubt be involved in some of your training while he is here. He is a remarkable swordsman and skilled at hand-to-hand combat.'

Jed looked up with interest at this warrior, but the man just nodded his greeting, without making eye contact, and pulled up a chair at the table before helping himself to the food that was upon it, seemingly ravenous. His clothes and face were stained with dirt and Jed wondered if he had come from a battle.

'How was your journey here?' the man asked politely as he bit into some bread and then drank before he had even swallowed.

'Eventful.' Jed replied with his own mouth full.

'That doesn't surprise me,' the man commented before asking how they had managed to get off the Island.

Prompted by Nathan's questions, Jed retold the story of their departure, their wrestle with the Sand Serpent, Amos, and their adventure within the Tunnels of Tamore. The man had momentarily stopped chewing and looked up at Reniah and then Asaph when Jed retold the moment when the Masquerader had appeared. Asaph had tightened his lips as he gave a pronounced nod, confirming that the account was a true one. Nathan kept his expression neutral and returned his attention to Jed.

Ethan found himself staring at this new person in their midst. There was something about him that seemed familiar, but he couldn't figure out why. He also noticed that this stranger, for all his questions, appeared distracted and sad. The tanned face with the blue eyes and blonde hair looked back at him and Ethan quickly turned away, embarrassed at having been caught staring.

'And then we just ran at it with the dagger and the whole thing disintegrated into a massive swarm of flies.' Ethan's mind re-joined the conversation just as Jed was recounting their escape out of the tunnel.

'A scheme of the Underworld to prevent you from reaching here,' Nathan said. 'You did well to handle that. Well done.'

Ethan and Jed both glowed under the praise.

'What will we do today?' Jed enquired, pushing his plate away and already eager to move.

'I thought it would be wise to not do too much,' Asaph replied. 'The past few days have tested us all and we should rest.'

Jed frowned. The idea of just sitting around talking did not appeal to him in the slightest.

Asaph smiled at him. 'That does not mean we won't do anything,' he added and saw Jed regain some interest. 'We are going to visit a friend of mine. He's a wood carver.'

Ethan's interest was immediately drawn. 'Amos had some carvings in his shed. They were really good.'

'You should see what Levi makes. He is incredibly skilful. His family have been craftsmen for years, and the techniques and skills he uses have been passed down from generation to generation,' Nathan told them.

'Is this part of a Cherithite training?' Jed spoke up, confused by how any of this was relevant to him personally so was already disinterested.

Reniah rose from her chair and laid a hand on his arm as she walked past him. 'Everything has a purpose, Jed. Do not take any path you travel here for granted or dismiss the lesson that is there to be learned and applied,' she said gently as she left the room.

Jed pursed his lips and shrugged with an air of resignation, unconvinced that the day was going to be beneficial to him in any way whatsoever.

Barlkron was glowering as he sat upon his throne, his fingers tapping against the cushioned arm rests. He could not see what was happening within the East Gates, and this was filling him with immense frustration. His people should have infiltrated there by now, which would have allowed him access. The small creatures that usually sidled up close around him were keeping their distance, knowing that the mood he was in did not bode well for their wellbeing.

The robed figure entered the throne room, flinching at the bridled anger he could sense from the Underworld's ruler.

'Why is it that you are you here and not there?' Barlkron hissed.

'There is something that needs to be done my Lord,' the figure replied.

Barlkron looked up, eyes narrowed and his expression calculating.

'It had better have something to do with the delay you have imposed upon me without my permission,' he said menacingly.

'It does my Lord. And it will work to your advantage I promise you.'

'I am listening,' Barlkron said as he leaned forward, his hands clasped with his forefingers touching, creating a steeple. The robed figure noted that Barlkron always looked at him in such a way as to make him feel he was under constant appraisal. It was an intimidating tactic and he swallowed down his fear and sense of inferiority. He needed to keep focussed on the task in hand for Barlkron would not tolerate any failure.

The boys were stood on a jetty by the River Tamore, waiting for Asaph to untie the small boat that was tethered there. The river stretched wide and long, punctuated now and then by circles of bubbles as a fish neared the surface. The sun bounced off the water causing it to glisten and sparkle, highlighting the flies that flickered about over it.

'If you two sit next to each other and take an oar, you can both row us to where we are going,' Asaph had commented.

Jed had immediately climbed on board, the small craft rocking precariously as he did so, causing Ethan to feel nervous about stepping into it.

'It's quite safe,' Asaph had encouraged him, noticing his hesitation. 'Just take your time.'

Ethan waited for the boat and Jed to be still before he placed one foot tentatively into the boat, holding his arms out to the side as he steadied himself and waited for it to stop rocking before bringing his other foot in and quickly sitting down on the small wooden seat next to Jed. He reached for the oar and positioned it so that it lay just above the water. Asaph pushed the boat out and then nimbly jumped in to join them.

'Right boys, we are going straight down the river. I will tell you when to stop.' And with that, the Cherithite warrior leaned back, put his hands behind his head and closed his eyes.

Jed directed Ethan to row so that the boat moved further into the middle of the river, but the boy smacked his oar flat into the water and they both got splashed.

'You need to angle the oar,' Jed told him, already irritated at Ethan's incompetence. 'Bend your knees, dip the oar and then pull back.'

Ethan tried again and this time did manage to turn the boat in the right direction without further incident. Once further over, Jed told him to stop rowing while he straightened the craft up. 'Right, now we both dip and pull at the same time,' he instructed. 'Ready?' Ethan nodded and both boys leaned forward, pushed their oar into the water and pulled back, but the boat turned off at an angle as Jed was much stronger than Ethan. Jed waited for Ethan to straighten up the boat and they tried again but the same thing happened.

'Do you want to try on your own?' Ethan asked, already feeling inadequate and not wanting to tempt Jed's frustration further.

'Pass me your oar,' Jed said impatiently. 'You'd better sit over there.'

Asaph observed without getting involved, reflecting on how the Island had influenced the boy's characters and behaviours. Re-setting some of these things was always the biggest part of the

Cherithite training and it was also the most challenging. People were often so set in their ways that they could not see how their attitudes or reactions were wrong, or how they could change.

He leaned forward. 'Ethan, you should watch out for Kingfishers. They are often seen around here,' he said to distract him. 'Jed, keep rowing. We aren't too far away.'

Reniah was arranging some fresh flowers in a jug, reflecting once again on the vision she had seen at the waterfall. She kept trying to understand its meaning, but it remained out of reach of her insight. She sighed.

'Waiting, poised on the edge of danger was extremely uncomfortable and it takes a lot of will power to hold one's nerve,' she pondered to herself. She wondered how the city of Wynere was doing with all that was going on there and how Nathan was faring in his fresh search for his wife. 'I will be glad when Shakirah returns so that I can talk to her about some of this,' Reniah thought to herself as she placed the jug on a small table in the entrance hall.

Asaph had moved next to Jed and taken the oars so that he could steer the boat towards the jetty that lay near to land. Jumping out, he had moored it securely so that the boys could climb out and then the three of them had walked down the landing and into the wood that lay beyond.

The grove they found themselves walking through was home to trees with thinnish trunks and slender branches which held delicate leaves that quivered and danced with the breeze.

'What kind of trees are these,' Ethan asked Asaph who was strolling along beside him. Jed had long bounded off in front.

'They're called Aspens.'

Ethan noticed some stumps where trees had been felled for use by the wood carvers.

'They share a common root system,' Asaph continued, 'so are all connected even though they appear to stand alone. The oars you used on the way here were made from these.'

Ethan was surprised. 'They don't look strong enough to make anything that sturdy,' he commented.

'Ahh, don't let their seeming frailty deceive you on that. Their wood is strong, and their roots are secure. They were often used for making shields. You know, there's a certain myth surrounding them, that a crown made of Aspen leaves will enable the wearer to descend into the Underworld and return unharmed.'

'I will take your word for that,' Ethan remarked wryly as he grasped one of the boughs and let go of it allowing it to spring gracefully back into position.

The grove opened into a wide-open field that stretched out before them, wide and green, lined by hedges. Flowers sprouted up through the grass giving accents of colour and holding court, in the centre of the space, grew one huge tree. The trunk was thick, cloaked with ancient bark from which large branches grew, each covered with vibrant green leaves that were dense in its foliage.

'Where's Jed gone?' Ethan asked, looking around and not seeing him anywhere.

Asaph laughed, 'Look up,' he suggested as he called out Jed's name.

From way up the tree, Jed's curly head emerged. He was grinning as he gripped a thick branch with one hand and waved to them with the other, his body extended as his legs wrapped securely around another sturdy branch. As the other two approached, he nimbly swung himself down until he was back on the ground.

Ethan gazed at the thick trunk and the wide-reaching branches. Little grew around it. Even the grass at its base was bald and brown, the gnarled roots poking up from beneath the surface of the ground. 'It looks like it has been here for a long time,' he thought to himself and wondered what secrets it had to tell.

'The oak,' Asaph said as he patted its trunk fondly. 'This is one of the oldest trees around. Can you not sense its ancient wisdom?'

Ethan immediately nodded whereas Jed looked from one to the other as though they were both a little crazed.

'They grow slowly but their roots grow wide causing them to be incredibly sturdy and strong. Much like you, Jed.'

Jed looked again at the ancient tree. 'Maybe,' he said, 'except I don't have any roots.'

Asaph didn't comment but smiled at the boy. 'The oak represents wisdom, stability and honour,' he continued.

'It reminds me of Amos,' Ethan remarked.

'You two are talking in riddles,' Jed said, interrupting their conversation. He felt uncomfortable with this mystical talk. 'Where's Levi's place, Asaph?'

Asaph grinned at him. 'Just over on the edge of the field. I'll race you.' Jed, his attention returned, immediately took off in a sprint with the warrior fast beside him. Ethan watched them go and then took one last stare at the oak. 'How lonely you look, sat in your own expanse of space,' he thought to himself, feeling a little sorry for it. But as he watched, a small bird swooped in and alighted onto one of its branches, closely followed by another. They looked at Ethan with twinkling eyes as they whistled and trilled to one another in the language of their kind. The branches of the tree embraced their tiny frames, covering, protecting, and Ethan changed his mind about this sturdy oak. It was not alone after all, rather it had its own special place and purpose to protect and watch over those around it.

From within the Underworld, Barlkron watched the retreating back of the robed figure as he strode out of the throne room. His mind was already plotting his next move. It appeared that the delay he had suffered was going to work to his advantage after all. He just needed to wait for all the pieces to align. His eyes stalked Ethan as he gazed at the old tree and noticed that there was a weakness in the boy's sensitivity that he would be able to manipulate, given time and the right set of circumstances. Jed, he could not see. Clearly, he must be close to Asaph. This thought triggered the beginnings of an idea, and he sat back on his throne, calculating how to weave this new step into his existing plot.

Levi's workshop smelt comfortingly of wood shavings and sawdust. All around the floor, and on the shelves surrounding the shed, were numerous items. The shields, oars, paddles, bows and arrows caught Jed's attention straight away and he hoped that he would be given something as a souvenir. Ethan was drawn to the smaller items that had been intricately carved into animals and people. There was one that was very similar to the one he had seen in Amos' shed of a woman holding the hand of a small boy. He picked it up to examine it more closely, again sensing the same sadness as he had before.

Levi, himself, was not to be seen but they could hear the chop of axe against wood, indicating that he was around the back of the shed somewhere, hard at work.

'Come on,' Asaph said as he walked out of the shed calling out Levi's name. Ethan quickly put down the carving and followed Jed and Asaph around the back of the workshop. The sound of chopping stopped and the first sight the boys had of the wood carver was of a tall, brown skinned man, his muscular arms raised as he held his axe in the air, suspended mid swing.

Seeing Asaph, his face broke into a grin, and bringing the axe down, he left it embedded into a log as he came forward to greet them.

'Word has reached me of you two already,' he said as he reached forward to clasp his hand around each forearm of the boys. It was not a greeting that Jed or Ethan was practised at, and it felt awkward and strange to them. Levi's hands were rough and calloused against their skin and his grip was strong.

He was younger than Jed had imagined he would be. The idea of a wood carver had given him the impression of someone much older, but he realised that Levi was far from old, maybe mid 20s, with dark eyes and long, black, braided hair that was tied back with a red cloth. He looked fun and dangerous, athletic and wise all at the same time.

'Come, you must be in need of refreshment if you have rowed down river,' he said as he strode back to the entrance of his shed. He gestured for the boys to enter in front of him before turning back round to Asaph, 'Is there any news of Naomi?' he whispered. Asaph shook his head.

'Levi, can I hold one of the shields?' Jed's voice called out, interrupting them.

'Sure,' the wood carver said, leaving the conversation in suspense as he strode ahead to lift one of the shields down from its display.

THE UNSEEN DIMENSION

Melchi and Japhron were aware of the rumbling from the depths of the Underworld. The plans of the enemy had been unobtrusive, gently simmering away but they sensed the heat had intensified and that things were reaching a boiling point. The intentions of Barlkron would soon be revealed.

Mia was wondering if she could possibly go back to the Library.

'I think I had better accompany her this time,' Melchi thought.

CHAPTER ELEVEN

CONNECTIONS

CHERITH

Jed held the shield close against his body. 'How do you get this from that?' he remarked, pointing to a log that lay next to the work bench, ready for use.

'Knowing what it will become before making the first cut is key,' the wood carver replied. 'The image is already there in the block of wood. I just have to carve it out.'

'Why do you do it?' Ethan asked, intrigued.

'It is what my family have done for generations. I was brought up around the trees and learnt to carve from being a young boy. It's instinctive in me. But I also love it,' Levi replied. 'I love the idea of forming something that will remain long after I have left the earth.'

'Does it bother you that you cut down the trees though?'

'I see it as an extension of its life. I reform it to give it further purpose. The trees that line the woods you walked through have defended many through the shields, bows and arrows that have been made from them.'

Jed picked up one of the bows.

'I see you are drawn to weaponry, Jeduthun,' Levi remarked. 'Are you from a clan of warriors?'

Jed immediately put the bow back down and shrugged. 'Who knows,' he said nonchalantly.

'Yes, he is,' Asaph spoke up causing Jed to quickly look up, immediately on his guard.

'What do you mean?' he said roughly, cross that Asaph clearly knew something about his past that he himself did not know.

'Your family were part of the Espionite clan, Jed,' Asaph said gently. 'Your great grandpa was a skilful hunter and swordsman and your mother a master at crafting bows and arrows. Your father was one of the greatest strategists that the clan had.

'How did they end up on the Island?' Ethan asked. Jed scowled at him. He was not comfortable that his personal life was being discussed with those he considered strangers or that Ethan felt he could ask a question about his life.

'There was a particular war that your parents wanted no part of, and they were sold to Sharaaim for their rebellion,' Asaph replied. 'But maybe the rest of that story is for Jed's ears only.'

Jed was grateful for this. The conversation was unsettling him and he didn't like it. The idea that he was part of the Espionite tribe panicked him, especially knowing what they had tried to do to Wynere. It made him feel inferior, as though he had no right to be here. He turned away from the others, pretending to examine his shield whilst trying to absorb this fresh piece of information.

'What about me?' Ethan asked. Ever since Sharaaim had revealed something of his lineage, he had been desperate to know more.

'Your father ruled the city of Jachin, which is not far from the Capital.'

Levi looked up with interest. 'I had heard that the heir had managed to escape. I had no idea you would still be alive,' he commented. 'My Uncle was part of the search for you.'

'What happened?' Jed asked, partly to get back at Ethan for asking questions about himself earlier. 'How did Ethan end up on the Island?'

'Ethan and his grandpa were captured and sold as they escaped from the battle that was being waged against Jachin by the Edomites,' Asaph replied. 'It was not long after your mother had died.'

'I think Noah spoke about this,' Jed spoke up. 'Are you saying Ethan actually is the son of a King? I thought Shaaraim was lying.'

'But what of my father? Is he still alive then? Where is he?' Ethan's questions were loaded with emotion and confusion. 'Why did he never come to find me?'

'The battle that he sent you away from waged for many days. And your father, the King, was captured and the city burned,' Asaph said gently, knowing that this part of Ethan's story was going to impact him greatly.

'But where is he? Why did no one try to find him?'

'They did remember!' Jed interjected. Asaph shot him a warning look and he shrugged and turned to look at the other shields on the walls.

'The trail went cold,' Levi continued the account. 'Wynere went to the aid of the city and managed to track your father to the tents of Edom, but he was not found among them.'

'So, he must have escaped?' Ethan pushed for clarity.

'His men continued to search for a long time Ethan. He has never been found.'

'But that doesn't mean he isn't alive. We must try and find him, Asaph!' he appealed to the warrior who stood watching him as these revelations fell like darts, piercing Ethan's world.

'We have tried, Ethan. For many years. If he is alive, he does not want to be found. Even those who can see into the realms of the unknown have no insight as to where he is.'

Asaph put his hands on Ethan's shoulders. 'I do not believe that this is the end of the story,' he said gently, 'but for now, it is not the path we are on. The order in which things happen are always significant. Do not underestimate what you have been told but hold it carefully for now. When the time is right, the path before you will be clear.'

The atmosphere in the workshop had become subdued with the revelations that had been unveiled. It was as though a knife had cut into the boys, exposing the grain of who they were. It was a cut that would mark and change them forever but, for now, it just felt raw and vulnerable.

Levi put down the small dog that he had been chiselling away at while the others had talked. 'Here,' he said to Jed as he lifted down one of the shields. 'Take this. Let it be a reminder of where you have come from and, as you hold it, may it also show you what you yourself carry. You may not see it yet but it's there, being formed, just like this shield was from the tree.'

He then reached for the sculpture of the woman holding hands with the child and gave it to Ethan. 'You may have never known your mother, but she gave you birth, and you carry some of her insight. Something of her lives in you. Remember that and find comfort!'

📖 THE UNSEEN DIMENSION

Melchi and Japhron looked in on this poignant moment that was happening in the wood carver's workshop. It was more significant than the boys knew. By being introduced to their past, and to their roots, the image of who they were was being more intricately defined, exposing the truth of, not just who they currently were, but of who they could become.

Mia found her face was wet with water flowing from her eyes. She put her finger against the drips, confused as to what this, and the weight that had settled on her heart, was.

'Melchi?' she questioned as she showed him the droplets that were glistening in her hand.

He reached out and gently caught her tears, holding them up to the light. They sparkled silver and blue.

'You have just glimpsed the pain of a human heart,' he explained to her. 'Your tears are not for yourself, Mia. You have experienced something called compassion. It is a beautiful trait in a Seer and maybe why you were assigned to us.'

Mia wiped her eyes. 'I am so glad that we get to help them,' she said, beaming her big smile, her joy already returned.

🗡 CHERITH

The journey back up the river to Twyndale was quiet. Asaph had suggested that he and Jed row back having sensed that the boy needed the distraction, and that Ethan would want to quietly reflect on what he had been told.

Asaph matched his strength to Jed's so that the boat easily glided through the water and the young apprentice noted this and was grateful, although he also felt a bit bad knowing that this is what he had deliberately not done for Ethan earlier. The truth was, he was so used to doing things by himself, that relying on anyone else made him feel weak and out of control.

Ethan sat behind the other two, holding the sculpture and gazing at its image. He had never known his parents but, somehow, he felt that he had made a connection with them today and this knowledge seemed to strengthen his sense of identity, as though the ingredients of who they were had been added into the mix of who he was, adding richness and depth. I feel like the Aspen tree, he thought to himself. Standing alone but connected to an unseen root.

Jed was in more inner turmoil and had questions he desperately wanted to ask but did not want to voice them in front of Ethan. His knowledge of the Espionites was mixed and the fact that they were part of his own lineage caused him to feel uncertain. He concentrated on the mindless task of rowing, tuning in to the sound of the oars striding through the river and the movement of his knees and arms so that he could avoid thinking about it.

Asaph allowed the quietness to continue until they arrived back at the landing near the East Gates. Alighting from the boat, he had moored it and helped Ethan jump out. Jed leapt from the boat without assistance, but Asaph gently caught at his arm holding him back. Ethan saw this and subtly went ahead to give them some privacy.

'Jed, your parents were both good people as were their parents before them. There is a great legacy that they have passed on to you that you are yet to discover and understand. The environment they lived in did not hold them back from doing what was right or from being the Cherithite warriors that they were.'

'But the Espionites have caused so much trouble,' Jed commented, shrugging off Asaph's hand. 'Maybe not directly in my family line, but certainly in my clan. Is that tendency for evil in me too?'

'The truth is, it's in all of us, Jed. Not one of us is perfect. We all have the ability to choose right or wrong and every day we make the choices that will either help us grow or hold us back. Just hold on to the fact that the roots of your family were strong in what was good and noble so, when trouble came, they were not swayed. That strength is in you too. You just have to allow yourself to become more securely rooted.'

Jed begrudgingly nodded admitting that this was true.

'You have come from a strong line of warriors and strategists. You just need to find a cause worth fighting for rather than using all that skill in purely defending yourself and keeping the world at bay.'

Jed looked at him. 'That's why I'm here, right?' He said this as a comment, but really, he was asking the question, wanting the reassurance.

'One of many reasons,' Asaph answered with a smile. 'Now, pick up your shield and let's go find some food.'

'Asaph,' Jed said but he was too late. The warrior was already striding towards Ethan. He had missed the opportunity to ask the other questions that were persistently prodding at him and leaving small indentations of distrust.

Nathan had returned from yet another fruitless search. He was perplexed and increasingly anxious as to the safety of his wife.

'There are no clues to point us in the right direction,' he said to Reniah as she came to sit beside him by the fountain in the courtyard. 'Every search I make has no direction to it, but I can't not look.'

'It's much like the whereabouts of the Oil and Sword,' Reniah said thoughtfully. 'All is veiled behind an invisible shield for some reason.'

'What do we do?' the warrior asked her, hoping that she had some wisdom.

'For now, we wait,' was the unwelcome response. 'We wait and we watch, and we keep alert. The enemy's plans will, in time, be exposed and we must trust that we will all be ready for when this happens.'

The meal that night was quiet compared to the celebratory noise of the night before but all were grateful for this respite. The conversation was peppered with stories of life in Twyndale and Wynere, as though there was an unspoken agreement to lay down all the deep things of the day and let them rest. Ethan felt that there were things the adults in the room wished to discuss but were waiting until the boys were not there. There was a tenseness in the atmosphere despite the easy chatting and humorous stories that were being shared. He was glad when it was suggested that the boys retire for the night as he was tired and wrung out with physical exertion and emotional turmoil. On reaching his room, he had immediately fallen asleep fully clothed on top of his bed.

Jed was not tired. His mind was whirring with everything that had happened and the people he had met. He had tried to sleep but was too restless. In the end, he had got up, opened the door, and crept out into the corridor intent on exploring Twyndale a little more on his own.

He quietly walked down the spiral staircase that led into the entrance hall. Tall, white marble pillars stood here creating a grand first impression for any visitor, but they held no interest for the young explorer. Instead, he made his way down one of the corridors which branched off from the entrance. He walked quickly, hoping that he wouldn't be seen and asked to go back to his room. The wall to his left was pure white, lit by flaming torches which were held in brackets. The flames flickered and danced with the breeze that blew in from across the courtyard and through the open archways that flanked the right side of the corridor. Jed shivered. He kept walking past many doors and was about to open one, when he heard voices coming from beyond it. He paused, his fingers gripping the handle. One voice grew louder as someone walked close by the door. Jed released his grip and stealthily kept walking. He was not in the mood for conversation. Eventually, the long corridor ended with just one last door. Jed pressed his ear against it but heard no sound. He carefully turned the handle, pushed open the door and peered inside. The room was empty; lit by both a fire and more of the flaming torches. Both gave welcome warmth and an orange glow, highlighting the many weapons that were hung there. Fascinated, Jed entered the room to take a closer look at them. Bows and arrows, swords and spears, daggers and knives of various shapes and sizes were displayed. All were beautifully crafted, and some were incredibly ornate. He unhooked one of the daggers and held it in his hand, making a few movements with it, twisting it around and lunging at an imaginary foe.

'I see you have the makings of a swordsman,' a voice spoke from behind him. Jed jumped and quickly replaced the dagger back in its place on the wall.

The man laughed. 'You need not worry. I will not tell anyone. I came here many nights as a boy to look and to play at war.'

'Who are you?' Jed asked nervously.

'I think I should be asking that question,' the man said, not unkindly.

'I'm Jed, Jeduthun,' he corrected. It seemed out of place to not use his whole name, although he usually didn't like to.

'Well Jed, Jeduthun,' the man laughed, 'pull up a chair and let us get acquainted.'

Feeling flattered, Jed did what the man suggested. There was something about this stranger that Jed found interesting. He was younger than Asaph and Nathan, tall, lean, and brown skinned like himself with dark, wavy hair that fell to his shoulders. He had a closely shaven beard and carried a sense of boldness and energy that appealed to Jed's own reckless, adventurous spirit. The eyes were dark and stared intently at Jed when he spoke as though what he was saying was hugely significant or important. He carried a sword which he drew from its sheath and laid down so that he could sit on the chair opposite Jed by the fire.

'Do you live here?' Jed asked.

'I do indeed. My family have lived here for many generations. We are part of one of the oldest clans of the Cherithite people.'

'So, you know Asaph and Nathan?'

The man smiled. 'Indeed yes. They are as brothers to me. My name is Abbir-Qualal but, Jed, if you should see them, do not let it be known that I am here just yet.'

Jed frowned. This place seemed full of secrets, and he didn't like to not know what they were.

Abbir-Qualal saw the frown. 'Do not worry my young friend, it is for no other reason than I would like a little time to myself. I have been out on a mission for a few days and am tired and not in the mood for questions or conversation.'

Jed smiled and nodded. He understood that only too well.

'Is that your own sword?' he asked.

'It is, yes. Would you like to hold it?'

Jed's eyes gleamed. 'Yes, I definitely would,' he replied eagerly.

Abbir-Qualal stood to his feet and picked up the weapon. He handed it to Jed, adjusting the boys grip so that he held it more securely. 'This is an Espionite sword. They are very rare and incredibly well made,' he informed Jed. 'You would be the envy of many a trained warrior right now if they could see you.'

Jed turned it around in his hands. He liked the feel of it under his fingers. The idea that this may have been made by someone in his own family came to his mind, but he dismissed the thought, not ready to align himself with his past just yet.

'It has seen much blood shed and saved the lives of our people many times,' the warrior continued to speak.

In the flicker of the firelight, Jed imagined the ground littered with bodies that this sword had slain. He twirled it around above his head and pretended to thrust it into someone. The sound of battle was loud in his imagination.

Abbir-Qualal laughed and steadied his arm, removing the sword from his grasp. 'Steady now or you will be beheading a fellow kinsman.'

Jed looked sheepish. 'Sorry.'

'I see you already have some skill in swordsmanship. Maybe while you are here, I will give you some tuition,' Abbir-Qualal said as he safely placed the sword back down on the floor.

As he did this, Jed noted the numerous marks on the man's forearms and hands. 'Battles are not without their scars,' the warrior said noting the fix of Jed's eyes upon his wounds.

'Have you just come from one?' Jed enquired, increasingly curious by this stranger.

'Of sorts,' Abbir-Qualal replied as he undid his cloak and flung it down on a chair. Jed's attention was immediately drawn to the clasp that was pinned onto it.

'I found one of those,' he said, pointing. 'It was in the Tunnels of Tamore lying on the ground. It had a different engraving on it though.'

Abbir-Qualal stared intently at Jed. The dark eyes seemed to be looking deep into the heart of him and Jed squirmed under the scrutiny.

'What did you do with it?'

'I picked it up and put it in the bag that Asaph gave us.'

'And it was in the tunnels you say?'

'Yes,' Jed replied, perplexed by the man's sudden intensity.

'Did you see anyone else while you were down there?'

'I'm not sure. I thought I did but now I don't know. We were chased by these bat-like creatures and now I'm not certain what was real and what wasn't.'

Abbir-Qualal's seriousness evaporated with a sudden smile. 'You have had quite the adventures it seems and now it's time you went back to bed. You have training tomorrow and it is not for those who are weary, believe me.'

Jed nodded as he got to his feet.

'Remember, you haven't seen me.'

Jed grinned and nodded. The fighter in him felt he had met a kindred spirit and he liked having a secret of his own.

Nathan paced the floor as he recalled and retold the happenings of the past few days. Asaph watched him, aware that his friend was ill at ease and so listened without interruption unless to clarify a point.

'There was a woman in Wynere who saw the one who extinguished the flame. She said that it was me and I have been under house arrest since that time until I escaped here. We knew then that a Masquerader had to be involved.' Nathan paused. 'Did you sense who it might have been?'

'There was something about them… but I have been unable to put my finger on what it was,' Asaph replied. 'I am sure it is someone I know or have met. He or she had a way about them that I found familiar.' He gave a small snort at the irony of his comment. 'Beyond them looking and sounding like me,' he clarified.

Reniah smiled at him and nodded her head. 'We understand.'

'You just said, "he or she". Do you think it possible that Naomi is responsible? That she is the betrayer?' Nathan was agitated by the implication, even though it only voiced what he himself was thinking.

Asaph looked at him, 'We do not know who it is,' he said gently. 'Have you any reason to believe that Naomi is involved?'

'No. Of course not. Except…' Nathan sighed, 'the night that the flame was extinguished, I awoke unsettled and uneasy and, as I went down the stairs to investigate, Naomi was coming up them. I have no idea where she had been. I cannot believe that she would be involved in this treachery, but it is this question that pushed me to come in search of her.'

'Is there anything else? Do not hold back any information however small,' Asaph said gently.

Nathan hesitated before answering, 'There was also the clasp.'

'What clasp?'

'One of my clasps, bearing my family crest, was in the clenched fist of one of the dead guards.' Nathan slumped down into a chair, his head between his hands. The idea that his wife was involved in any of this was an unbearable concept.

Asaph went and sat beside him, placing a comforting hand on his friends' shoulder. 'There are many things that, as yet, we do not know but remember that there was certainly no time for Naomi to have taken the Oil and the Sword and hidden them outside of Wynere and they would have been discovered by now if they were within the city. Also, why would she have been attacked as the evidence suggests? All these are facts in her defence, do you not think?'

Nathan looked up, hope returning to his heart with these thoughts.

'One thing I am certain of is that there appears to be a web of deception that the Underworld is weaving that is deliberately trying to turn us against each other. Trust that nothing appears what it seems.'

At that moment, Reniah entered the room bearing a tray of warm drinks. They each took one and then all sat by the light of the fire continuing to outline what they knew and place it in some kind of order.

'So, Naomi left over four days ago - two days after the flame had been extinguished?' Asaph clarified.

'Yes. We found her boots on the moorland. The trackers believe she was attacked by a multitude of Scorpion Wasps. There were two sets of hoof marks appearing to head towards Hymangees but there was no trace of anything there.'

'But it would appear she was in the company of someone else,' Asaph said thoughtfully. 'Reniah, have you sensed anything?'

Reniah hesitated before shaking her head. 'No, all is veiled,' she answered.

Asaph noticed the slight pause and looked at her questioningly, but she slightly moved her head, warning him to not ask her anything more.

'Ephron and the elders are preparing for attack,' Nathan blew out his cheeks not noticing the covert exchange between them. He had been carrying much weight and was glad to be able to offload it onto trusted people and find some counsel.

Reniah leaned forward. 'I sense that the attack is not going to be the one they imagine,' she said quietly

The two men looked at her expectantly as she continued, 'The age-old prophecies have spoken in part of these times and of two boys. If this is the time, let us not forget the role that they must play, both here and back on the Island. The extinguished flame may have more to do with them than an attack on Wynere.'

From outside the room in which they were sat talking, Jed stood listening. He had not intended to eavesdrop, but as he had walked by, he had overheard part of the conversation and it had intrigued him, so he had stayed there for longer than he should have. He heard someone coming towards the door, their footsteps getting louder. He turned and ran back to his room, his heart hammering in his chest and his mind overrun with questions and suspicions. The flame was extinguished! This was a frightening thought given what Amos had said. And what did they mean by "back on the Island?". 'I'm never going back there,' he vowed to himself as he slammed his door shut.

Asaph peered into the corridor.

'Is anyone there?' Nathan called from behind him.

'Not now,' Asaph said shutting the door thoughtfully and returning to his chair.

THE UNSEEN DIMENSION

The Seers looked at Ethan fast asleep in his bed and then at Jed fleeing back to the safety of his own room.

'He knows too much, too soon,' Japhron stated.

'Asaph knows he was there. He will know what to do,' Melchi replied, although his mind was elsewhere. He had sensed that something dark had permeated the atmosphere of Twyndale but could not yet see as to which direction this had come from. It had been a long time since his sight into the realms had been this veiled and his heart was deeply troubled.

'You are unusually quiet, Mia.' Japhron smiled at her. 'Is everything alright?'

The young Seer-ling sighed. 'Do you think that Asaph is right about Naomi?'

Melchi turned to face his young apprentice. 'What do you mean exactly?'

'Well, he said that the betrayer couldn't be her as she wouldn't have had time to take the Oil and the Sword and hide them outside of Wynere. But what if she was working with someone else! She could have done it then and it would explain about the clasp and why she was wandering about on the night everything happened.'

'Good point. But how would you explain the attack on her life by the Scorpion Wasps?' Japhron questioned her. 'Why would that have happened if she were involved?'

'But maybe she knew it was going to happen? Why else would she have removed her boots? It was an odd thing to do don't you think? Remember when you asked me what I saw, Melchi? And I said it looked like she knew that something was about to happen? Well, maybe she did know. Maybe the attack was planned, and it has been a way to keep suspicion away from herself.' Mia face was flushed as she expressed her thoughts out loud. She had been holding onto them ever since she had seen the grey mark on Naomi's forehead.

Melchi turned away. His own forehead was furrowed in concentration as he searched through his memories, looking to see what may align with Mia's theories.

'I think that it is time for you and I to both visit the Library,' he announced unexpectedly.

Mia's face lit up.

'Really? That would be the most exciting thing ever.'

Melchi smiled to himself. 'We will see,' he was thinking.

'When will we go?' Mia was already on her feet, eager to find out more.

Melchi patted her pink cushion, implying she should sit back down.

'Noy yet, Mia. Not yet.'

CHAPTER TWELVE

THE HEART OF A MAN

CHERITH

In Cherith, the morning gradually eased out of its slumber with the trilling melodies of the birds calling to each other from the leafy branches and bushes of the gardens. White clouds appeared like delicate brush marks against the canvas of what promised to be a blue sky but was currently tinged with the palest pink and everywhere glistened with silvery morning dew.

Jed was stirred by a hand gently shaking him awake. He shrugged it away, still half asleep, but, when the realisation drifted through his subconscious that someone was in his room, he sat up quickly, alert and ready to fight. He relaxed on seeing Abbir-Qualal stood there, fully dressed.

'You scared me! Is it time to get up already?' he yawned and swiped a hand over his eyes.

'No, not yet. It's still very early and no-one is currently about. I've been thinking about the clasp you found Jed. Have you got it?'

'It's in the bag that Asaph gave us, but Ethan has it. Why?'

'Could you go and retrieve it for me?' Abbir-Qualal asked without answering Jed's question.

'I guess so. Can it not wait?'

Abbir-Qualal looked about him as if checking that no-one could hear. 'It may be very important. Someone's life may depend on it, but I can say no more at present.'

Jed stirred. It was a very dramatic statement, but his new-found friend seemed in earnest. He shrugged. 'I'll go now.'

Ethan was sound asleep, still laid fully clothed on top of his bed. Jed quietly searched for the bag, eventually finding it resting under a cushion on the bed by the sleeping boy's head. Carefully, so as not to waken him, Jed reached inside and felt about for the clasp. Grasping it, he crept out of Ethan's room and back to his own where he handed it over to Abbir-Qualal who examined it closely.

'Jed, try and describe exactly where you found this?' he said intensely.

Jed screwed up his face trying to remember. 'Well, we had been walking down the main tunnel when it began to branch out into others either side of us. I went down one on the left. It had drawings on the walls…' he paused. 'That's all I can tell you. Oh, except my lamp will be down there. It went out when the bats started appearing and I forgot about it.'

Abbir-Qualal smiled. 'You've done well, Jed. Keep this to yourself my young friend. I have something I need to do but I will see you later. Maybe I'll give you a lesson in combat!'

With that, he abruptly left the room, quietly shutting the door behind him.

Jed got back into bed and lay on his back, clasping his hands behind his head and wishing he had been able to talk about the things he had overheard the night before. 'I'll ask him later,' he thought to himself as he closed his eyes and promptly fell back to sleep.

THE UNSEEN DIMENSION

Melchi had left Japhron and Mia to watch Ethan and Jed and was now sat within the vastness of the universe, waiting for the morning stars to begin their song. It was a place that he often came to when he needed some time alone to try and order the activities happening in the realms of men.

He had lived through many, many years now and had seen much. But this current string of events he knew to be particularly significant, and it was important he had time on his own to process them.

He recalled with intricate detail all that had been happening and studied the various threads that were weaving in and out of his view. The shout from the Underground, when the flame had been extinguished, still made his heart shudder, as did the sight of the Masquerader on the Island. The robed figure remained anonymous which was disconcerting to say the least as was some of Mia's thoughts on the subject. The invisible shield of protection, which surrounded Wynere, when the flame was lit, had disintegrated, leaving them easily exposed to the enemy. But then, into all this chaos was the arrival of Ethan and Jed.

Around him, others from the dimension had gathered. Each took their place amidst the stars and the patterns and colours of the galaxies. There was a hush of expectation. And then the song began. The melody was new, as it always was, every day. This one rang out, small at first as one star sang just one note that echoed into the distance. It was pure and resonant in its tone. A call to listen. An encouragement to be still. Gradually, more and more joined in. The harmonies adding rich layers of sound until the skies resounded with joy. Despite everything, Melchi found excitement stirring within his being and his hope steadied.

CHERITH

Over in Wynere, Ephron stood gazing at the Tower of the Lighted Flame. Rain had seemingly abandoned them and the dried blood from the slain guards could still be seen, an indelible mark in the earth.

A soldier approached. 'My lord,'

Ephron turned, startled out of his thoughts by the interruption.

'There's been word from the East Gate. Asaph along with the new apprentices have arrived. I was also to tell you that Nathan has sought shelter there and that Naomi never arrived. A search for her is underway.'

Ephron took this information in without giving anything away to the young officer as to what he was feeling. He just nodded his head and the soldier left to return to his post on the city wall. The sound of shouting reached the older man's ears and he sighed before pulling back his shoulders and taking a deep breath. Another day, another fight and still no advance from the enemy. It was no wonder the city was on edge, tense with waiting for an impending war that never seemed to arrive. That, in itself, was wearing, sucking the energy out of them. He took one last look at the Tower before turning to see where the latest brawl had broken out, his thoughts only partly on the matter in hand due to his concern for his friends and the whereabouts of Naomi.

❧ THE ISLAND

From back on the Island, Sharaaim stood inside the finished tower smiling with contentment. It was the exact replica.

'All is ready,' he said out loud to himself.

He turned his attention to the package that lay on the central pedestal and carefully removed the leather skin of the outer layer. Dropping it to the floor he began to peel back the next piece of cloth that was protecting what was hidden beneath. His eyes gleamed with excitement for he had longed for this moment since the day he had been inaugurated.

Gazing at the object before him he gasped. It was more beautiful than he could have ever imagined. Reaching out with trembling fingers he went to touch it. Immediately, a strong current coursed through his body knocking him to the floor and sending him spinning across the room. He closed his eyes in fear. Gradually, all came to a standstill. He lay, flat on his back, unable to move, his heart pounding. The object glowed as though a fire burned from within its very being. Sharaaim covered his face unable to gaze upon it. Filled with fear, he got to his feet and fled from its presence, trembling. He did not look back.

⚑ CHERITH

The boys stood together in the entrance hall waiting for Asaph, wondering what the day was going to hold.

'I hope we get taught about sword fights,' Jed said, the memory of the previous night was still alive in his imagination.

'I don't,' Ethan murmured under his breath remembering the last time he and Jed had fought against each other. Physical combat was something he was neither skilled at nor inclined to do.

Suddenly from outside the door there was a commotion. Reniah's voice could be heard over the sound of horse's hooves. Nathan and Asaph came bounding down the stairs, followed swiftly by Shakirah who had arrived back in the early hours of the morning. Jed and Ethan hurriedly stood back to let them all by. Through the open door they saw Nathan lifting down an unconscious woman from the horse where she had been held by the rider. He quickly bore her through the hallway and up the stairs, closely followed by Reniah.

'Abbir-Qualal,' Ethan heard Asaph say to the rider as he dismounted. The two men hugged, clapping each other on the back.

'It is good to see you. Where did you discover her?'

'In the Tunnels of Tamore.'

'So near to us,' Asaph said, almost to himself. 'There is much to fill you in on and much we need to talk about.'

'I have sensed it,' Abbir-Qualal said. 'But come, let us first see how Naomi is.' He entered the hallway. Ethan noticed Jed step forward as though to speak but the strange man ran past them and up the stairs. Jed stepped back.

'I am sorry boys. As you can see there is much going on this morning. I will need to postpone our plans for today,' Asaph paused to speak to them.

'I could take them,' Shakirah said as she stood in the hallway next to the boys. 'It is Reniah that has the healing hands and there is little that I can do here at present.'

Asaph paused briefly before saying, 'Alright. But just to the "Heart of a Man" today. No further. And boys, remember what I said on the way here. Some lessons may not be what you expect but they all have an important purpose. Embrace each with courage and an open mind.'

Shakira smiled. 'Come, young warriors. We have a way to go. We must stop by the kitchens on the way for some supplies.'

'I will see you on your return,' Asaph said to them, particularly catching Jed's eye. The boy looked away, the strains of what he had overheard the night before was still ringing in his ears and he didn't want Asaph to see his growing distrust.

'Asaph,' Reniah called down to him, 'hurry.' As the Cherithite warrior turned away from the retreating backs of the boys, something caught his attention out of the corner of his eye and his hand immediately started to draw his sword. He saw a small creature skuttle away into the shadows behind the marble pillars and out of view. He slowly took his hand off the hilt of his weapon, still staring in the direction the creature had gone but all was quiet and there were no others. Hearing Reniah call his name again, he turned and swiftly made his way up the spiral staircase. His mind was disturbed by what he had just seen and by what he was beginning to sense had invaded the walls of Twyndale. He was confused as to when and how this had managed to happen but was glad that something was beginning to stir that may point to what was truly going on.

Barlkron snarled as he surveyed the Northern part of his kingdom. Stark, broken down iron structures defined the landscape of this formidable place. Fires constantly burned in metal braziers fuelled by some foul-smelling substance and everywhere was ash.

The bottom levels were inhabited by the lowest ranking creatures. They swarmed in dark masses or lay huddled together in the shadows. His lieutenants kept order to a degree with whips of nails that flamed red as they slashed through the air. Sounds of shrieks and hisses and screams of torment filled the stagnant atmosphere.

The middle tiers were where larger, more terrifying creatures dwelt. They had some level of ruling powers and, when given a chance, could dominate and control whole cities among the realms of men. Among these were the Hunters and Invaders. Barlkron often sent these creatures ahead of an attack to try and ensnare people by casting their hooks into any bitter thoughts, fears or old resentments. Whenever these hooks embedded themselves into someone, these creatures could manipulate the thoughts and actions of whoever they had caught. Their victims rarely knew what was happening and would unwittingly end up playing into the Underworld's schemes.

Barlkron stood calculating his next move. He had managed to infiltrate both Wynere and Twyndale, but knew that Asaph would be increasingly aware of this, and he was a force to be reckoned with. And then there were the two apprentices. Barlkron growled. He knew there was enough deception to keep things confused for a little while longer, but he still needed to rework part of his plan.

The boys had walked through the City of Twyndale and towards the mountains they had seen when they had first arrived at the East Gate. They were still shrouded in pale mist, creating a mystical but beautiful image. Along the way Shakirah had pointed out various plants that held healing properties. 'Myrtle moss is very good for bringing down a fever,' she was just saying, as she pointed out a purple-coloured bush. She bent down and pulled a sprig off it, rubbed it between her fingers and gave it to the boys to smell, 'No doubt Reniah will be using if for Naomi.'

'Is that the woman who was on the horse?' Ethan asked. 'Who is she?'

'Naomi is Nathan's wife and a relation of mine,' was the reply. 'She went missing a few days ago.'

'What is wrong with her?'

Shakirah let the remaining myrtle moss rub through her fingers and fall to the ground. 'I am not sure. She possibly was stung by a Scorpion Wasp. We understand that she was under attack from them on her way from Wynere to the East Gate. But where she has been, and why, we do not know.'

'And the man who found her, Abbir-Qualal, who is he?'

'A descendant of Cherith and as a brother to Asaph and Nathan. They were brought up together and were trained under the same mentor, though he is some years younger than them.' She smiled. 'We have known each other all our lives.'

Jed kept quiet not wanting it to be known that he and Abbir-Qualal had already met or that he had overheard the circumstances surrounding Naomi already. Shakirah turned and looked at him and he lowered his eyes. He somehow felt that she could read his inmost thoughts and he didn't want to give anything away.

The sound of thunderous rushing water had gradually become louder as they had travelled, and they increasingly found themselves having to raise their voices to be heard over the roar of it.

'The waterfall of the veiled mountain,' Shakirah shouted. 'This will lead us to the "Heart of a Man". It will reveal some things that your heart believes that, as yet, your mind does not understand.'

'What do you mean?' Jed shouted back at her, not liking the

sound of this at all.

'You will see,' Shakira answered, but her voice was scarcely heard. A sheen of spray was settling over them as they followed her across a wide stone ledge that lay behind the drop of water. The boys had to concentrate on where to put their feet as it was slightly uneven. Once they reached the middle, they all stopped so that the three now stood side by side, behind the waterfall, facing towards it.

Shakirah brought her hand to her eyes and gestured towards the view indicating that the boys should look forward into it. She, however, looked away. Today was not about her.

Jed stared, fascinated by the fierce beauty of what he saw. But as he looked, the sound gradually faded into silence and the waterfall parted as though it was just a curtain allowing him to see the stage beyond it. Scenes began to play out in front of him of experiences he had lived through. There was himself as a very young child at the door of a family who were going to look after him after his parents had died in an accident. He saw himself leaving that house and standing at another where the man who lived there was shaking his head and shutting the door in his face. He saw himself hiding in shadow, pinching food from the market sellers. He was now in the home where Sianna lived, eating food at the table served by the comforting face of her mother. The sight of Shalimar, the older sister, came into focus. She was smiling as she handed him a basket of bread. Suddenly the scene changed, and he saw himself running as though being chased, his eyes were darting around frantically as he kept glancing back behind him, the world around him grey and empty. He was then hiding in a hole in the ground. The hole became a prison. He was looking through iron bars above him and then the image changed direction and he realised he was gazing into a prison and Sianna, Shalimar and their mother were all in it. They looked sick and defeated, stained with dirt. He now saw Abbir-Qualal holding a sword and laughing as he fought with Asaph. But then Asaph turned around and Jed was shocked as his features became distorted and Asaph transformed into a grimacing, mocking image. Both men were beckoning for Jed to come join them. Jed drew a sword and a fight ensued. The movements were fast and blurred and then Jed saw his own shocked face looking down at his sword that was now embedded in Asaph. Horrified at what he had done he knelt and turned the limp body over. Then the curtain fell.

Ethan had first seen his reflection as though he was gazing into a mirror. The image of himself had then gradually altered so that it was now the face of a young man that gazed back at him. A crown sat upon his head and a tear was running down his cheek as he handed a small bundle to an older man. As this man turned around, Ethan saw that it was his grandpa and realised that the small bundle he held was a crying baby. As they walked away, the crown slipped off the young man's head and shattered into smithereens upon the floor. The scene changed and he saw a picture of his grandpa and himself in a boat. His grandpa held the oars and was trying to row towards land, but the current was too strong, and the boat kept getting pushed further away from where they were headed. He then saw himself drifting on his own in an expanse of sea – his grandpa was nowhere to be seen. He was now in Sharaaim's court, sat on a smaller throne next to the governors own. A crown was being placed upon his head and, around his feet, strange, black creatures lurked. He was then stood holding a sword upright in both his hands. The sword flickered and danced as though it was on fire and within the flame, he saw the face of Sharaaim. The scene swiftly altered, and he was now standing in a vast wilderness. He knew he had been searching for something or someone, but there was no one anywhere. He was all alone.

The vision came to an end as the image of the mirror suddenly shattered into shards, each piece caught in the rushing water of the waterfall until they became part of the crystal droplets that fell into the torrents and were carried away.

Naomi was in a fever. Reniah had left in search for some myrtle moss to make into a medicine that would help to bring this down. She was confused by what was happening for she sensed that there was some kind of darkness surrounding Naomi that she was not familiar with.

'Where did you find her?' Nathan demanded of Abbir-Qualal, 'and how did you know she was missing?'

'Word travels,' Abbir Qualal answered calmly. 'But it was the clasp that Jed found in the tunnels that alerted me.'

'Jed? How have you two met already?' Asaph enquired, keeping his expression neutral as he took hold of Naomi's hand and felt her forehead.

'Oh, I arrived last night and found him in the weaponry room brandishing a dagger.' He grinned at the memory.

'And?' Nathan interjected forcefully, unhappy at being kept in the dark about all that had happened.

Abbir-Qualal turned to look at him, 'And,' he over exaggerated the word, mimicking Nathan, 'he commented on my clasp and said he had found one just like it in the tunnels. I got him to show it to me, realised it was one like Naomi's and went to check it out. And here we are.' The younger man was casual in how he told the story, and this riled Nathan even further.

'You should have woken me.'

'Why? She might not have been there,' came the angry retort.

'That is not the point. She is MY wife. As much as you would have liked her for yourself.' He said this last statement almost to himself, but Abbir-Qualal heard.

Asaph put a restraining hand on Nathan's arm. 'Come now,' he intervened, 'She is found and that is the important thing. Abbir-Qualal you did well. We must send word to Ephron to let him know.'

'I'll see to it,' Abbir-Qualal strode angrily out of the room.

'You were hard on him,' Asaph said gently, after the door had closed.

'I know. But he is always so independent and impetuous. He should have let us know. What if he had walked into a trap!'

'This is Abbir-Qualal we are talking about,' Asaph said to his friend. 'Impetuous and independent, strong willed and lacking thought I agree, but he is also strong and astute, a skilled warrior and well able to handle a trap from the enemy.'

Nathan relented. 'Alright, alright, I will make amends when I see him.'

'Good,' Asaph said. 'You should go and rest a while. Let Reniah and I care for Naomi. Hopefully the fever will abate soon, and we can find out more as to what has happened.'

Nathan, deeply fatigued from the search and the worry, nodded. 'But let me know the minute she is awake,' he said as he left the room leaving Asaph deep in thought.

Pushing them all aside for a moment, he went and stood by Naomi. Her feet were lying bare on top of the bed, and he took them in his hands to examine them for any puncture wound. He traced his finger across a long, bloodied cut that was on her right foot, but it did not appear that the sting from the Scorpion Wasp was there. He frowned. Something was not quite right about all of this.

As he stood looking at her, her eyes flickered open, and her pale lips parted as she tried to speak. Asaph bent down close to her.

'What are you trying to say?' Asaph quietly asked.

Suddenly, without warning, Naomi's eyes went dark, and her features contorted. She sat up a little and hissed in Asaph's face. 'I saw fire and blood and burning,' she shrieked.

Asaph put his hand on her head. 'Come back to us Naomi,' he whispered. 'Be at peace.'

She immediately calmed down. Her eyes gradually returned to their usual vivid green colour, and she fell back upon the bed, her hair matted and wet around her face.

'Asaph,' she said weakly with a small smile as though seeing him for the first time.

'It is I,' he said smoothing back the hair from her eyes. 'Sleep now. You are safe, here at the East Gate.'

She closed her eyes and slept.

The boys and Shakirah had reached the grassy incline of the mountainside that would lead them back down into Twyndale. Ethan had been subdued since they had left the waterfall and Jed had stomped off in front of the other two, disturbed and angry by what he had seen and not wanting to talk about it. Shakirah had needed to call him back at one point so that they stayed together and had then suggested they stop for a while to dry off in the sun before making their descent back down into the city.

She handed them some bread, flavoured with fruit and spices, and then poured something from a leather water pouch into three small bowls. 'Drink this,' she had encouraged them, 'it will settle your heart and your minds.'

The liquid was sweet and tasted of pomegranates and lime and something else that neither boy recognised. As they drank, both felt the unsettling effects of what they had seen begin to abate and their minds began to clear from the tumultuous thoughts each had been left with.

'Why did you take us there?' Ethan eventually asked.

'It is the first lesson for apprentices and an important one. Every one of us have lived through experiences and made choices that have defined how we see the world and how we view ourselves and others. Because of this we sometimes learn a way of thinking and behaving that is contrary to the Cherithite way. The "Heart of a Man" will have shown you some of this. It may also have shown you some things that may happen if you continue to live governed by these incorrect concepts or, possibly, have given you some insight as to what may happen if you turn from them.

'Our up bringing isn't our fault though,' Jed interrupted harshly. 'We can't help being who we are.'

'That is true in part, Jeduthun,' Shakirah said softly. 'We all live through things that are not our fault, our choice, or desire. But recognising when those things have influenced us in a way that is not right and learning a different, truer way is the route to great freedom. Remember this, the past can either restrain or propel you depending on how you allow it to define you.'

'Is that true of you too?' Ethan asked.

Shakirah brought her green eyes to meet Ethan's own and held his stare. He looked away, uncomfortable with the scrutiny, and began winding strands of grass around his fingers, pulling them up from the roots.

'Like I said, we have all lived through things that have affected us for better and for worse. I am no exception.' Shakirah spoke softly.

The tone of her voice caused him to look up again and, in doing so, he thought he caught an expression of sadness upon Shakirah's face. He wondered what had happened to her to cause such pain and found himself wishing he could help her in some way.

Noticing his gaze, Shakirah smiled, and the cloud lifted. 'Now, enough talk,' she said with a laugh as she gathered their things. 'Come, I will race you to the bottom,' and jumping to her feet she started to run gracefully through the tall grass to the city below, her hair trailing behind her in the breeze. Ethan followed. For once, Jed did not rush to join in but walked casually on behind, weighed down by the increasing number of conflicting thoughts gathering in his head.

Reniah walked back into the room and immediately sensed that something disturbing had happened. She looked enquiringly at Asaph who raised his eyebrows at her and pursed his lips.

'The enemy has infiltrated us here,' he answered her unspoken question. 'There is somebody or something that is allowing him access.'

'Naomi?' Reniah enquired, frowning as she still couldn't see clearly into the past few days.

'I am not sure. Maybe inadvertently. I see no sting in her so the enemies poison should not be still affecting her, but she is saying some dark things. Yesterday evening, you seemed to have something to say but you felt unable to. Are you…'

At this moment, Abbir-Qualal entered the room causing further conversation on the subject to be lost.

'I have sent a messenger to Ephron with the news of Naomi. Is there any change?'

'Not yet, although she sleeps peacefully enough,' Reniah answered him. 'The myrtle moss should bring down her fever and then we will see.'

'How long will that take?'

'Usually within a few hours,' Reniah replied as she put a hand on Naomi's forehead, before reaching for a cool, damp cloth to wipe her face.

'Why don't you both go and eat with the boys. I will stay with her,' Abbir Qualal offered.

Reniah hesitated. 'I will go and get something and come back,' she said, 'I do not like to leave her for long.'

THE UNSEEN DIMENSION

Japhron sat analysing all that he had seen so that he could relay it to Melchi and Mia when they returned from the Library. Although they had all sensed that some evil had permeated the land of Twyndale, the enemy had left a few deceptive trails, each one designed to confuse and mislead. Untying each strand was proving difficult. But Barlkron could not do this forever. Sooner or later, the truth would be unveiled, and the prophecies would be fulfilled. Japhron both longed for and dreaded this happening.

Melchi and Mia were stood surrounded by images of the East Gate.

'You see the grey mark on Naomi's forehead?' Mia was saying to her mentor with conviction, when she was distracted by the sound of a brush sweeping against the floor.

Sshhhhwerp went the brush followed by footsteps. Sshhhwerp. The light grew brighter as the sound grew nearer.

Mia paused mid flow unable to discern which direction the sweeping was coming from.

Melchi was apparently not distracted in any way but was examining the said mark on Naomi. 'You are right young Mia. But look. That mark is on most humans,' he pointed out. 'Look, there,' he jabbed his finger towards the hearts or minds of numerous people who were living in Twyndale and also in Wynere. 'And there, and there. Nearly all have some area of unresolved pain or misaligned thinking that affects their behaviour. That's what causes those marks to appear. Why are you so set on Naomi?'

Sshhhwerp came the sound of the brush. Sshhhwerp. It was sounding very close now which caused Mia to wait before answering.

'Why are you not as convinced about say… Shakirah or Nathan or…' Melchi continued.

Sshhhwerp. The brush was pushed into view from the end of the aisle in which they were both stood, followed by the head and shoulders of one of the Seekers. Although dressed in grey overalls, the bright light made it appear silver which matched the long, bushy hair that surrounded his jolly face.

'I thought I heard voices,' the Seeker said, grinning with pleasure at the sight of them. 'Ooh. Wait one minute.' He bent down and extracted a word that had got caught between the bristles of the brush. Cupping it gently in his hands, he then flung it up into the air where it fluttered happily, creating a spark of colour before it flew away to find its place within the book it had come from.

'I thought you were sweeping up dirt, not finding lost words,' Mia smiled.

Melchi and the Seeker both laughed but not in a way that made Mia feel stupid, just in delight that she was learning new things and that they could teach her.

'I have never seen dirt anywhere,' the Seeker said. 'I don't think I would know what it looked like.'

'No. Me neither,' Melchi added, 'Except for what I have seen in the other realms. The Seekers job is not to keep things clean, Mia, but to seek out anything that has got lost and put it back in its place.'

'It would not do for any word to be lost or unaccounted for in someone's story now, would it? That is not in the Author's plan.' The Seeker winked at Mia and shook hands with Melchi before excusing himself to continue with his sweeping.

Sshhwerp… Sshhwerp… Sshhhwerp. The sound grew fainter.

Mia clicked her fingers. 'Of course,' she exclaimed. 'Let us just look at the end of Naomi's story to find out if I am right.'

The book in front of her obediently turned its pages. Mia waited for the words to jump out as had happened before. But all was still.

'Why is there no picture?' she asked in surprise. Walking over, she stood on tiptoes and peered into the open book. What she saw caused her to turn and look at Melchi in confusion.

'I don't understand,' she said, her brow wrinkled. 'There's nothing there.'

Melchi nodded his head. 'Well of course. The end hasn't happened yet, Mia. And only the Author knows the end from the beginning of someone's story. It is written to him but not known to us until it happens.'

'That makes sense, I guess. I did think that it would make our lives way too easy,' the young Seer-ling responded, slightly despondently.

'You will have to learn to be content with what you are allowed to see, knowing that it will always be revealed in its time.'

Mia sighed. 'I guess so,' she replied. 'I still think it's Naomi though.' She added in a whisper as she followed Melchi out of the Library. In the distance she could hear a faint Sshhhwerp and again the light dimmed leaving all in natural shadow.

CHAPTER THIRTEEN

THE IMAGE OF A THOUGHT

⚓ CHERITH

That third evening at the East Gate felt disjointed and fragmented to Ethan as there was so much coming and going that few people were in the same place at the same time. The evening meal had only been attended by himself, Jed and Shakira. Although, Nathan had briefly come in, loaded a platter with food and left again with very few words having been exchanged. Asaph and Reniah had also made a brief appearance but the strange man he had seen that morning did not come down at all. Jed and Shakira had, in turn, excused themselves and Ethan felt a bit like a guest who, having been invited to dinner, had been left to entertain himself.

He sat, gazing at the flames of the roaring fire and found his thoughts drifting back to his first day in Sharaaim's castle where, sat in front of another fire, he had discovered the truth of his lineage and been seduced by the idea of wealth and control. As he revisited his thoughts and actions during those few days, a sense of immense shame came over him and, unseen by his eyes, a small, black creature came sidling up close to him, its eyes wide and calculating.

'All alone?' Asaph's voice interrupted the moment, and the creature ran off with a shriek, its feet skidding on the wooden floor in its haste to get away. Asaph's eyes flitted to the shadows where it had gone and then back to Ethan.

'Yes, everyone else seems to have somewhere to be.'

Asaph poured something from a wooden jug into two goblets,

handed one to Ethan and then pulled up a chair by the fire with the other in his hand.

'Do you want to talk?' the Cherithite warrior asked. 'I sense that you are carrying a burden that need not be yours.'

Ethan paused and looked down at the goblet in his hand. 'There's such a lot that I don't understand, and I don't really know where to begin,' he paused briefly before forcing himself to continue. 'The night you came to get us and the other man appeared who looked like you and I couldn't move...'

'You want to know why that was?' Asaph asked gently.

'Well, yes. It's just that Jed was stood with you and I don't understand why it was hard for me to get to you and not for him? And why I was unsure who was who. Also, why was there someone else who looked like you and knew our names and everything?' his jumbled questions tailed off.

'Tell me about the days leading up to my arrival Ethan.'

The boy paused and looked away. He could feel Asaph's gaze was still on him but couldn't bear to meet it. He sighed and then spoke in a low voice. 'When the Cherithite people were being put under house arrest or in the cells, I wasn't. I was taken to Sharaaim and he told me that I was of royal descent and should train as his apprentice and become his heir.'

'How did you feel about that?'

'At first, I was scared but then really relieved that I wasn't going to be put in the cells. I had been waiting for you for so long and then Sharaaim said you were a myth and weren't coming and I think I began to believe that.'

'And then?' Asaph's voice remained gentle but still Ethan couldn't bear to look at him. He felt an increasing sense of shame envelop him.

'And then what he said seemed to make sense and I began to enjoy it,' his voice choked up a bit.

'What did you enjoy?'

'Oh, I don't know. The wealth maybe and the feeling I was important and had a connection to something. It made me less scared of everything. I began to think that I could change things for the better but I think, looking back, that it was me that was beginning to change and not for the better.' He stopped and turned to face Asaph. 'I was really foul to Jed. He doesn't like me,' he added.

Asaph surprised him by laughing out loud. 'He will learn to in time,' he said, 'Don't you trouble yourself about that.'

Ethan wasn't so sure. 'Maybe,' he said.

'The ways of the Underworld are shrouded in deceit and lies, Ethan, and they are always trying to trap us. When we choose to believe those lies or even consider them, they can cause us to act in ways that are not in keeping with those of the Cherithite people and that gives the Underworld power over us. Do you understand what I am saying?'

'I think so,' Ethan answered quietly.

'Because you started to doubt my existence and entertain a way of life that you were not called to, the more you would have struggled to discern what was right.'

For the first time, Ethan turned to look at Asaph as he talked. There was no reproach in his face and Ethan began to believe that everything was going to be alright after all. He had wondered if he would be allowed to stay once he had confessed to what he had done.

'So why could I not move that night? What was happening?'

'Because you had aligned yourself with some lies, the darkness of the Underworld began to have some power over you. It brought confusion and doubt and would have tried everything in its power to keep you bound to a future that was not yours. It was only when you chose me over the Masquerader and asked me to help you that those lies started to loosen and the Underworld's hold on you broke.'

Ethan looked at him, the shame he carried felt like a physical weight on his shoulders, but he could sense it was beginning to lift a little.

'I think I understand but, Asaph, who was the Masquerader? How will I recognise them again if I see them?'

Asaph took another sip from his goblet. 'I'm not yet certain of who it is but, as long as you keep applying what you are being taught, the more you will begin to sense the truth from the lies,' was the reply. 'And the light is always more powerful than the darkness, remember that.'

'That helps,' Ethan visibly relaxed. 'I'm really sorry for doubting you and for, well, everything.'

'I know. And it is done. No more dwelling on it.' Asaph smiled as he raised his goblet to Ethan and they both drank in companiable silence.

Jed had gone back to the weapons room after dinner hoping to find Abbir-Qualal. He was in luck for the Cherithite warrior was there, eyes closed and with his legs stretched out in front of a roaring fire. Jed noted an expression of anger on the man's face and was wondering if he should leave when Abbir-Qualal's eyes looked up and saw him standing there. Immediately the anger was replaced with a welcoming grin causing Jed to wonder if he had been mistaken.

'Jed! Come in. You're just the company I need after such a day. How was the waterfall?'

'Not what I was expecting,' Jed replied pointedly. He was still smarting from the revelations that had been shown him.

Abbir-Qualal sensed that Jed was not in the best of moods. 'I know what you need,' he said suddenly jumping to his feet. He went round the room, looking at the weapons that hung there and then lifted a sword from its place and handed it to Jed. 'Come on.'

Jed did not need to be asked twice.

Reniah stood with Nathan and Shakira watching Naomi sleep. She seemed peaceful enough even though the fever had not yet abated.

'I don't understand why she remains in this unconscious, feverish state,' Nathan said, frustrated at the fact that there was no seeming improvement.

'It will be revealed in time,' Shakirah answered, 'Let us see what tomorrow brings. She is not getting any worse so let us be hopeful in that.'

Reniah remained silent. Hidden in Naomi's sleeping form were some of the answers that they were all needing to help unlock the mysteries of the last few days. 'I just wish we understood the evil that is preventing her from regaining consciousness,' she thought to herself.

 THE UNSEEN DIMENSION

Mia turned and looked at Melchi and Japhron to see if they were convinced yet as to her suspicions.

Melchi turned to her.

'You are right in as much as the Underworld does have some hold over Naomi,' he admitted. 'The agitation her dreams create show us that much, but we must be careful to interpret things correctly otherwise we could end up being side tracked and looking at the wrong thing. Keep watching.'

CHERITH

Abbir-Qualal had paused, sword in the air and stared at Jed. 'So, are you telling me that you saw Asaph arrive on the Island three days before you were rescued? And that there were two of him on the night you left?'

Jed nodded, feeling better for both the physical fight he had just had and for being able to talk about what was troubling him.

Abbir-Qualal lowered his sword and looked at Jed. 'Did Asaph explain?'

'No. Ethan asked who the other person who looked like him was, but he just changed the subject and I've not found a time to ask him where he had been for those three days. There's something else. I overheard Asaph and the others talking last night after I left you. They said the flame had been extinguished and then talked about Naomi for ages but then also mentioned about me being sent back to the Island.' Jed's voice was bitter.

The trained Cherithite put his sword back in its sheath and held out his hand for Jed's weapon.

'Jed, there are a few things going on that even I have not heard about yet. Will you let me draw out the answers from Asaph myself? I will let you know what I find out, but it would be best if you did not speak to him directly. Can you trust me with that?'

Jed nodded.

Abbir-Qualal grinned at him. 'By the way, you have the makings of an excellent swordsman. You learn fast young warrior. In fact,' he handed the sword back to Jed, 'You keep this.'

Jed grinned, his eyes sparkling with excitement as he reached out and took the sword.

Far in the South of Cherith, from their homes in the mountains of Evernebulis, the Espionite people were preparing to wage war on Wynere. If anyone had enquired as to where this desire to attack had suddenly come from, they would have been unable to say, so subtle had the work of the Underworld forces been.

Barlkron watched. It never ceased to amaze him how easily the hearts of men could be swayed and manipulated, especially if bitterness or entitlement existed in them somewhere. He smiled, pleased with his success. Tomorrow was going to be interesting.

Tomorrow arrived and it was muggy and warm, even from the early hours of the morning. The lack of rain was causing pressure to build in the atmosphere and everything was beginning to wilt. Asaph stood looking at the drooping plants, wondering if any ploy of the Underworld was at work in all this. It was just one of many thoughts running through his mind for he was burdened with all that was happening in Wynere and he was well aware that his presence there would be greatly desired. However, he just couldn't shake the sense that some of the answers he was looking for were close by him here, at the East Gate, and, until more was revealed, he knew he needed to stay.

'Asaph?' Ethan interrupted his thoughts.

The man turned round to see the two boys approaching, dressed and ready for the third day of training. He grinned at them. 'You two are early!'

'Earlier we start, the earlier we finish, right?' Jed said.

Asaph glanced at him. There was something in the boy's attitude that was not quite right and that would not help in the day's challenge. 'Is everything alright, Jed?'

Jed nodded without making eye contact. 'Yes. Where are we going today?' he answered abruptly, steering the subject away from himself. Ethan looked at him, surprised at his tone of voice.

'Actually, we are going back inside the house,' Asaph said leading the way back into the entrance hall and to a side of the building that the boys had not yet seen. Stretching in front of them was a long, empty corridor, leading off from which were many doors.

'The first thing I would like you to do is choose a door,' Asaph informed them.

Jed immediately chose a huge, heavy looking, wooden door which was decorated with large iron studs. 'It looks like a warrior's door,' the boy thought.

Ethan took longer deciding but, in the end, he chose the simplest looking door. 'This one looks safe,' he thought.

Asaph looked at them. 'Today's training is a continuation from yesterday so bear in mind some of the things that you were shown. Remember, whatever happens, I am not far away so if you need me, just call.' The boys nodded.

'When you are ready, you can enter,' Asaph said to them.

Ethan turned the handle of his door and hesitantly stepped inside. It swung shut behind him and he immediately found himself standing in an expanse of desert. All he could see were ripples of sand dunes stretching out into the horizon. He turned back around but the door was no longer in sight. Ethan's heart began to pound with the old, familiar panic. This was his worst nightmare, trapped, with nowhere to hide and all alone.

He began to walk, wishing there was something he could put over his head to protect him from the scorching heat. Looking down, his eyes caught sight of a piece of cloth poking up from just below the surface of the sand. Bending down, he grabbed it and pulled. It happened to be a large piece of flimsy material that he used to wrap around his head like a turban and then over his mouth. Feeling slightly more protected he continued to walk.

'Maybe there are pirates beyond those dunes,' he thought, his imagination beginning to get the better of him.

Suddenly, he heard the clamour of hooves and the sound of shouts and whistles. Galloping towards him was the very thing that he had feared. A band of pirates, dressed in black with turbans on their heads and brandishing swords, were heading straight towards him.

'They are going to capture me,' the boy thought, rooted to the spot in fear.

No sooner had he thought this when he felt a hand grab him from his shirt collar and swing him up onto the back of a horse behind its rider. Ethan clung on for dear life. It was all happening so fast that he couldn't gather his thoughts quick enough to work out what to do. He was being jolted all over the place. 'I'm going to fall off,' the boy thought to himself. Immediately, he slid off the animals back and landed unhurt in the soft sand. The other horses galloped past him as he curled up in a ball with his hands over his head to protect himself from their thundering hooves.

As the sound of them grew faint, Ethan stood to his feet. 'I need water and shade,' he thought to himself beginning to panic.

In that very moment, way in the distance, his eyes began to make out the outline of a palm tree which looked like it was standing next to a pool of water. Trudging through the sand towards it, growing hotter and more uncomfortable with each step, he wondered if it was real or his imagination playing tricks on him. 'I guess it will just be a mirage,' he thought to himself as he reached out towards the pool. As he did this, it all disintegrated into sand. He could have wept.

Sitting down, the heat burning through his clothes, he took a deep breath and tried to shut down the jumble of cluttered thoughts that were causing him to panic. It was as he did this that a memory came back to him of something that Jed had mentioned in the tunnels. 'Amos said that Asaph wouldn't ask us to do anything without giving us all we need to do it.'

'But I haven't got anything,' Ethan thought, confusion causing him to frown. 'I'm here on my own. Just me with my thoughts.' In that moment, an idea began to take shape in Ethan's mind. He traced back to what had happened since he had entered through the door. He had thought about needing a head covering and then there it was, hidden, waiting for him to discover it. He had thought there may be pirates and there they were. He had thought he would be captured, and he was. He had imagined falling off the horse, and he did. He had thought about shade and water and, once again, there they had been.

Slowly, he stood to his feet and looked about him. 'It is shade and water that I need the most,' he said out loud and immediately, for the second time, there was the palm tree with the pool of water next to it. Without hesitation, Ethan jumped into the pool, fully clothed and this time, it held its substance. He laughed as he splashed about in the cool water, immensely grateful for the shade of the tree.

'It would be good to know that I'm not on my own,' he was thinking to himself, when his eyes caught the outline of a figure standing a little way off. The figure was surrounded in a haze of light so he was unable to clearly identify their features, but he could make out the short stocky build, the brown skin and the muscled arms holding a sword.

Ethan laughed.

'If only Asaph were here to see me now,' he thought.

'I see you have begun to recognise the power of your thoughts,' a voice came from behind the tree and Asaph's grinning face came into view.

Ethan splashed to the edge of the pool and Asaph reached down to help pull him out.

'Does what I think carry that much power?' Ethan asked as he stood dripping onto the sand, wringing out his shirt as best he could.

Asaph nodded. 'It will not always be as virtual as what you have just experienced to the natural eye but yes. Remember, all the greatest inventions and creative ideas of the world have started as an image in our thoughts. It is also where our fears and expectations begin. False expectation has the power to attract around us the very thing we would wish to avoid but of course, the opposite is also true as you have just discovered. Learning to control our minds is a big lesson to learn and one that a Cherithite Warrior must understand. Now, come, let's go and see how Jed is faring.'

Ethan nodded and immediately the desert disappeared from around him and he found himself facing the door he had come through. Pushing it open, he walked back into the corridor to wait for Jed. His clothes immediately dried.

Jed had watched as Ethan disappeared through his door before turning to push hard against the one that he had chosen for himself. Just as he was about to enter, Asaph caught his arm.

'Be careful where you allow your thoughts to settle, Jed. Remember on the Island when you discerned that I was Asaph even when Ethan was thinking the opposite? You have an ability to know what the truth is, even when no one has taught you. Trust that!'

Jed shrugged Asaph's hand off. 'Sure,' he said as he entered through the door.

He immediately found himself in a room that was pitch black. He held out his hand in front of his face, but he couldn't see it. The quietness was deafening, and he found himself clearing his throat just to break the unnerving silence. Standing with his feet slightly apart, he circled around trying to work out if he there was anyone else in the room with him.

'I wish I had a sword he thought,' and immediately he felt the substance of one in his hand. He held it out in front of himself. 'I wish I knew if someone else is here with me,' he thought and immediately the blade of his sword hit against the metal of another.

Jed tried to centre his balance as he fought against this invisible foe, but he found it impossible to read his opponent when he couldn't see them. His every move was outwitted, and he would find himself with the blade of a sword pressed against his throat or tripped up and sprawled out on the floor. The other person did not once speak to him which Jed found unnerving and just fuelled his anger.

'I don't want to fight someone I can't see, or battle someone I can't beat,' he thought to himself and immediately sensed that he was on his own.

'Hello,' he called out, just to make sure. But was greeted by silence.

He sat on the floor, knees against his chest with his head burrowed into his arms trying to think how this test related to yesterday. He realised that he did not respond well when he felt trapped, or in a fight that he could not win, but he couldn't work out how knowing this helped him with the current challenge he was facing.

'It would be easier if there was some light,' he thought to himself and immediately a candle appeared in the centre of the room casting a comforting glow around him and he now saw that he was alone in a locked room. Nothing was in it apart from himself and a key lying on the floor next to the candle.

Getting to his feet, Jed examined the walls of the room but there was no door or lock that he could see. The key, however, reminded him of his experience in the Tunnels of Tamore and the reality that something could appear real and yet not actually be so.

'I just need to see the door,' he thought to himself and, as soon as this idea came to him, the outline of a door came clearly into view.

By now, Jed was beginning to realise that the environment around him was responding to his thoughts and ideas. 'Lesson learnt,' he said to himself proudly as he went to let himself out of the room. 'Time to go.' He inserted the key into the lock and turned it. The door however would not open.

Jed kicked it, rattled the handle and tried the key again. Nothing worked.

'There must be another door,' he thought to himself and immediately around the walls, one after the other, several doors appeared in military succession. Jed tried the key in each lock of each door but found that none of them opened.

'This is the wrong key,' he said to himself. 'I need a different one.' Hearing a rattle, he glanced down at the floor and found a whole pile of keys lying next to the flicker of the burning candle. He picked up a few and went round the room, inserting every one of them into the locks until he was fed up and confused as to which keys he had tried and which he hadn't.

'I don't know what to do,' he said out loud, frustrated with himself. 'Asaph,' he shouted, just wanting to escape the confines of this prison he felt himself trapped in.

Immediately one of the doors opened and there was Asaph and Ethan peering in at him.

Even though this exercise had not been a competition, Jed felt like Ethan had won and this fuelled his increasing sense of frustration and anger. He barged through the middle of them without speaking, and stormed off down the corridor, leaving Ethan looking horrified at his rudeness to Asaph.

"Jed…' he called after the angry boy.

'Let him go,' Asaph told him. 'He is not in the frame of mind at present to listen.'

Asaph watched as the creature he had glimpsed yesterday followed Jed, its black body appearing as a shadow against the boy's feet. His heart was heavy with the weight of what he was beginning to sense was happening around him. 'The enemy has been cunning,' he thought to himself.

THE UNSEEN DIMENSION

Melchi had also noticed something in the events of the day that had deeply burdened his heart. 'I hope this is another misdirection,' he thought to himself, unwilling to acknowledge that what he had seen could possibly be true. Japhron stood and placed his hand on the older Seer's shoulder.

Mia saw this and wondered what it was they were seeing that she was not.

CHAPTER FOURTEEN

THE BONDS OF TRUST

CHERITH

Jed was sat by the pool near the East Gates, fingering the iron key in his hands and pondering whether he dared use it to leave, when he heard someone approaching. Turning around, he was surprised to see Ethan coming towards him holding a platter of food.

'I thought you might be hungry as you missed dinner.'

Jed stared for a second before reaching out for the platter and grunting a begrudging thanks.

Ethan hesitated, not knowing whether to stay or leave. It was the first time the boys had been on their own since arriving at the East Gate and it felt awkward. Two strangers, thrown into the same story but with no personal history to link them together. He glanced at the key in Jed's hand and wondered what he could do or say to help.

'It seems a long time since we left the Island,' he remarked eventually. 'Do you remember when we first met? You completely thrashed me.'

Jed surprisingly laughed. His mouth was so full of food, that crumbs sprayed everywhere. Ethan laughed too.

'And then you had me put in the pit for it,' Jed said rolling his eyes.

'True. Sorry.'

'I guess it puts us even,' Jed said unexpectedly. His unresolved issue with Asaph currently overshadowed other offences and he felt in need of an ally.

'Could you show me what I'm doing wrong? Apart from a few lessons at the Castle, I've had no practise at combat.'

'I can tell!' Jed remarked but with a grin so that the sting of the statement didn't hurt. 'Yes, I can show you. From what I saw, you've been taught to fight from a place of anger. That will always cloud your ability to think clearly.' He shoved another piece of bread in his mouth and then jumped to his feet. 'Right, stand like you were taught. Now, come at me like you were shown and I'll show you what I do to block an attack.'

Abbir-Qualal poked his head around the door of Naomi's room. 'How is she?' he whispered.

'No change,' Reniah answered, looking up. 'I am perplexed by her lack of response to our remedies.' She sat back in her chair and looked at him. 'We have hardly seen you since you returned from your journey South. Did all go well?'

'As well as can be expected,' Abbir-Qualal answered without elaborating any further.

'Have you met our two apprentices yet?'

'Only Jed. He reminds me of myself at his age,' he said with a grin.

Reniah smiled. 'Yes, I can see that.' She turned her attention once more to Naomi who had stirred in her sleep. 'Did Asaph find you? He came looking for you just a few moments ago.'

She looked up just in time to see a strange expression cross the young warriors face but, seeing she was staring questioningly at him, Abbir-Qualal immediately smiled.

'I will go and seek him out then,' he said withdrawing his head and shutting the door behind him.

Reniah was thoughtful as she once more wrung out a cloth in cool water to bathe Naomi's face.

Ethan had, at last, managed to dodge Jed's fist by turning away from the punch and bringing the flat of his hand to block a further move.

'That's good,' Jed said, 'You're getting there. Try again.'

This time Ethan managed to not only block the attack but also grab and twist Jed's arm behind his back. Releasing him from his grasp, Ethan grinned. 'Yes!' he shouted punching the air with gratification. He didn't see Jed creep up behind him and use his foot to trip Ethan up and bring him to the ground.

'Final lesson of the day,' Jed said grinning, 'Do not take your eye off your opponent.' He helped pull Ethan to his feet. 'That was good. I'll show you more tomorrow. Maybe Abbir-Qualal will teach us something new.'

'I've not met him yet,' Ethan said before adding hesitantly, 'Does that mean you're staying? It's just that I saw the key to the gates in your hand.'

Jed sat down, cross legged on the floor and picked up an apple. Rubbing it on his sleeve to bring out the shine, he took a bite, chewed and swallowed before asking, 'Do you wonder why Asaph chose us? I mean, why leave so many behind and take only us?'

Ethan took his time replying as this was a question he hadn't thought of before.

'Maybe it's because we were the ones looking for him,' he replied eventually. 'You and I were often sat, watching, waiting, when no one else was.'

'Do you wish we hadn't come or wonder if we have chosen the wrong side?' Jed said looking at Ethan. The boy flinched in seeing Jed's expression. It was so hard and bitter.

'What's happened Jed? You were the one convinced that Asaph was real even when I wasn't and you were the one who could tell him from the Masquerader when I couldn't. Why are you doubting him now?'

Jed threw the apple core into the pool before turning to face Ethan. 'There's some things you should know,' he said, picking at the grass. Ethan sat quietly as Jed told him of all that he had overheard on their second night at Wynere and of the fact that Asaph had been on the Island for three days before they had seen him.

'If he knows things before we tell him, I don't understand why he left me in that stinking prison for so long.'

Ethan surprised himself as he listened for, instead of the familiar sense of panic and fear that he usually felt, he was calm and clear minded.

'There will be a reason we weren't told about the flame,

Jed. And we don't yet know the context of the conversation you overheard. Maybe one day we will go back to the Island, maybe to help rescue our people. Asaph promised me I would see my grandpa again so that does make sense. And maybe it wasn't him you saw pull up on the Island that night? I think we should find Asaph and ask him outright about all of this.'

Jed nodded. 'Maybe you're right. Let's do that first thing in the morning,' he said as he got to his feet.

The trees on the other side of the pool shimmered in shadows as the daylight had surreptitiously passed its baton to the dusk. From between them, a robed figure retreated, their expression fierce and calculating. Time was running out faster than they had anticipated, and they couldn't wait any longer.

THE UNSEEN DIMENSION

Melchi and Japhron closed their eyes. The veil was lifting and what it showed them was unbearable to watch.

'We should send the Guardians back to the East Gate. The boys will need their assistance,' Melchi said. 'And send others to Wynere. The people will also need all the help we can give them.'

'I will send word,' Japhron quietly answered.

Mia stood to her feet and stretched. 'I think I will just go for a little wander,' she announced to the other two.

Melchi looked at her, knowing what was on her mind.

'Don't be too long, Mia,' was all he said.

CHERITH

Ephron was awakened from his sleep by a loud knocking on his door.

'What is it?' he called out while reaching for his robe.

A young soldier entered; his face grim with the news he had to tell.

'We have news that an army from Evernebulis is marching towards Hymangees,' he informed the elder. 'They are carrying weapons and are less than two days travel from here my Lord,' the soldier informed him.

'Send a rider to the East Gate and have them request Asaph,

157

Nathan and Abbir-Qualal return immediately,' he ordered.

The soldier bowed his head and hurriedly left the room.

'And so it begins,' the older man thought. 'Although, I wonder why it is the Espionites that wage war against us after all this time. Is this really the Underworld's plan? For Wynere to be overthrown by the Espionites?' The more he thought about this, the more unconvinced he was that this was the reason the flame had been extinguished. 'There's more to this than I understand,' he said out loud before adding to himself, 'I hope that Asaph has more insight than me.'

Asaph awoke with a start. His dreams had been filled with the sound of marching feet and the sight of large, ancient creatures swooping over Wynere with their leathery wings. A robed figure was riding on the back of one of them and the wind had caught at the hood they wore, lifting it for a brief second to partially reveal the face that lay concealed beneath it. Disturbed, Asaph rose and dressed and strapped his sword around his waist. Leaving his room, he crossed the landing to where Naomi lay sleeping and pushed open the door. Reniah immediately stirred in her chair.

'Asaph, what is it?'

'Can you check again that no sting rests in Naomi's flesh,' he said urgently. I am confused by the wound on her foot. I just can't shake the feeling that she has been used as a decoy this whole time to mask where the evil really lies. Maybe, once this deception is dealt with, we will have a clearer understanding as to where the betrayal really is.'

'I will check,' Reniah said, quickly rising to her feet. 'Have you yet talked with Abbir-Qualal?'

'No. I searched for him after I left here earlier but I couldn't find him.'

'He said he was going to look for you.'

'I will go now and see if he is still awake. I have not been on my own with him since he arrived and there is much we need to talk about.' As he turned to go, Reniah spoke again.

'I have seen an army camped at Hymangees in my dreams.'

'Yes. I too have sensed that invaders are heading towards Wynere,' Asaph confirmed what she was saying. 'Although, I wonder how much of that is a distraction to turn our attention away from where we should really be focussing.'

'Yes, I agree,' Reniah said, nodding. 'It's important that we keep reminding ourselves of the prophecies concerning the boys and the flame, if this is indeed the fulfilment of that particular prophecy.'

Asaph nodded. 'I am more and more convinced that it is,' he said as he left the room.

The Espionites had set up camp among the pillars of Hymangees. Fires blazed and crackled on the dried-out earth and the smell of roasting meat wafted across the open plains. Among them lurked the dark shadows of creatures from the Underworld, their job was to incite anger and resentment among the hearts of these warriors so that they did not turn back. They snaked in and around the fires where the men sat talking and slid over their feet and around their shoulders. Everywhere they went, the conversation turned to the past and to all that had occurred between them and the Cherithite people from Wynere. Age old offences, passed on from generation to generation, were revisited until the whole company were filled with the desire for revenge. Barlkron smiled. 'This will do very well,' he thought to himself as he watched.

Unable to sleep, Jed had got out of bed and wandered down the stairs in search of something to eat. He was just helping himself to some bread and cheese, still laid out in the dining hall from dinner, when the door opened and Asaph peered in as though looking for someone. He appeared surprised to see Jed sat there.

'Trouble sleeping?'

Jed nodded.

Asaph looked behind him, paused briefly, and then purposefully entered the room. He pulled up a chair and reached for an orange from a bowl. He scored the skin with a small knife so that he could peel back the layers and pull apart the segments of fruit beneath. While engaged in this, he turned to Jed.

'I have sensed a growing distrust in you, young warrior. Is all well?'

Jed, unafraid of confrontation, did not hesitate to answer.

'Do you know everything, Asaph? I mean, do you see everything before it happens?'

'I know of many things,' Asaph replied. 'And what I don't see I can often sense. You will learn the same as you continue your training. Some things though have to wait in line to be revealed.'

'So, what I don't understand is, if you knew that I was in the cells at the Castle, why did you leave me there for three days? What were you doing on the Island all that time and why didn't you rescue me sooner?'

Asaph looked up sharply. 'What do you mean for three days? I arrived on the Island the same night that we left it together?'

'But I saw you arrive by boat three nights before,' Jed faltered, suddenly uncertain.

Asaph shook his head, laid down the orange and leaned forward. His whole posture was charged, the warrior in him was on alert. 'It wasn't me, Jed. But this information is vitally important. Tell me again what you saw and leave nothing out, however insignificant.'

Behind the door, the robed figure listened in. Everything was unravelling fast and it would only be a matter of time now before he was discovered. Hastily, he retreated causing the small, frog like creatures to dodge out of his way as he strode up the stairs. It was time to make his move.

Reniah had examined Naomi's feet again. As she did this, she was reminded of the image she had seen in the waterfall and of Naomi raising her hand to wave. 'Was there something about that which was a clue?' she wondered. She had learned over the years that insight often came to her through daily events that seemed insignificant at the time.

Picking up Naomi's hands, she searched for any other puncture wound. There was nothing on the left hand but, on closer examination, she noticed on the palm of the right was a small red line running up to the thumb. Tracing it, Reniah gasped. There, under the nail, was the stinger that they had missed. This was the reason that Naomi was not recovering. The poison of the enemy was still infecting her.

Hastily, she gathered around her all she would need to extract this thorn from Naomi's flesh, all the time wondering how it had managed to lodge itself in such a hidden, difficult place. 'It's almost as if someone has pushed this into you deliberately,' she spoke out loud to Naomi, her thoughts already concluding that, if this was the case, her friend had indeed been used as a decoy. Reniah instinctively knew that someone must be close by if they needed attention to be diverted away from themselves.

She frowned as she turned her full attention to the task in hand.

Jed sat pondering on what Asaph had told him. There seemed to be a link between who had extinguished the flame and the person he had seen arrive on the Island. This information had to be particularly important for Asaph had immediately taken his leave, telling Jed to get some rest for, early tomorrow, they would be leaving for Wynere.

'Asaph,' Jed had called, causing the warrior to stop and turn. 'What was the point of the darkened room and the invisible foe?'

Asaph smiled at him, 'If you can learn to trust when you can't see, you will never be at the mercy of the darkness.' With that reply, he left the room, shutting the door behind him.

Jed sat there for a few more minutes pondering on what he had been told. The relief he felt on learning that Asaph had not abandoned him to the cells had dislodged the doubt he had begun to feel but with this relief came the revelation that his judgements had been increasingly clouded by his lack of trust. This understanding began to unravel many scenarios in his life and, for the first time, Jed saw that he had hidden behind natural strength and the ability to fight because he didn't trust people to help him or be on his side. He recalled what had happened to Ethan when he had started to doubt Asaph and, wanting to talk about it more, he went up the stairs to Ethan's room to wake him up.

🐺 THE ISLAND

It was late and Ethan's grandpa stood before Sharaaim in the tower, bleary eyed and confused as to why he had been awoken and brought here.

'So, old man. There is something I would have you do,' Sharaaim said, his eyes hard.

'What is it?'

'Pick that up,' the governor demanded, pointing to the package that lay on the floor from where it had dropped when he had fled from its presence. It now lay quiet and cold on the stone slabs.

Slowly, Ethan's grandpa bent down and lifted it up, removing the remaining covering to reveal what lay beneath. He gasped when he saw it and fingered it carefully, in awe at its beauty and craftsmanship. Sharaaim smiled his disfigured smile as he realised that the older man could touch it without any adverse reaction.

'Is this what I think it is?' the older man enquired, not quite able to believe what he was seeing.

Sharaaim did not answer the question, 'I need you to use it.'

The older man trembled as he placed the object on the pedestal and slowly withdrew his hand.

'That I cannot do,' he said resolutely, looking the governor in the eye.

'Is that so,' Sharaaim snarled. 'Let me see what I can do to have you change your mind.' He turned to the soldier at the door, 'Take this man to the cells.'

THE UNSEEN DIMENSION

Mia stood once more in the great Library. It's vastness still overwhelmed her. Resolutely, she went and stood in one of the aisles.

'I'd like to know about Nathan, Abbir Qualal and Asaph,' she spoke out clearly.

She waited. The book seemed to come out of nowhere, hurtling towards her at great speed. She actually thought it was going to crash into her but it managed to come to an abrupt halt just under her nose. She and the book stared at each other for a moment. Mia realised she was holding her breath.

'I appreciate your fast response, but do you think you can step back a little?' she asked. 'Also, please show me the past regarding the three men I mentioned.'

The book obediently moved away from Mia's face and its pages fluttered open. The words spilled out into the air, turning and swirling until the images began to play out in front of her. Everything was moving very fast though and Mia struggled to keep up.

'Why is this happening so quickly?' she asked.

'Because you have chosen to know something that is relevant right now,' the sing-song voice from her first visit to the Library echoed down the aisle. 'Pay close attention, Mia.'

Mia watched, trying to not even blink in case she missed something.

The lives of the three warriors held her in fascination. Of all three, Asaph was the one who captivated her the most. He was always surrounded by a glow of light and had held insight into the unseen realms even from when he was a baby. Strong, resolute, kind but fierce - he had been special since the beginning she realised.

Nathan and Abbir-Qualal were fighters. Nathan was always ready for battle. Strong, determined and not to be argued with, he did not lose to a fight easily. Abbir-Qualal was different, Mia thought as she watched. There was much hidden about him for he was a great thinker and calculated his moves carefully. Some would say he was highly strategic. And this was probably true. She realised she could not easily read him as she could the other two.

The images began to slow down, and Mia looked up from them. She felt uneasy and wondered why and when she had started to feel this.

'Maybe you have seen all you need to know,' the sing-song voice answered her thoughts.

Mia was jolted with a sudden revelation and without hesitation she turned and ran back to Melchi and Japhron as fast as her short legs could take her.

⚬ CHERITH

Jed sat on Ethan's bed relaying his conversation with Asaph.

'So, the man you saw that night with the boat, was he the one who extinguished the flame?' Ethan said, wide eyed.

'I think that's what Asaph believes,' Jed replied.

'If that's true, it's very possible that the Oil and Sword are on the Island!' Ethan added thoughtfully. 'I wonder why they were taken there!'

Their conversation was interrupted by a knock on the door

and Asaph strode purposefully into the room. His sword was sheathed and a shield was set upon his back.

'Jed, I know I said we would leave for Wynere tomorrow, but we need to leave now for the Island instead. Be as quick as you can. You too, Ethan. I'll meet you by the gates.' Asaph left the room without another word.

Ethan immediately jumped up, pulled on his clothes and grabbed the bag that Asaph had first given them. Jed returned to his own room for his sword, shield and cloak and then they both quietly descended the staircase and went out the front door into the night.

Crossing through the gardens they followed the white brick path that led down to the East Gates and to where Asaph stood waiting for them. He unlocked the gates with a key identical to the one that the boys had been given and, pushing them open, the small party walked out of the beauty of Twyndale and into the expanse of the night.

'Are Nathan and Abbir-Qualal not coming too?' Jed asked.

'I do not know if I can trust either of them,' was the reply. The boys looked at each other in confusion but Asaph did not elaborate any further and they could sense that this was not the time for conversation.

Unseen, Oholiab and Nehari followed, their hands resting on the hilt of their swords, and their expressions fierce. They were ready for battle.

THE UNSEEN DIMENSION

Melchi and Japhron were grateful that the two warriors were there. The boys' training was nowhere near complete and the circumstances they were walking into would challenge the most competent of warriors, never mind untrained apprentices.

'Where is Mia?' Japhron asked.

'She will be back with us any sec…' the word was not even completed before Mia came flying into the space, her pigtails bobbing around her face.

'I know who it is,' she said as she tried to get her breath. 'I don't know why I didn't see it before.'

CHAPTER FIFTEEN

TO THE BEATING OF DRUMS

CHERITH

The fever had at last broken and Naomi was sleeping peacefully. Nathan sat watching her, having told Reniah to get some much-needed sleep. This was, in part, being kind to Reniah but mostly it was because he wanted to be on his own when Naomi woke up. He needed to ask her where she had been on the night the flame went out and what she remembered about her journey to the East Gate.

'How alike you are to Shakirah. The family resemblance is so strong among you women of the East Gate,' he thought fondly as he gazed at her. Naomi stirred and opened her eyes and Nathan swiftly rose from his chair and went to sit on the side of the bed next to her.

Seeing her husband, Naomi's eyes filled with tears.

'Sssshhh,' he said to her, wiping her eyes. 'What is it my love? Are you in pain?'

'I think I have done something terrible,' she half whispered, a tear falling down her face.

Nathan gently lifted her hand and held it in his own.

'Why do you say that?' he quietly asked her.

'I have strange memories, ones filled with darkness and fire.' Her eyes were troubled, and her voice trembled as she spoke. 'I keep seeing my face reflected in it all.'

The door opened and Reniah entered. She smiled on seeing Naomi was awake but then caught sight of her tears and Nathan's worried expression.

'I think you should try to get some more sleep,' she said lightly, setting down the lamp she carried. 'The night always distorts reality and the truth will be much clearer in the morning and less frightening than it appears now.'

Naomi obediently closed her eyes, too weak to argue, and Reniah beckoned Nathan to follow her out onto the landing.

'What is she saying to you?' she asked.

Nathan shook his head, unwilling to voice his own fears.

Reniah put her hand on his arm, 'Asaph does not believe she is involved in this except, perhaps, unwittingly,' she said quietly.

'Naomi herself seems to think that she is,' Nathan replied, glancing about him to check no one else was about and could overhear.

'That is perhaps part of the Underworld's ploy do you not think?' Reniah said as she raised an eyebrow and put her head on one side to emphasise her point. 'Barlkron will constantly want to mislead and misdirect until confusion reigns and deceptions rule. I am also confused as to how the stinger got under Naomi's fingernail. That is not something I believe she would have done to herself. It all leads towards Naomi being used as a decoy.'

Nathan breathed a sigh of relief. 'Yes, you are right. Hopefully, she will be clearer minded in the morning. I do not like seeing her so distressed.' He paused before adding, 'Why a decoy though, especially here at the East Gates?'

Reniah sighed. 'It is a question that both Asaph and I have been wondering about too. But the truth will become clear. It always does when there are those who are willing to hear it and embrace its revelation, however painful that may be. You should go and rest for a while. I will stay with Naomi.'

The boys had followed Asaph for nearly an hour, struggling to keep up with the large strides that he was taking. No one had said a word. Only the occasional hoot of an owl or the rustle of some small creature as it dodged into hedgerows to escape the feet of the three travellers interrupted the silence.

'Why do we always leave at night?' Jed grumbled at one point.

Ethan didn't reply. He was using all his energy trying to keep up with Asaph, remembering that the Underworld couldn't see him if he kept close by the seasoned warrior.

They had passed by the Tunnels of Tamore on their left and followed the path away from the East Gates and down by the side of fields, lit only by the light of the moon and the occasional lamp from the windows of farmhouses.

'Are we not going back to the Island the way we came?' Jed asked. 'We could see Amos again if we do.'

'See who?' was the reply.

'Amos.'

'Why would we do that?'

Ethan glanced at Jed with raised eyebrows, confused by Asaph's response. Surely, he didn't believe that Amos was on the side of the enemy. Jed just shrugged his shoulders and pulled an 'I don't know' face.

The fields had eventually given way to the wider open space of wasteland. Asaph kept glancing up and behind them, watchful and alert. Every now and then he would stop suddenly in his tracks and raise his hand for the boys to keep still whilst he listened intently before relaxing and continuing to lead the way. The tension in the atmosphere was palpable. Ethan found the old familiar anxiety creeping back around his heart and tried even harder to keep as close to Asaph as possible. Jed's face was grim, his hand resting on his sword as he half jogged along.

Oholiab and Nehari kept close, their own swords in their hands, ready to strike within seconds if needed.

Shakirah was sat out in the gardens when she heard the sound of horse hooves from beyond the gates.

'Who bids entrance?' she called out as she placed the key in the lock.

'I have come with a message from Ephron of Wynere for Asaph, my lady.'

She hastily swung the gates open, and the young soldier quickly dismounted his horse.

'What is the message you bear?' Shakirah enquired.

'An army advances from Evernebulis and will be upon us in less than two days. His presence along with Abbir-Qualal and

Nathan is urgently required back in the city.'

'I will go myself to find him and relay the message. Will you not stay for some refreshment before returning?'

'Thank you, my lady, but no, I must immediately take my leave.'

Shakirah watched as the soldier swiftly mounted his horse and, with a slight bow of his head, turned and cantered away. Slowly, she closed and locked the gates before thoughtfully making her way back to the house.

Asaph and the boys had now approached a settlement on which many tents were set. Despite the hour, some people were still sat around small campfires, talking and eating. As the boys followed Asaph through the camp, they were aware of suspicious and wary eyes watching them and that all conversation became suspended in mid-sentence as they approached and remained so until they had walked past. It gave the distinct impression that they were not welcome and caused both Ethan and Jed to feel nervous and ill at ease. One older lady, partially bent over with age, caught Ethan's arm as he walked past her, restraining him. Her grip was strong as she grabbed his hand and turned it over, staring down into it as she traced the lines on it with her finger.

'I will tell you of your past,' she began to say in a soft, beguiling manner, 'and then of your future.'

Ethan snatched his hand away, 'I don't need you to, thank you,' he said as he ran to catch up with the other two who seemingly had not noticed what had just happened. He felt somehow defiled and wiped his hand on his tunic.

'I wonder why the insight of the Cherithite people doesn't make me feel like that?' he thought and made a mental note to ask someone about it when he got the chance.

Asaph led them to a tent in the middle of the settlement that was much larger than the rest and undoing the flap, he ducked inside telling the boys to wait for him until he called for them to enter.

Ethan quickly opened the bag and took out the map. He held it up trying to let the light of the moon illuminate it so that he could work out where abouts they were.

'I think we are at the tents of Edom,' he said quietly to Jed, passing the map for him to have a look.

'Edom,' Jed whispered in disbelief. 'But aren't they the ones that...'

'I know,' Ethan said shortly, cutting off Jed's comment. He was well aware that these were the people responsible for capturing his father and for what had happened to him and his grandpa.

'But why would Asaph...'

'Jed, Ethan, you can come in,' Asaph called out to them, interrupting any further discussion on the matter. Glancing at each other, they both pushed back the flap that covered the opening and cautiously stepped inside.

'This is Edom, who has kindly offered us shelter,' Asaph introduced them.

'So, these are the two apprentices everyone's talking about!' a large man, with a dark bushy beard and bald head spoke. He wore a fur garment that covered his upper body and leather trousers on the lower. Edom smiled at the boys, a blackened toothed smile that didn't quite reach his eyes. The air in the tent smelt of stale smoke and some strange sickly substance that made the boys feel lightheaded. He stared at the boys, his eyes settling on Ethan slightly longer before turning away, his expression neutral.

'Rest here for a few hours tonight,' he said to Asaph. 'I can lend you horses to take you to Evernebulis from where you can borrow a ship for the Island once the tide is in.'

Ethan stood, watching Edom as he spoke. There was nothing about this man that was trustworthy or likeable and he was confused as to why Asaph appeared to have an alliance with him.

'Why didn't Asaph warn me we were coming here?' he was thinking, feeling an unfamiliar rise of anger surge through his being.

'There is a tent on the outside of the camp that is unoccupied. I will have someone show it to you,' he heard Edom saying.

At this moment, a young woman entered the tent carrying cushions and blankets. The light from the lamps bounced off the many bracelets that circled her arms and the large, golden hoops in her ears. She did not look up, but kept her head bowed so that her dark eyes remained firmly fixed on the floor.

'Tamar will show you where to go,' Edom told them and the eyes of the woman briefly flickered up at him in acknowledgement of the order.

'Please, to come with me,' she said quietly, her voice low and almost musical in its rise and fall of the words. She turned and led them through the camp to a smaller tent where she set down what she was carrying, bowed her head and exited backwards without glancing up. As she did this, her foot caught on an edge of a sheepskin lying on the floor, and she stumbled. Ethan ran to help her regain her balance and, for a fleeting moment, her eyes lifted and settled on him. The expression on her face altered between recognition, fear and then confusion.

'What is it?' Ethan asked her, not understanding, but the shutters had come back down, and her eyes lowered back to the floor.

'Please to excuse me,' she said quietly as she fled, leaving Ethan staring in bewilderment after her.

'Everything alright?' Asaph asked him.

Ethan nodded despite feeling unsettled by what he was seeing. He was becoming more and more confused as to why Asaph would bring them here, especially given the history this clan had with his own.

'When will we leave?' Jed's question to Asaph interrupted his jumbled thoughts.

'In a few hours. You should try and get some sleep,' Asaph said as he went over to a corner of the tent and pulled out two long, wide benches which he proceeded to drag into the middle of the space.

'You boys take the cushions and furs from the floor and make yourselves comfortable on these. I'm going to go out and check that we haven't been followed.' He hastily left, leaving the boys alone.

Ethan looked at Jed. The boy had a frozen expression on his face and his eyes were wide as he looked at the tent entrance Asaph had just left by.

'What is it?' Ethan asked him, puzzled.

Oholiab went and stood next to Jed. His presence would give the boy strength and help keep him clear minded.

'Ethan, we need to get out of here,' Jed said fiercely.

'You don't think we are with Asaph, do you?' Ethan stated, confirming his own growing suspicions.

Jed shook his head, his mouth set in a grim line.

Barlkron snarled and kicked at the small creatures that were sat around him. He summoned one of his lieutenants to send him the Hunters. He had hoped the boys would be deceived for much longer than this but he had underestimated the environment the boys had been in and the impact that it had already had on them. He needed to move fast.

Shakirah went to wake up Nathan to relay the message from Wynere.

'I have yet to tell Asaph and Abbir-Qualal,' she said.

'Go and do that. I will meet them in the entrance hall as soon as I have spoken to Reniah about Naomi.'

'What of the boys?'

'Ask Asaph what he wants to do. I can't imagine he would have them accompany us but he may have some insight that I do not.'

She nodded and left the room, leaving Nathan to dress.

Quickly she went and knocked on Asaph's door.

'Do you know who it is?' Ethan glanced furtively around him as Jed was looking around the tent for anything that they might need. 'It must be someone from the East Gate.'

'I don't know. But the way he just dragged those benches into the middle of the room reminded me of the man who brought the boat ashore that night on the Island. I'm sure it's the same person.'

'I haven't felt right since we left the East Gate. Asaph, I mean, the Masquerader doesn't talk like Asaph would talk and what he said about Amos was strange. Also, I don't understand why he would bring us here. This place feels really dark.'

Jed paused from his search. 'Ethan, you aren't going to like this but I think we need a different plan than both of us just escaping from here. We don't know what he is up to yet and it may be good if one of us stays close to him so we can find out.'

Ethan sat down on one of the benches. 'What are you thinking?'

Jed told him.

Oholiab and Nehari listened in. Their faces were like flint, their stature straight and unyielding.

'I think the plan is a good one,' Nehari said as he listened.

'He has the makings of a strategist as well as a warrior,' Oholiab smiled. 'Be on high alert though, my friend. Barlkron will not settle until his plan is outworked.'

Nehari nodded as he followed Ethan out into the night. He quickly put his shield over the boy so that he would remain unseen as he exited the camp. Ethan kept watchful, hoping to see Tamar again so that he could question her as to why she had reacted like she had on seeing his face. He wondered if he had reminded her of someone, and if it could possibly be his father, but she was nowhere to be seen and he didn't dare risk being caught by lingering. He had to trust that Asaph was right when he had said there would be a right time to pursue these things.

Once Ethan had left, Jed quickly bundled cushions under a blanket on one of the benches to imitate the shape of someone lying there, before quietly lying down on the other and pretending to sleep.

Oholiab went and stood close by, his unseen presence provided both comfort and strength to Jed, which enabled the boy to keep alert and clear minded whilst he remained in this lifeless, heavy atmosphere.

Asaph was quickly dressing wondering what he should do. He remained convinced that the battle heading towards Wynere was a distraction, incited by the Underworld, and so it did not seem to him the right course of action for him to go there, despite Ephron sending word for them to return. The prophecies along with what Jed had told him kept circling around in his head.

'I am sure that the Oil and Sword are on the Island,' he thought as he placed daggers into straps around his ankles and sheathed his sword. Straightening up, he quickly left his room and went to the boys' quarters.

Nathan had gone to inform Reniah of what was happening. His heart was heavy with leaving Naomi but there was little choice when their city was under attack.

'Do not be anxious, Nathan,' the lady of the East Gate said to him when he had told her what was happening, 'She is safe here and I am sure that Naomi will soon return to being herself. You go.'

As Nathan turned to leave, Reniah put out her hand to stop him. 'The battle is not the one you think, Nathan. Be alert,' she said intensely.

He squeezed her hand in acknowledgement of what she had said before turning and leaving the room. The warrior in him was already focussed on the battle he was heading towards and he did not look back. As he closed the door behind him, he saw Asaph running from the boys' rooms and down the stairs, leaping over them a few at a time.

'Asaph, what's wrong,' he called out.

'The boys are gone,' came the shouted reply. 'Have you seen Abbir-Qualal?'

Nathan sprinted down the stairs behind his friend.

'Shall I check the grounds?' he asked.

Asaph looked at him. 'I don't think they are here. I should have been more watchful,' he chided himself.

'Where do you think they have gone?'

Asaph looked at him intently. 'I don't believe they would just leave. I'm thinking they went with someone they trust.'

'What do you want to do?'

'About what?' Abbir-Qualal's voice came from behind them.

'The boys are missing.' Nathan told him unaware of the expression on Asaph's face. If he had seen it, he would have questioned him as to what he was thinking.

Asaph himself was questioning what he was thinking. He stared intently at Abbir-Qualal.

'What is the matter, brother?' the younger man asked him with a quizzical look.

'I am wondering as to what the best plan is,' was the reply. 'I think we may need to split up into different directions. Nathan, you go to Wynere to help there, Abbir-Qualal you should stay here to protect Twyndale.'

'Where will you go?'

'To find the boys of course,' Asaph replied, staring intensely at the young warrior.

'Are you sure I would not be best served going to Wynere?' the younger man said. 'What is the point of me staying here when we are needed in battle?' his voice was slightly petulant.

'I am positive this is the better plan,' Asaph replied emphatically with a hard expression on his face. It was one the other two had rarely seen and signified that Asaph was not only ready for battle but was also not about to be argued with.

THE UNSEEN DIMENSION

Mia stared in disbelief. 'But… but…'

'Remember what I have been saying all along Mia,' Melchi said as he laid a hand on her arm. 'There are many deceptions that the enemy is weaving to confuse us. Sometimes we have to look past what we see and go by what we sense, to find the truth.'

Japhron watched as the young apprentice nodded, pushed back her shoulders and drew up her chair to watch what was happening. Already, even after such a short time, she was growing in knowledge and understanding and poise. He smiled, feeling a little nostalgic for the chatty Seer-ling that was even now talking less and watching more.

The Underworld was a swarm of activity. Barlkron addressed the two large creatures that stood in front of him. They had the bearings of men, but their skin was scaled, and their foreheads held deep ridges that drew down to their eyebrows, causing them to look almost reptilian. Behind their backs were massive wings which folded behind them in leathery neatness.

'You wish us to go hunting, oh mighty one?'

Barlkron paused and then slowly looked at them with narrowed, calculating eyes. 'Yes and no,' he replied. 'You know the boy's weaknesses. Use them to your advantage!'

'One travels alone, yes?' the other creature spoke, its voice was gravelly and hoarse.

'You and I both know that Cherithites do not travel alone, so stay hidden and make no advance upon them unless you are sure of your success.'

Barlkron watched as these two hideous beings left his presence before turning his attention back to what was happening in Cherith.

⚬ CHERITH

Ethan was running over the open wasteland towards what he hoped was the River Tamore. The plan was for him to return to the East Gate to find Asaph and the river was a clear guide for him to do that as it wound down from near the East Gate and towards the bottom of Wynere. Far in the distance, he could hear what sounded like the steady beat of drums. The noise resonated over the open ground like rumbling thunder. He stopped, hands on his knees, trying to catch his breath for a moment. Yet again, the scene reminded him of his desert experience and he paused for a second as he considered some of what he had learnt from it.

'Expectation is a powerful thing,' he recalled Asaph saying something to that effect.

He remembered how he had wanted to know that he was not alone and had seen the image of somebody standing just beyond him.

'I am not alone,' he said out loud. The words seemed empty and out of place and he felt ridiculous voicing them. To all intents and purposes, he was alone, standing in open space, an easy target for anyone.

'I am not alone,' he said the words out loud again. 'I have been given all I need,' he gripped the bag that Jed had insisted he take. 'You may need this more than me,' he had said pressing it into Ethan's hand. 'Asaph promised me I would see my grandpa again,' he also said out loud, 'so I must be safe.'

The more that Ethan addressed these thoughts out loud to himself, the more he found his resolve strengthening. He could almost physically feel courage and energy returning.

He stood up, straightened his shoulders and, once more, started to jog towards where he hoped the river lay.

Nehari smiled as he ran alongside. 'He is learning well,' he thought proudly.

Jed heard the Masquerader come back into the tent. He peered through barely opened eyes, but the man did not seem to be suspicious of anything as he merely sank into a chair and pulled a fur covering over him. A few minutes later and the slight sound of snoring reached his ears. Jed breathed a sigh of relief. This would hopefully buy Ethan the time that he needed to find Asaph and to get to the Island before they did.

Nathan had already left on horseback from the East Gate. He had taken a different route to the one that had brought him there as that space was too open for him to ride through safely. Asaph was still in the grounds of Twyndale deciding on his own course of action. His instinct was telling him that the boys were likely being taken back to the Island. However, he had a strong feeling to travel by way of the River Tamore, which made little sense as it was not near the coastal paths.

Reniah found him standing in the entrance hall.

'You are to leave Abbir-Qualal here?' she questioned. 'Is that wise?'

'I think it is for the best if you are agreeable?'

She paused before nodding and saying, yet again, 'Nothing is as it seems, Asaph. We must all be on our guard.'

'That is true,' was the reply. 'I am now going to follow a path that seems contrary to what makes sense.'

Reniah smiled, 'You must always follow your heart. You are highly trained so trust your instincts.'

Asaph smiled. That encouragement gave him the reassurance he needed. 'Reniah, on our first evening here when we were all talking, I was sure you wished to say something to me but felt restrained to do so. Can you tell me now?'

She paused before replying. 'I was sensing the betrayer was closer to home than we would have liked to believe although I did not know who it was then,' she confided sadly.

'And you know now?'

Reniah nodded and told him what she had noticed, her eyes brimming with pain.

Asaph nodded. 'Yes. I thought you may say it was them,' he replied, his own heart heavy with grief. 'Are you sure you will be alright here?'

'I too have my part to play. Do not be anxious for me.'

Unexpectedly, he leaned forward and gathered her to him. 'Be very careful my lady,' he said quietly before releasing her. Reniah watched him as he strode out of the house. She was a while before turning back around and walking slowly back up the stairs to Naomi's room. She had never felt the need for wisdom and courage as she currently did. And she had never quite felt so alone.

THE UNSEEN DIMENSION

Melchi and Japhron watched all the threads of the night unfold. Everything was fast advancing to its conclusion and they were grateful that warriors had been released to wage war in the middle realms over Hymangees. That alone would help to weaken the power of the Underworld in its schemes and give Asaph and the boys the time they needed to get into position and outwork the written plan.

Mia hardly dared blink in case she missed anything.

CHAPTER SIXTEEN

RACE AGAINST TIME

CHERITH

Ethan stared transfixed at the sky that lay over in the distance. A few moments ago, red and orange clouds had started to roll in, as though carried on a tide, and they were rising and falling, ebbing and flowing like crashing waves. Every now and then, there was a flash of white light which streaked across the space like lightning along with a menacing crackle. Mists appeared, moulding into strange, mystical, ghostly shapes that would suddenly vanish into nothing and, all the while, the steady, hypnotic beating of drums from the Espionite army continued, pounding into the night.

Ethan dragged his attention away and turned back to what lay in front of him. He could see where the wasteland was coming to an end and what looked like a forest began. He started to sprint towards it, hopeful that through the forest was the River Tamore. Every now and then he glanced again at the strange happenings centred in that one particular part of Cherith and wondered what was causing it.

Melchi, Japhron and Mia watched intensely from their vantage point.

Mia was enthralled with the battle she could see happening. 'So, that is what the Guardians do?' she said in wonder. 'They are magnificent.'

Despite himself, Melchi smiled. Mia's ability for joy was a beautiful thing.

'Ethan can see some of what is happening,' Japhron remarked to him.

Melchi turned to look at him. 'His sensitivity will give him some insight into the unseen realms as he becomes more aware of it,' he pointed out. 'It's one of the reasons why Barlkron would want to keep his attention turned towards the darkness. His desire would be for that to be more real to Ethan than the Cherithite ways.'

Japhron turned his attention back to Hymangees while Melchi kept his eyes firmly fixed on Ethan as he entered the dense forest. He had noticed that a Hunter from the Underworld was already skulking in there; its dark, scaly form merging against the dark bark of the tree trunks, making it almost invisible.

In the middle realm, above the Espionite army, a battle waged between the Guardians and the middle ranking creatures from the Underworld. They had arrived at virtually the same time and had advanced against each other, meeting in a clash of fire and electrical currents. Hunters and Invaders, sent by Barlkron, were wielding huge iron balls, in which poisonous spikes were embedded. These were attached to chains that the creatures used to swing above their heads, before unleashing them towards the Guardians. Every time the hit was blocked by fire from the Guardian's swords, lightning would flash across the sky with a deafening crack.

The Guardians flew across the space, always aiming for the heads of the creatures from the Underworld. Whenever they managed to decapitate one, the creature would melt away to skeleton, before reforming in mid-air, but each time they grew back, they were smaller and weaker than before. A second hit was usually enough to destroy them altogether.

As the battle raged unseen above them, the Espionite camp was being thrown into confusion beneath. Some were starting to question the plan to wage war against Wynere and others continued to be convinced that this was the right course of action. The army was beginning to turn on each other as small factions were breaking away and wanting to head back home but were being prevented from doing so by those who wanted to fight the Cherithites from Wynere. The lower ranking creatures that were crawling around on the ground found that they could no longer get near to some of the men and they turned their attention to those who they could still manipulate in the hope that they would overpower those who wanted to turn back.

Mia was completely enthralled as she watched all of this happening. It made so much more sense of the realms of men and the struggles they faced.

Ethan walked among the tall, pine trees of the forest, the smell of the needles under his feet emitting a comforting fragrance. The sound of the drums had lessened somewhat, blocked by the depth of the forest, and he had slowed his pace as the protection of the trees and the deepening quiet had diminished his sense of urgency.

'Maybe I can stop for a while,' he thought to himself.

Nehari looked around him. He sensed all was not well.

'Why do I think that I can help with all of this?' Ethan began to wonder. 'Even if I find Asaph, there's little that I can do. They're probably all better off without me.'

Nehari stood a little bit closer and Ethan blinked as though coming round from a trance.

'Come on,' he encouraged himself, 'you need to keep going. There isn't much time.'

The Hunter stayed hidden in the shadows. It had been stalking the young Cherithite for a while now, watching and waiting for a chance to attack. It carried something that resembled a fishing rod and every now and then it would cast this towards Ethan trying to embed the hook into him so that a negative thought would be allowed to attack the boys mind. Whenever Ethan ignored the thought and continued to move forward, Nehari was able to unhook it and hurl the sinister weapon back in the direction it had come from.

Ethan had just begun to pick up his pace when another thought came at him out of nowhere.

'What are you doing walking through a forest. You don't know what lies in here. You're just going to get lost and die in here alone.' Images of the bears from the walls of Sharaaim's Castle came flooding back to him and he looked about nervously, stopping and holding his breath at the slightest sound, his eyes wide. He found he was dragging his feet and that everything was becoming an effort. The Hunter smirked as it tried to reel him, in like a fish caught on the end of a line, realising that Ethan was susceptible to these negative thoughts, especially while he was tired and anxious.

'What is wrong with me,' Ethan wondered. 'I think I must be sick.'

Nehari raised his shield over the boy's head and, again, Ethan found a spurt of renewed energy and picked up his pace.

'You're just tired,' he spoke to himself. 'You must get to the East Gate and find Asaph. Jed is depending on you.'

Nehari unhooked him and, using his sword, batted it powerfully back in the direction it had come from. The Hunter yelped as the hook caught him in the eye. This gave Ethan a bit of time to get further ahead, spurred on even faster by the sound of water he could now hear ahead of him. However, before he could reach the riverbed, the hook, once again, came whizzing through the air, landing on his boot. Triumphantly, the creature from the Underworld began to reel in its prey yet again. Ethan tried to lift his caught foot, but it felt weighted to the ground. It was the best thing that could have happened for, immediately, he was reminded of the moment back on the Island when the Underworld had tried to prevent him from leaving with Asaph.

'Oh no you don't,' he said out loud. Reaching into the backpack, he grabbed the small dagger wondering whether it could somehow help him. He stood, knife in hand, with his feet slightly apart and his body tense and alert, ready for attack, not really sure what to do as last time, Asaph had been there to help.

'Asaph, where are you when I need you?' he said out loud to himself.

As he said this, a number of things happened all at the same time. Nehari stepped forward and slashed the line in half which caused the Hunter to lose its balance and fall backwards onto the forest floor. Then, before it had scrambled back to its feet, Asaph appeared through the trees, his sword glowing with fire and light which seemed to also reflect in his face, illuminating the strength and resolve that he carried. He advanced straight towards the Hunter, hurling a lasso around its head and yanking the creature towards him before thrusting his sword between its eyes. The creature howled, a piercing shriek that reverberated around the forest. Asaph pulled his sword out from the Hunter's head and thrust it into the creature's heart before withdrawing it again and slashing across its neck so that the head came clean off the body. The whole being crumpled into a mass on the forest floor before disintegrating, leaving nothing behind but a stale smell. The power of the Espionite sword did not allow the creature to reform.

Ethan watched, unable to see this invisible foe, though he could sense when it had been defeated, even before Asaph had wiped his sword.

'I'm so glad to see you,' he said as he sat on the forest floor, examining his boot. Nehari bent down and removed the unseen hook that was still embedded into the leather.

Asaph came and stood next to Ethan, putting a hand on his shoulder. Immediately, the boy felt strength returning and the fatigue and confusion that he had been feeling seemed to lift off him leaving him intensely alert and energised.

'Are you alright?' Asaph asked him.

'Yes, I'm fine.' He paused before adding, 'You are the real Asaph, aren't you?'

Asaph helped Ethan to his feet.

'I am,' he replied, smiling. 'Where's Jed?'

'With the Masquerader. When we realised it wasn't you who we were with, Jed came up with a plan.'

'You had better tell me of it,' Asaph said, his features strong and intense with resolve. For all the gentleness that Ethan had known from this man in the last few days, he was suddenly reminded of the fierce warrior he actually was, and was glad.

Jed had fallen asleep. He had tried hard not to, aware that he needed to keep alert, but his eyes had eventually grown heavy and the next thing he knew, a hand was shaking him on the shoulder.

'Wake up. We need to get moving,' the Masquerader said.

Jed opened his eyes and sat up, reaching for his boots. The man went over to where he thought Ethan slept but as he went to shake the sleeping boy, his hand met with nothing but the cushions and fur coverings. He frantically threw them onto the floor before kicking at the bench, overturning it in a rage. The man stormed over to Jed, placing his face close to the boys own. 'Where is he?' he snarled, his breath slightly stale.

'I don't know,' came the reply. 'He must have left while I was asleep.'

'Why would he do that?' the voice was sinister, low and threatening.

'How should I know?'

The Masquerader suddenly stood up and turned, his cloak billowing out behind him.

'Get up and come with me,' he commanded.

'Where are we going?'

'To Evernebulis to charter a ship. Ethan will have to suffer his own fate.'

Jed was surprised at how little restraint the Masquerader was now showing. He wasn't even trying to behave like Asaph anymore. He hoped that Ethan had gotten enough of a head start. He reached for his sword and shield, somehow finding courage not just in the things themselves but in the knowledge of where they had come from. It reminded him that he was from a family of warriors who were skilful in battle.

'You just need to find a cause,' Asaph had said.

'I think this may be it...' the boy thought grimly as he followed the Masquerader out into the camp.

Melchi and Japhron saw that the evil was beginning to take a permanent hold on the betrayer. The veil was slipping and soon he would be exposed for who he really was. Melchi's heart ached.

Back at the East Gate, Naomi was stood at the window in her room looking out on the gardens. It was all in shadow but some lamps were still burning, casting their glow in and around the contours of the bushes and plants and of the sculpture of the hands. She shivered.

'You are up.' Reniah stirred in the chair in which she had slept, waiting for Naomi to wake up. 'Are you cold?'

'No,' Naomi answered. 'A little weak still. I was just looking at the sculpture of the hands. I've always seen it as two friends reaching out to help one another but, tonight, it looks different to me as though one hand was reaching out to lead the other into danger.'

'Why do you say that?' Reniah prodded gently, coming to stand next to Naomi at the window.

A lone tear escaped from Naomi's eye and rolled down her cheek. 'It reminds me of a dream I keep having. I was lying on the moors, unable to move. There was a great weight pressing down against me and then someone rescued me. They reached down to lift me up and carried me to safety, but I actually found myself imprisoned and in darkness, in and out of conscious thought, attacked by dreams of fire and flame.'

'Why do you think all this this was a dream?'

'Because it is all so blurred and out of focus.'

'Can you remember who it was that rescued you on the moor?' Reniah asked.

Naomi turned and looked at her. 'Well, yes and no. Sometimes I think I remember a familiar face being there but then, the next time, it is someone completely different, someone I do not recognise. That's why I think what I remember was a dream and not a reality.' She stopped as another tear fell, closely followed by another until a steady stream rolled down her face. 'But I fear if it wasn't, then I am somehow to blame for what is happening and maybe these aren't dreams at all. Maybe I am going mad!'

'Look at me,' Reniah said, taking Naomi's hand in her own. 'You are no more to blame than I and you are certainly in your right mind. The betrayer found a way to implicate you and to throw suspicion away from themselves, that is all. Maybe it was the Masquerader you saw, transformed into an image of someone you trust. Now tell me all you can remember and let us look for the truth among the riddles.'

Asaph and Ethan were on horseback, cantering towards the Tunnels of Tamore. They needed to reach the shore while the tide was still out so that the land linking Cherith with the Island would be clearly visible. It was their only chance of reaching the Island before Jed and the Masquerader did. Ethan felt the heaviness of the night lifting as they moved farther away from the South and back towards the East Gates. He hoped that Jed was alright and that everything was unfolding as they had planned.

Jed was glad that he had learnt to ride. The Masquerader was not slowing down for anybody, and they were now galloping over the wastelands towards Evernebulis at a great speed. He was aware of the sound of drums getting louder and that slight spots of rain were beginning to occasionally hit against his face and found himself wishing that he and Ethan had stayed together. The thought made him snort in surprise. He had never been one for either wanting or needing anyone else so this was a new concept to him.

Oholiab was sat behind him, his hands around Jed's waist to keep him from falling off. He sensed that Jed was becoming more aware of his need for help and smiled. Somehow the unlearnt lesson from behind the locked door had still managed to impact him, even though he had not seen it at the time. 'Trust is a powerful thing,' he pondered, remembering something he had once been told. 'If you can learn to trust in the dark, the darkness itself will not overcome you.'

'May this be your revelation, young warrior,' he said out loud.

Naomi and Reniah had continued to talk for some time realising that the vision Reniah had seen in the waterfall and the dreams that Naomi had been having were very similar. They had gone in circles trying to figure out what everything may mean but were finding themselves confused and frustrated.

'I feel we are trying to put an interpretation on something that is not real,' Naomi had said at one point, 'almost like we are looking at an image of something that is distorted or the wrong way round.'

Reniah looked up sharply. An idea began to take shape in her mind, fuelled by the image of the hands in the garden, the face in the vision of the waterfall, the flame being snuffed out, Naomi's face within it all. She drew in her breath.

'What is it?' Naomi asked, concerned at how pale the woman of the East Gate had gone.

'Oh. We have been blind!' she said, her voice distraught.

'Reniah, whatever is it?' Naomi pressed, beginning to feel

anxious.

'Naomi, I need to go.'

'I'll come with you.'

'No. You are not yet strong enough. But if I don't return by midday tomorrow, do not stay here. Take one of the horses and find refuge in one of the towns near Wynere. And Naomi, trust no one.'

With that, she swiftly left the room leaving Naomi confused and wondering what she could possibly have said to cause this reaction.

Asaph and Ethan had made good time. They had left the horses at one of the farms near the East Gate and had travelled on foot through the Tunnels of Tamore. There was nothing to distract them this time, Ethan noted, and surmised it was the presence of Asaph that had accomplished this. Once out on the other side, to his surprise, he saw Amos was there waiting for them.

'Well, young 'un,' he smiled, 'I guess t' adventure be not ended.'

'When does it ever end, my friend,' Asaph grinned as he grasped the forearm of the old gardener. 'Now, all speed. We have little time before the tide turns.'

'All is taken care of for t'journey,' Amos responded as they all climbed into the horse and cart.

It was not yet dawn, but Ethan wasn't sure they were going to make it to the Island in time. He felt a wet splash fall on his nose, and he wiped it away before holding out his hand, palm up in the air. He waited until another splash fell into it.

'This is just what we need,' he tutted to himself.

'That's right now. You shed your tears upon t'earth,' Amos laughed, his face turned to the sky. 'Wash away t'evil and make things grow.'

'It will need more than a shower to wash these lands clean of the current evil,' Asaph said.

'Aye. I 'ave sensed it, but t'light will always win in't end,' Amos turned and smiled. 'We will yet talk of these times and t' prophecies bein' fulfilled. They will become t' tales told to t' next lot of young 'uns, you mark my words.'

Asaph laughed as the rain began to heavily pour down, the

drops dripping off his hair and beard.

Ethan never knew what happened on that journey. He remembered closing his eyes for what felt like a mere second when he heard Asaph calling to him to wake up for they were at the sea.

'I didn't think I had been asleep,' he said completely confused. 'I only shut my eyes for a moment.'

He climbed out of the cart to the sound of Amos chuckling and Asaph shouting his thanks.

'Make haste now,' the old gardener called out before making clicking sounds to his horse who began to trot obediently away.

Ethan was still feeling puzzled and disorientated as he followed Asaph across the grass and back down the precarious steps that he had climbed up, just a few days ago. It did occur to him that he was not quite so cautious about them as he had been when he had first arrived, even though the rain had made them more slippery and was obscuring his view. He climbed down backwards so that he could try and steady himself by grabbing hold of the shrubs and bushes. His movements reminded him of Jed and wondered how he was faring and if the plan was succeeding.

As his feet met the pebbles of the beach, he turned around and then looked at Asaph in amazement for, in front of them was what looked like a chariot hitched up to a team of large, long haired, dark eyed dogs.

'How did they manage to get here?' he asked, bewildered.

'Amos arranged it.'

'But how?'

Asaph didn't answer. 'Come on,' he shouted through the sheet of rain that was descending in a steady torrent.

Ethan climbed into the chariot.

'Hold on,' Asaph instructed, showing Ethan where to place his feet and hands so that he maintained his balance. 'These boys fly like the wind.'

Picking up the reins, Asaph made a whistling sound to the dogs, and they smoothly took off with howls and whines and barks and the rain glistening off their backs. Ethan held on tightly, using all his concentration to keep his balance, unaware that Nehari was right behind him to help keep him from falling. The wind and the rain lashed around his face, and he felt a sudden rush of exhilaration. 'Woohoo!' he shouted. The wind whipped his words and carried them away. 'Yessss,' Ethan shouted again, laughing. 'This is amazing!'

Asaph turned and laughed with him. 'Where's the timid boy that was last seen on these shores gone?' he shouted.

'Left in the desert with the pirates,' was the reply.

Evernebulis was unlike anything that Jed had ever seen. The mountains towered in their natural formations, craggy and strong and dangerous, creating a magnificent backdrop to the city that had been built among them, but it was the man-made structures he saw that held his fascination. Bridges linked mountain to mountain over precarious drops and huge towers stood, made of a substance that he had never seen. They looked like they had been carved out of one massive rock, so smooth was the appearance, so grey in colour. The air around him smelt of chemicals and metals and smoke. Around certain areas, fences were erected with spikes built into the metal lattices so that anyone touching them would be pierced by the thorns. Soldiers stood near these, dressed in uniforms of dark green and black and grey, their faces set into stony, blank expressions that gave nothing away. Jed realised that the power the Espionite clan had to invent and create was clearly something far more formidable and advanced than he had ever been told. This place felt like it belonged many years into the future and, despite himself, the boy was somehow fascinated by it all. This was, after all, the city of his birth. The idea that his family had once walked the path he now rode on felt strangely comforting to him despite its intimidating scenery. The place felt empty though, for despite the presence of some soldiers in certain areas, he had only seen women and children.

'Asaph, where is everyone,' he shouted out to the Masquerader. He deliberately kept using Asaph's name in the hope that the betrayer wouldn't realise that Jed knew he was an imposter, but he wasn't sure if this was working or not.

'They are going into battle to reclaim what is rightfully theirs,' came the reply, shouted back at him.

Jed frowned at this. He could not imagine that this meant anything good for Wynere. He just hoped that Ethan had managed to get back to the East Gate and find Asaph. They needed to find the Oil and Sword before the Masquerader reached the Island and got to them first.

They rode through the city and down a sandy passageway which stretched between two mountains, the sides of which were so straight and smooth they looked man made. Beyond, he could see the sails of a ship, flapping around in the breeze, and some men standing on the deck. At that moment, without any warning, the heavens opened and it began to heavily rain, obscuring any further view.

Melchi and Japhron watched Asaph and Ethan as they raced across the sandy pathway and then at Jed as he boarded the ship with the Masquerader.

'The events are all beginning to collide,' Japhron remarked.

Melchi nodded. 'Yes. Everything is moving towards its conclusion,' he said. 'It is now all a question of timing and of choices.'

'I think I would like to ride a chariot pulled by those beautiful dogs,' Mia said.

CHAPTER SEVENTEEN

THE OIL AND THE SWORD

 **THE ISLAND**

The rain was lashing down as though it was unleashing pent-up rage at being held back for so long. Ethan stood on the shore completely drenched and trying to acclimatise to being back in the very place he had waited so long to get away from. He found that he didn't feel the same about it somehow and realised that, somewhere on the journey, the fear that his history had bound him to had lost its grip.

'Ethan,' Asaph shouted through the downpour, 'We need to move.'

The boy nodded and went to help untie the dogs and drag the chariot as far up the beach as they could.

From within his private chambers, Sharaaim suddenly awoke. He felt uneasy and didn't know why, as though he had been jolted from a bad dream that he couldn't now remember. He rose from his bed, his heart racing, and went over to the window where he gazed out at the rain as it pounded against the ground. The grey and tempestuous sight matched his mood and he felt his racing heart begin to settle into its usual beat. He looked towards the tower and wondered if the old man had come to his senses yet.

'I have no leverage against him without the boy,' he thought to himself as he clenched his fist. 'I hope that the plan has worked and that they are on their way. I am sure that one of them will comply if the other's life is in the balance.'

SOMEWHERE BETWEEN CHERITH AND THE ISLAND

Jed stood on deck, clinging to a rope that was pinned around the side of the ship, watching the sailors as they struggled to keep it steady. The wind had picked up, but it was seemingly working in their favour, propelling them through the waves for they were approaching land much faster than he had anticipated. The Island was now clearly in view, a bruised mark through the grey and dismal landscape.

He hoped that Ethan had managed to complete his part of the plan as Jed had no idea what he was going to do if he was alone on the Island with the Masquerader and Sharaaim.

Oholiab held his position next to Jed and watched the beast from the Underworld as it reared over them. Its scaled, ancient body was almost camouflaged against the underside of a wave, but he could still make out the jagged outline of its head and the gnarled claw like hands as it pushed them through the waves, granting them an unearthly speed to their journey. The Guardian was very aware that the incidents of the past few days were now beginning to align like some epic piece of music that was building with increasing pace towards its final crescendo.

THE ISLAND

Ethan kept as close to Asaph as he could without being trodden on.

'Asaph, what is the plan? Have you any idea where the Oil and the Sword are?'

'No, not yet. But I imagine that they will not be too far from Sharaaim himself, although he will be unable to handle them.'

'Then why are they here?'

'He may not be able to touch them but a true Cherithite can.'

An idea began to formulate in Ethan's mind that started to make sense of something that had been confusing him for a while.

'Is that why Sharaaim tried to make an alliance with me?'

'Yes. I believe that was his plan.'

'But there are a number of Cherithites on the Island. Why did he choose me?'

'He knows of your lineage, and some of what your future holds, so would have wanted to misdirect that and use it to his own advantage.'

'But, if that had happened, I wouldn't have been able to handle the sacred things!'

'There would have been a window of opportunity when you would have been able to.'

'But Ethan continued, still confused, 'there are still other Cherithites who could touch the Oil and the Sword!'

'True. They could hold them. But only someone of royal lineage can use them to relight the flame. There are many things Barlkron has underestimated and misunderstood and what he intended for evil will yet turn for good.'

Ethan hoped so.

CHERITH

The Espionite army continued to be fractious. As the Guardians had destroyed one after another of the Underworld creatures, more and more men had begun to question the wisdom of the plan to attack the Capital of Cherith and the army was now divided into two groups. Each side had tried, in vain, to convince the other of what they should do, and the arguments had now given way to anger which, in turn, had fuelled deep rage and frustration. One man had begun pushing his friend whilst yelling in his face that he was wrong and insisting he advance with them into battle. The response had been volatile and a fight had ensued that had then broken out amongst the whole camp. No-one was sure whose side anyone was on which meant the battle was confused and chaotic; each man fighting for his life and yet uncertain of what he was fighting for anymore. All around them the rain fell relentlessly, causing the ground to become slippery and unhelpful as though even the earth was warring against them, or perhaps issuing a warning to cease.

Ephron stood on the city walls watching and waiting. From the high places, men were ready to sound the horns as soon as they saw the Espionite army reach the borders of Wynere.

'Once Asaph has the Oil and Sword and we relight the flame, the army will be defeated,' Nathan shouted to Ephron through the downpour.

'If you are right and they have managed to reach the Island, it will still be hours before they return. There will have been many losses by then.'

'Then we will do all we can to hold our ground and defend the city until they arrive,' Nathan said resolutely. 'Whatever Barlkron's plan is, it cannot stand against us. It will yet turn to our advantage, of that, I'm sure.'

Ephron didn't reply out loud. He wanted to have the same strength of conviction as Nathan but he wasn't certain what he believed anymore.

🐺 THE ISLAND

Ethan looked around the empty cottage and wiped his finger over the table. It left a clear line through the dust that had gathered there.

'He hasn't been here for a while,' he remarked. 'Do you think Sharaaim has him?'

'I think it likely,' was the reply. 'He would want to use him as leverage.'

'Then we must go to the Castle and find him,' Ethan said with panic in his voice as he made for the door.

Asaph went and put his hand on the boy's shoulder.

'We will, but we need to do everything in the right order. How long has the tower been here?'

Ethan looked confused by the question, 'The tower in the town?'

Asaph nodded.

'It was started a few months ago. Sharaaim ordered it to be built although none of us know why. Only Cherithites have been allowed to work on it though,' Ethan pondered this as he said it.

'The tower is an exact replica of the one in Wynere where the flame was lit. Did you know that?'

Ethan's eyes widened with the revelation of this.

'Then that must be where the Oil and Sword are,' he said excitedly. 'Let's go and get them, rescue grandpa and get out of here.'

Ethan realised that Asaph wasn't moving towards the door.

'What are you waiting for?' he asked, frustrated by the slowness of Asaph's response.

'Do you trust me?'

Ethan stared at him. 'Why are you asking me that? What is going on?' he asked crossly.

'Do you trust me?' Asaph said again.

Ethan closed his eyes and let out a breath that was a mix between a sigh and frustration.

'Yeeees,' he said a little reluctantly. 'Although that doesn't mean I'm going to like what you are about to do, does it?'

Asaph laughed. 'That's the beauty of trust,' he stated. 'Besides, this is about what we are both about to do.'

Ethan pursed his lips and shook his head. 'What's the plan?' he asked with a resigned tone although he did notice that there was also a very unfamiliar sense of excitement bubbling up in him too.

Nehari smiled.

The ship had been run aground onto the stretch of beach that lay below the city gates. Jed wasn't sure how this had happened for he felt like they had almost been pushed up and onto the sand by some invisible force.

'I wonder how they will manage to get it back into the water,' he was thinking as he stared around him at the vessel. It looked like it had been shipwrecked, thrown up out of the ocean and cast away.

The Masquerader came to stand next to him.

'Stay close to me when we disembark,' he ordered without smiling. 'Our priority is to get to the Oil and the Sword.'

'Do you know where they are?'

The Masquerader didn't answer but looked at the boy with narrowed eyes as though trying to work something out. Jed held the man's gaze without looking away and eventually the Masquerader nodded his head as though satisfied that all was well.

'Follow me,' he said abruptly as he jumped down over the side of the ship onto the beach.

CHERITH

The battle amongst the pillars of Hymangees continued to rage, the rain diluting the blood that ran across the earth, leaving a reddened hue upon it. Most of the creatures from the Underworld had been defeated and the Guardians had now withdrawn to the Capital. One man had bravely broken away from the battle and begun to resolutely march over the muddy wasteland towards the pine forests that marked the boundary lines of Wynere. Another man noticed the solitary figure leave and ran to join him. In turn, someone else noticed both men heading towards the boundary lines and, within a few minutes, a number had joined ranks and were now advancing together. Those left behind looked at the bodies that lay lifeless on the ground around them. They knew there were two choices ahead of them. Either return to their homes and explain that some men had fallen by the hands of their own clan or join the advancing army so that they could let the impending battle be blamed for the losses of life. Swords in hand they hastily went after their kinsmen, and the army of men marched on in silence, confused by what had just happened and subdued by both the rain and remorse.

From the high places around the city of Wynere, the horns blasted out its warning. As one sounded, another responded until the surrounding areas reverberated with the echoing call.

Nathan rode through the city, shouting to the troops along the wall.

'Today is not a day we thought we would face but, today, we fight for our lands, our children. Today, we call on the courage that our forefathers bore when fighting for peace, for peace we will have again. Remember, in the moments when your hearts may fail you, that there are more with us than against us.'

Some of the younger warriors looked confused by this statement. The Espionite clan was much larger and more powerful than their own and they already felt at a disadvantage.

'Take heart and be strong,' Nathan continued.

From the unseen dimensions, the Guardians moved among the troops. They were already in battle against the low-ranking creatures that moved around the feet and shoulders of the men. Every time one was overpowered, the heart of that warrior was strengthened and their minds became clearer.

Benaniah, the leader of that host stood, surrounded in light, giving orders, as Melchi and Jahron looked on, nodding their approval.

Mia's attention was firmly fixed on the journey Reniah was making. Her clothes were drenched from the pounding rain, her hair clung in a sodden sheet down her back. But it was the sadness on her features, dimming her natural radiance which Mia noticed the most.

Reniah had climbed over the hills of Twyndale and was now nearing the waterfall. She would normally stop and pause in these moments, taking time to be still and allow the beauty of the land to imprint itself upon her mind but, today, she could hardly see for the rain that was falling and the tears that rolled down her cheeks.

'How could I have been so blind?' she thought. 'All along, we knew that the danger was closer than we thought. All along we said to trust no-one. How could I have missed what was so obvious… what was right in front of me.' The self-doubt was stabbing at her brain, attacking her courage. She moved swifter, the roar of the waterfall growing louder and fiercer as she drew closer to it. She usually found great exhilaration from this but not today. She felt for the sword that she had taken from the weaponry room before she left the house and gripped its handle. 'Please may I be wrong, please may I be wrong,' she said over and over as she reached the ledge that led behind the thunderous drop of water. As she had feared, she was not the only one who stood there. The robed figure turned and looked at her, their eyes darkened with bitter rage.

🐺 THE ISLAND

Asaph and Ethan had made their way around the outside of the city through the back streets. The rain had delayed the start of the day for many, and this had worked in their favour for, as yet, no-one was about, and they had managed to reach the tower without being seen.

Ethan pushed against the door and found it open but, as he entered, he heard a shout and turned back around to be met with a sight he had seen before. Asaph was stood, sword drawn and, opposite him, an identical figure stood facing him. Jed came running up and stopped, already confused as to who was who. He looked over at Ethan who shrugged.

'And so, it ends here,' the one nearest to Ethan said.

'It should never have begun,' the other replied. The boys looked at each other, reassured that this man must be Asaph.

'Many things should never have been,' the first figure commented and then the boys were not so sure again.

While the two men spoke, they circled around each other, swords poised waiting for the first thrust of a strike. Jed tried to move closer to Ethan but one of the men pointed his sword at him and told him to stay still. He froze in his tracks, uncertain of what to do.

'It doesn't have to end this way,' one man said.

'You have made your choice,' said the other and then moved forward to attack.

The swordsmanship of both was skilled and fast. The movements almost blurred by the rain and the speed in which the two fought. Jed saw his opportunity and ran over to where Ethan stood.

'What should we do?'

'Find the Oil and Sword,' Ethan replied. 'Asaph reckons they are in the tower.'

'You go in and get them and I will keep watch down here,' Jed ordered as he drew his own sword.

Ethan nodded and quickly entered the tower. He ran up the steps that spiralled around to the top and then froze. Sharaaim stood in front of him with a knife to the throat of his grandpa.

'I thought you would come,' the governor said as he smiled his twisted smile.

'Don't do anything he says,' the older man said to Ethan.

'Oh, but you will – won't you?' Sharaaim said in a coaxing tone. 'After all, who else do you have in the world?'

Ethan stepped forward.

'Don't you touch him,' he said fiercely.

'I would stay still if I were you,' Sharaaim snarled as he dragged his grandpa back, still with the knife to his throat. 'Now, listen closely to my instructions and no-one should get hurt.'

Ethan nodded with his hands held up to signify that he was unarmed.

'Slowly come and stand next to the pedestal,' Sharaaim ordered.

Ethan edged into the middle of the room still with his hands slightly raised and his eyes fixed on his grandpa and the knife that was against his neck.

'Now, undo the wrapping.' Sharaaim's eyes shined with crazed excitement and Ethan knew that he and his grandpa were in real danger. Nehari was stood, sword unsheathed and shoulders back. He would not hesitate to intervene.

Slowly, Ethan unwrapped the package that lay on the pedestal. As he pushed aside the coverings, he gasped at what lay in front of him. The Sword shimmered with light as though a flame burned from within its very core.

'Take the Oil and pour it into the bowl,' Sharaaim's voice was high and Ethan noticed that the man's hands were trembling.

Carefully, he lifted the large ornate bottle that stood next to the Sword and pulled out the stopper. Immediately the most beautiful fragrance filled the room. Sharaaim staggered back slightly.

Slowly, Ethan poured its contents into the bowl. The Oil appeared to have flecks of gold in it. It shimmered and glowed as it swirled around the bowl before settling into stillness.

'Now, lift up the Sword,' Sharaaim almost shouted. Ethan saw some spit settle at the corner of the governor's twisted mouth and knew he was becoming more maniacal.

'Ethan don't!' his grandpa shouted out. Sharaaim pushed the older man to the floor and kicked him in the stomach.

'Stop it,' Ethan shouted. 'Leave him be!'

'Then do as I say,' Sharaaim sneered as he came and stood closer.

Ethan paused. 'Tell me why?'

The governor looked at him. 'So that I hold the power of course,' he spoke in a condescending tone as though Ethan was stupid to have not understood. 'No-one will be able to come against me once the flame burns. I will finally be the most powerful ruler.'

Ethan held the man's gaze. He recalled what Asaph had said in the cottage and found himself almost smiling. Slowly he reached out for the handle of the Sword and carefully picked it up with both hands. As he did so, the blade appeared to catch fire. It blazed fiercely.

'Yes, yes,' Sharaaim came and gripped the sides of the pedestal.

'Light it, quickly, let me see it burn.'

'No. Don't do it,' Ethan's grandpa pleaded.

The Cherithite apprentice reached towards the Oil with the lighted flame that spurted from the sword.

The fight between the Masquerader and Asaph continued to be equally matched. Jed watched as they expertly twisted and turned away from each blow, neither able to get the upper hand on the other.

'This is your chance to stop this madness,' one said.

'Not until I have defeated the evil that has gripped you.'

Jed stood watching, still trying to discern who was who. He closed his eyes and was reminded of the moment in the darkened room where he had fought an invisible foe. 'What was it Asaph had said before he went through the door?' he racked his brains, somehow instinctively knowing that this was important. Oholiab came and put a hand on the boy's shoulder.

'You have an ability to know what the truth is, even when you have not been taught.' The words came back to him.

Jed opened his eyes and studied the actions of the two men as they battled; Both coming close to running their weapon into the other but never quite managing to do so. He watched the manoeuvres of each assailant, the clash of swords arguing against each other until, in a swift move, both brought their swords to the throat of the other, before pushing each other away.

'Jed,' one called out to him. 'You need to kill him. He will not stop until he has defeated me.'

Jed immediately drew his sword and without hesitation ran forward and thrust it into the side of the one who had just spoken. He watched as the man staggered forward, a look of disbelief on his face.

'What have you done?' he whispered as he dropped his sword and reached to put his hand over the wound. Blood dripped over his fingers as he fell to his knees and then onto his front. Jed stared, expecting the Masquerader to transform into his original form but nothing happened. He looked at the other man who stood there watching and horror gripped his heart as he realised his mistake.

To Melchi and Japhron, it felt as though everything had suddenly been suspended in time.

Mia found herself holding her breath

CHAPTER EIGHTEEN

THE UNSEEN MADE VISIBLE

CHERITH

Reniah stared for a moment at the face of Abbir-Qualal. The noise of the waterfall had retreated somewhat as she had arrived. It seemed to know they must not be interrupted.

'Why?' she asked, the sadness on her face was clear to see.

'When did you know?'

'Just a short while ago. It made no sense that only one person was involved in this. But why you? I don't understand.'

'No. You wouldn't, would you!'

The image of Abbir-Qualal slowly began to transform before Reniah's eyes. Transfixed, she watched as the figure in front of her materialised into the one she had expected to find and hoped that she wouldn't see.

'You never knew what it was to be in the shadows.' Shakirah's voice was filled with bitterness.

'You have never been in the shadows.'

'You do not know!' Shakirah shrieked. 'It was always you who had the visions and then it was Naomi who won Nathan's heart. It should have been me he chose. Me!'

'That is not true,' Reniah said gently as she moved further onto the ledge.

'Stay where you are. I'm warning you, if you come any nearer, I will jump.' Shakirah moved towards the drop of the waterfall.

Reniah stopped although her eyes never left Shakirah's face.

'But why make a pact with Barlkron? Why betray all you know?'

'Because I was promised all I have ever longed for and never found.'

'From the Underworld?' Reniah could not hide her utter confusion.

'No,' Shakirah turned and looked at her. 'From the one I love and who loves me. You have never understood but he did.'

'Then help me understand,' she said as she took a step forward, her hand outstretched.

The bitterness on Shakirah's face darkened her features, distorting her beauty.

'It's too late,' she hissed. 'Do not take another step or, I swear, I will throw myself off.'

'Did you know?' Mia turned to Melchi with a heavy heart.

'All was beginning to point to her being involved in the end.'

'But… but…'

Melchi laid his hand on her arm and she found her heart settled.

'It's just so sad,' she whispered. She looked at the two women of the East Gate. 'Can the ending be changed? Can we send the Guardians to help?'

'Someone's ending can always be changed if they are willing to turn from the wrong path. But, no, Mia. We cannot interfere with those choices.'

'Please choose right,' Mia said under her breath in Shakirah's direction. 'Please choose right.'

🐺 THE ISLAND

As Ethan stretched out his hand, his grandpa stared at him with fear in his eyes while Sharaaim laughed. The Sword felt heavy in his hand. It was as though the flame was pulling itself down towards the bowl, desiring to be reunited with the Oil that lay there. As they all watched, a spurt of fire flashed out from the Sword and the Oil caught it. Ethan fell backwards as a great light filled the tower. It grew brighter and brighter until he could no longer look upon it and covered his eyes.

Jed saw the flame as it burned through the tower windows. 'We've lost,' he thought and sank to his knees in despair. As he did this, he realised that the body lying near him began to change shape. Cautiously, he crawled over and stretched out his hand to turn the man onto his back. He gasped as he saw the features contort and then settle.

Asaph knelt beside him and placed a hand on his shoulder.

'Did you know?' Jed asked him, tears in his eyes.

Asaph nodded. 'For some time, although he will have had help and that other person remained a mystery until this morning.'

'But he was like a brother to you. Why would he do it?'

Abbir-Qualal groaned, and Jed reached for his sword. Asaph placed his hand over Jed's.

'Leave him be. You do not want his blood on your hands Jed. That is a great weight to bear and he has already lost.'

Jed shook his head. 'But he hasn't Asaph. The flame is lit. Look.'

Asaph didn't look. He just smiled.

Jed found himself smiling in response but he didn't know why. 'Asaph, what are you smiling at? Everything has gone wrong?'

Ethan tentatively peered through his fingers and saw that his grandpa was on his feet staring at the floor. He slowly got up, trying to not look directly at the burning flame, and went to see what the older man was staring at.

'He just disintegrated,' his grandpa said, looking a little shaken. 'He just crumpled into a heap and this is all that is left.'

Ethan looked down at the pile of dust lying on the floor, the fur robe in a heap next to it, and then looked at his grandpa.

'Have you a brush?' he said and then, whether from relief, fear or surprise, they both started to laugh and laugh until the tears rolled down their cheeks.

CHERITH

The Espionite army had reached Wynere and stood in defiant rows facing the city walls while those behind it held their positions. For a moment, all was silent and still except for the steady lashing of the rain that beat against them.

As all was held in a moment of suspense, one of the younger men saw some strange light hurtling towards them.

'Ephron!' he shouted, 'look.'

The light grew larger and more defined the nearer it got. It appeared like a huge flame glowing in red and orange hues. The Espionite army heard its approach for it was like a fiery furnace, roaring above them. They lowered their weapons and stood back as they watched it pass over their heads. As it made its journey over the wall, all the warriors in Wynere dropped to the floor and covered their heads except for the young man who had first seen it. Transfixed, he left his post and ran after the flame as it shot through the city and towards the Tower. The flame tore through the door of the Tower and alighted in the central room. The young man tentatively followed behind and watched in amazement as it settled on the bowl. As this happened, the room was filled with a blinding light that erupted through every window, more radiant than it had ever been before. He fell to the floor, unable to gaze at it any longer.

The glow from within the city caused the Espionites to stagger backwards, instinctively wanting to get away from it. They had heard of this before and knew that the light was no friend to those who were aligned with the darkness. Leaving their weapons on the ground, they turned and fled, watched by the astounded faces of the warriors of Wynere and the radiant faces from the Guardians of the unseen realms. The soldiers cheered, not just a celebratory cheer but a heart-felt, guttural, war-like sound that erupted from the depths of their being and reminded them of the warriors they actually were. Fear retreated with the Espionite army, along with the creatures from the Underworld. The shout went on and on.

And then the rain stopped.

'There is yet a way back if you will renounce the path you have chosen,' Reniah pleaded.

'There is no way back for me. I know we have lost. I sensed it the moment that Asaph left to find the boys and wouldn't let me leave. I was wrong in thinking that the prophecies could be overturned.'

'That is true but, please, do not let the darkness overshadow what you know to be truth.'

Reniah moved forward, her hand outstretched. 'Shakirah,

come home with me. Turn away from this evil. There is still time.'

Shakirah edged backwards, away from the treaties of her friend. 'I renounce nothing,' she hissed.

All that happened next was a blur. Through the waterfall, a blinding light shone. Shakirah brought up both arms to cover her face from its glare and, as she did, she lost her footing.

'Shakirah!' Reniah screamed. She ran forward only to see her friend tumbling, flailing down into the thunderous waters. Shakirah looked up and, for a second, it appeared that she was suspended, held up by the torrents. 'Forgive me,' she mouthed before all closed in around her in a burial of water and she was gone.

Reniah fell to her knees on the ledge and wept. The silence, that had been, was overpowered by the returning roar of the waterfall. It was as though, it too, grieved bitterly for a lost friend.

THE ISLAND

As the rain had ceased and the sun began to come out of hiding, the people came out of their dwellings to stare at the tower. The light that shone from it was something that they did not understand and many were fearful by the sight of it.

Asaph and Jed got to their feet, leaving Abbir-Qualal rolling in pain on the ground. Asaph dragged the betrayer to a standing position.

'Do not be so rough, brother,' the young warrior spoke to Asaph in a sullen tone.

'You would do well to not utter one more word,' the Cherithite warrior responded grimly.

Ethan came running out of the tower, stopping short when he saw the people standing there and Asaph gripping Abbir-Qulal by the arm. He stared at Jed in amazement. 'Did you know it was him?'

'Only at the end,' he replied. 'He used some of the sword skills that he himself had shown me and I recognised his sword. I had hoped I was wrong though.'

Asaph smiled. 'I told you that you would know!' he said to Jed, who responded with a grin. Ethan felt he had missed something.

'Where is the governor?' a woman's voice shouted from the crowd.

At that moment, Ethan's grandpa appeared at the doorway of the tower holding a bowl filled with, what looked like, ash. He held it out in front of him.

'He's in here,' he said, still perplexed by what he had witnessed. 'He just,' he paused before adding, 'disintegrated.'

Jed looked at Ethan. Ethan looked at Asaph. Asaph pulled a face. Then a cheer erupted from the crowd and Ethan and Jed found themselves doubled over with laughter and unable to stop.

Nehari went and stood next to Oholiab. 'All is well,' he said.

Oholiab smiled. 'Yes. All is better than good.'

Barlkron was destroying everything that was in his path. Bodies of dead creatures lay behind him as he had furiously wreaked his anger, throwing fire and poisonous darts everywhere as he overturned and pulled down structures until the Underworld looked even more like a war zone than it usually did.

'They will pay,' he hissed, still utterly confused that the plan had outworked like he had imagined but with the opposite results to what he had planned. The terror he felt coursed through his being, fuelling immense rage.

He had underestimated the power of the lighted flame and the fact that it would never submit to the darkness. He had imagined it would give him power but, instead, it had betrayed him.

He howled a menacing shriek of pain and torment, fear and anger. The rest of the Underworld froze for a second before joining in with the same deafening howls of defeat.

⎯⎯⎰⎯ CHERITH

At the East Gate, Nathan and Naomi were walking hand in hand through the gardens that lay behind the pool. The sun cast its rays around them causing everything to shimmer. It looked fresh and clean. The smell of grass and lavender, which hung in the air around them, gave a sense of peace.

'How is Reniah today?' Nathan asked his wife.

'She is still quiet. Her grief is deep, made more so by both betrayals and the fact that she was unable to save Shakirah.'

'How did she know in the end that it was her?'

'It was because of what she had seen in the waterfall. When

she knew I was missing, she had gone there hoping to discover more about what had happened to me so had assumed it was my face that she saw in the vision.'

'You and Shakira are - I mean - were so similar to look at.' Nathan said gently.

'Yes, we were. Apart from one thing. In the vision, the person she saw waved at her. She hadn't made the connection that the person was facing her and so was a mirror image. When she realised this, she knew that the vision had showed someone waving with their left hand.'

'Ahh,' Nathan sighed as he realised. 'And Shakirah was left-handed. I still can't believe that it was she who kept you prisoner.'

'I knew there was something familiar, but everything was so distorted and confused that I could not tell what was a dream and what was reality. Of course, capturing me wasn't planned. It was a question of making the most of an opportunity. Abbir-Qualal found me on the moor and used it to his advantage. I think that was when he approached Shakirah with his plan.'

'It certainly worked in their favour, for the sense of evil that we knew had invaded the East Gate was assumed to have come from you. It was no wonder that the pair of them were rarely around unless they were in your presence. But, still, to deliberately poison you!' Nathan stopped at a loss for words unable to believe that Shakirah had deliberately pushed the poisoned dart into Naomi's thumbnail so that the poison would keep her vulnerable.

'Reniah thinks that, when you chose me over her, a root of jealousy embedded deep in her heart and allowed the Underworld access.'

'Likely fuelled by the jealously Abbir-Qualal nurtured when you chose me over him!'

'Oh, he was never in the running for my affections,' Naomi said lightly. 'There was only ever one man for me.'

He smiled at her before continuing, 'That explains why they would try and incriminate us both but I still don't understand why they made an alliance with the Underworld,' Nathan commented. His heart was still heavy from all that had taken place and, as yet, he had refused to go to the Island to meet with Abbir-Qualal.

'Jealousy and resentment for being the youngest and wanting the power to rule their own Kingdom was the biggest reason, I think,' Naomi replied. 'It was easy for Barlkron to entice them when he offered what they both desired. Shakira's longing to be loved made her an easy target to Abbir-Qualal who needed an accomplice to outwork his plan.'

'They both should have known better. The power of the flame will not be bound to darkness.'

'What will become of Abbir-Qualal?'

Nathan frowned, 'That will be up to him,' he said grimly.

'Then let us hope he chooses redemption,' Naomi said quietly.

Nathan squeezed her hand. 'You have a pure heart, my love. That is one of the reasons I chose you.'

'One of many reasons, I hope,' his wife teased.

He laughed. 'I can think of a few,' he replied. 'But I do still have a question for you which remains unanswered.' He paused, turning her round to face him. 'Where were you on the night the flame was extinguished?'

Naomi smiled and looking into his eyes, with her face full of emotion, she told him.

Mia gazed at Melchi in delight, her face suffused with joy. 'Ahhhh. So that was why she was wandering about in the middle of the night? This is the most exciting thing ever!'

Melchi smiled at her. 'It is indeed,' he replied.

CHERITH

The Espionite army had returned to Evernebulis and retreated behind the strength of their high grey walls. Resentments had temporarily been displaced with a sense of shame and regret and they turned their attentions to their inventions and to keeping what had happened at the pillars of Hymangees a secret from all who had not witnessed it.

Barlkron watched them and smiled. He would wait a while and let their wounds and secrets fester until he could use them once more to his advantage. This may have been one battle that he had not won but there were yet other future victories to claim. This current defeat still stung but he ignored it as he turned his thoughts towards a new plan to overthrow the Cherithite people.

Wynere was welcoming back the families who had sought refuge in the West Country, but the city was far from being back to normal. It felt weakened, much like someone who had survived a great illness and now needed time to recover and grow strong. Ephron ensured that the watchmen still lined the city walls and the high places of their lands. They would not make the same mistake twice by becoming complaisant and allowing the enemy such easy access to their borders.

'Yes,' Ephron thought to himself, 'there has been much to learn from all of this, and we can only be better and stronger for it in the end.'

Melchi and Japhron watched the various scenes as they merged into one cohesive image. All was as it had been intended. All, that is, except for the losses they had incurred.

Melchi looked at Abbir-Qualal, imprisoned in the house of healing and was saddened that his fears had proven correct and that this Cherithite warrior had not only made a pact with the Underworld but had killed and betrayed his own people, including Shakirah.

'Can he be saved?' Japhron asked.

'The journey back from this will be long and not without consequence and it will be his choice whether to embrace it or not. But there is always hope. And there is always a way back if he desires it.'

'Do you think he does desire it?' Mia asked.

Melchi didn't reply. Just like when Abbir-Qualal was the robed figure, some things remained veiled to this old Seer. Man's choices were, in the end, their own to make.

EPILOGUE

Ethan stood in the scorched wood staring at the tiny shoots of green that were beginning to push up from the earth. It had been a week since the flame had been lit in the Island's tower and already there were subtle changes everywhere. Life was emerging again, even where you would have thought there was no hope.

Jed came to find him, carrying two spades.

'Are you ready?' he enquired.

Ethan tore his gaze away and grinned. 'Of course. Pass me one of those.'

The two apprentices walked over to 'The Pit'. The iron grate remained on the ground in the exact place where Ethan had placed it on the night they had left.

'I'll just move it out of the way,' he said as he bent down to pick it up. The grate did not budge. He pulled at it with all his strength but it was far too heavy. He straightened up, red in the face from his exertions.

Jed was grinning. 'You have grown weaker despite all the happenings of the last few weeks.'

'It was so easy before,' Ethan said highly confused.

'Maybe you had some unseen help?' Jed commented, his voice full of mischief. Ethan had mentioned some of the strange things he had seen and Jed often referred to it, teasing him for being mystical.

'Maybe you are right!' Ethan remarked, unfazed by Jed's flippancy. He looked around him, trying to imagine if there was some unseen being that stood close by. Although he didn't see anyone, he smiled to himself, feeling certain that this was the case. 'Anyway, come on. Let's get and bury this hole.'

Nehari laughed. 'My friend, I am sorry that you remain disbelieved in!'

Oholiab pursed his lips. 'His training is not yet complete. And anyway, credit is not for us to own.'

'Alright, alright,' Nehari put up his hands in mock surrender. 'No need to be so sensitive.'

Oholiab rolled his eyes.

Asaph stood in the tower, gazing at the lighted flame. He never grew tired of watching it as it flickered and moved, caught up in its own graceful dance. The light it exuded was bright around him and, as he remained there, he too started to glow and become more and more radiant as though the power of the flame was depositing its life into the being of the man.

The moment passed as he was interrupted by the sound of running footsteps coming up the tower steps. Turning around, he saw the sweaty, muddy bodies of his two apprentices, fresh from filling in 'The Pit' with earth.

Jed stared around him, oblivious to the radiance that shone from the face of the trained Cherithite warrior. 'One thing I still don't get is why Barlkron thought that his plan would work?' he blurted out.

'Well, the idea he had was right in part. The flame was intended for more places other than Cherith. Unfortunately, his motives were corrupt. He thought if he had royal Cherithite blood to light it for him, and to also govern here with Sharaaim, that it would be enough for him to be able to use its power without being hurt. His error was in thinking that he could rule the power of the flame.'

'So that day in my grandpa's cottage when you told me to trust you and to light the flame...'

'Yes,' Asaph interrupted. 'It was always the plan. It was what the prophecies foretold.'

'What did they say?' Ethan enquired.

'It spoke of two boys coming from another land during a time of darkness, to see the flame re-ignited across the oceans. When

I heard that the flame had been extinguished and you two were already in Cherith, we began to recognise that this particular prophecy was unfolding.'

'I wish you had told us sooner,' was Jed's response.

'Where's the fun in that?' Asaph said with a grin.

The boys rolled their eyes.

'What will happen here now?'

Asaph smiled. 'Nathan and Naomi are going to come and govern the Island.'

'Really?' Ethan couldn't hold back his excitement. He paused for a moment before continuing, 'Jed, do you remember Nathan ever being here before? I just keep thinking that he looks really familiar.'

Asaph and Jed looked at each other before looking back at Ethan with bemused expressions.

'Whaat?' Ethan said pulling a face.

'You do realise that he looks familiar because he looks like you?' Jed said grinning.

Ethan looked confused. 'No. No... He doesn't! Does he?'

Asaph laughed out loud. 'There is so much more to tell you yet,' he eventually said. 'But yes, Nathan is from the city of Jachin, although not a direct relation of yours.'

Ethan grinned. He felt as though he was constantly discovering new things about himself that were subtly changing the fabric of who he was, as though there had been pieces missing that were now slotting into place, making him more complete. His smile faded for a moment as his thoughts returned to his father and what could possibly have happened to him. 'I will find out,' he thought to himself and, with this thought, he returned his attention to the banter that was happening between Asaph and Jed.

The inauguration of Nathan and Naomi happened a week later. Every inhabitant of the Island lined the streets; some curious, some cynical and some excited to meet the new governors. It was going to take time to reset and rebuild what had been and not all believed that it was possible.

Nathan squeezed his wife's hand. 'Are you ready for this?'

She turned and smiled at him. Those who caught that moment

thought how beautiful she looked. The wisdom and peace that she held, passed on through her ancestors, seemed to be carried on the breeze as she walked through the streets.

When they reached the tower, a hush descended around the city.

Asaph stood there, regal and solemn as he held the Oil and the Sword. Carefully, he poured some of the Oil onto the hands of the new governors and then touched some to their foreheads. The fragrance from it reached far, pushing back the foulness that the air had carried, forcing it to move out of the way and to make room for the new. The couple then knelt side by side and opened out their hands, palm up, for Asaph to place the Sword into them.

'Today begins a new order here on the Island. No longer will this be known as the Island of exile but Mika meaning "beautiful fragrance". I charge you, Nathan, warrior of Cherith and Naomi, daughter from the East Gate, to govern with integrity, wisdom, justice and truth. And I charge you, the people of Mika, to embrace what is to come as you relearn, rebuild and reset the history of the past.'

As Nathan and Naomi rose to their feet, the gates of the city were opened, signifying that people were now free to leave or enter when they chose. It was a tiny change but symbolic, and many of the people were encouraged by the gesture. Those who had intended to leave, seeing that they now had the freedom to choose, felt inclined to stay.

As the celebrations continued, the boys went around saying their goodbyes. They were to return with Asaph to the East Gate to continue their training.

'Will you come back?' Shalimar asked Jed.

'Of course,' was his reply before adding, 'Did you know that you can walk into Cherith at low tide?'

Shalimar, Sianna and their mother looked at him, not sure whether to believe him or not.

'It's true,' he insisted. 'It's how we left.'

'Are you saying that in all the years we have been trapped here, that we could have just walked away?' the mother asked.

'Well, Sharaaim made sure that we would never find out by

enforcing curfews, but yes. There was always a way.'

'So, we can come and visit you too?' Sianna said excitedly, jumping up and down. 'We can go, can't we Mama?'

'Yes, we can all go,' her mother reassured her. Jed glanced at Shalimar and they both suddenly felt self-conscious and looked away.

It was very early in the morning. Asaph, the boys and Ethan's grandpa stood on the beach looking at the pathway that stretched towards Cherith.

'What will happen to Abbir-Qualal?' Jed asked.

'He will remain here at Mica until he has sufficiently healed enough to stand trial. He will then be brought back to Wynere.'

Jed looked away. He was still angry with himself for not seeing that Abbir-Qualal had been the Masquerader and the betrayal still stung.

'There is always a way back for him,' Asaph said gently.

'Only if he chooses it.'

'Yes, that is true,' Asaph agreed. He too was still saddened by the choices his friend and brother had made and by the loss of Shakirah. He desired with all his heart that Abbir-Qualal would choose to break his alliance with the Underworld but, as yet, remained unconvinced that this would be the case.

'Come on,' he said to his apprentices. 'Let's go home.'

The early morning sun caused the sand ahead to shimmer and sparkle with what looked like flecks of gold and all around them felt clean and fresh. Ethan looked at his grandpa.

'Are you ready?'

Grandpa looked at him, his eyes bright with excitement. He didn't reply with words but stepped resolutely forward, a smile on his face. He kept going without once looking back.

From behind them, the flame burned bright and strong, casting its seen light and unseen protection around Mika and the ocean that surrounded it and, from way beyond, in the city of Wynere, the same flame flickered. Neither was diminished by the existence of the other but, rather, the presence of both reinforced its power and beauty.

From their place outside of time, Melchi and Japhron continued to watch over the lands, aware of the various threads that would continue to wage war against each other. But, for now, they sat in the stillness that this one victory had won for them, humbled that they had been part of seeing the written plan unfold before their eyes.

From behind them, Oholiab and Nehari stood, their faces radiant.

'Well, brother. Shall we go and settle this current scuffle in the lower realm?' Nehari turned and asked the tall warrior.

'I am always ready for battle,' Oholiab answered, with a glint in his eye, as he reached for his sword.

Mia was on the Eastern side of the realm. With her, watching with great interest, were a group of Young-lings and in front of her was a chariot, hitched to a team of dogs.

Placing her feet where Asaph had shown Ethan to place his, she gave a shout. The dogs took off, their feet scarcely touching the ground. Mia laughed and laughed. Although she had seen this in the realms of men, the speed here was beyond what they would have experienced.

'This is the best thing ever!' she shouted to the wind.

Japhron nudged Melchi to watch.

The ancient Seer looked on, suddenly remembering what it was like to be young, with so much to learn and experience. A desire to feel the wind on his face and know the exhilaration of great speed overcame him.

'I think I will join her,' he said unexpectedly. And getting to his feet, he left the room, leaving a stunned Japhron behind him.

Moments later, the younger Seer watched as Melchi stood alongside Mia in the chariot, his hands on the reins and a grin upon his face. The shimmering sand stretched endlessly in front of them, glistening with gold, silver and copper accents. With a shout, they took off – becoming a blur with the speed at which they travelled.

'Well, that is one thing I never thought I would see,' Japhron said to himself, laughing in utter delight, before turning his eyes back to the realm of men. His attention was caught by the sight of an age-old monk standing amidst the ruins of an old monastery, set high within the mountains. 'That is interesting!' he thought to himself as he pulled up his chair for a closer look, his senses on high alert.

And from within the Library, a book fluttered from its place on the shelves, opened its pages and turned to a fresh chapter.

Acknowledgements:

The fact that this project has taken years to complete, means that there are countless people who have travelled this journey with me. So, to all those family members and friends who have invested in this, who listened as I shared my latest ideas, who championed me, and pushed me to finish – from the bottom of my heart – thank you!

An especial shout out to all the team at Spiffing Covers who turned my book into a reality. James, Joe, Stefan – you enabled me to put this out there and you did it with immense style, kindness, and creative genius. I'm so grateful. (Thanks, Tim Pettingale, for the heads up on these guys. You were right! They're good!)

To Annie Styles – for your creative editing, your encouragement, and your honesty. Thank you. It was fun!

To Adrian Davies. You are one of the most incredible, creative minds I know. To have you read that first draft, and believe in it, meant so much. Thank you for your insights and honest opinions. And to you, Jayne, and Jacob for helping create some funding – I am so grateful. Thank you!

Lastly, to my parents. I'm so glad you were there at the start of this process. I'm sad you aren't here at the end – but promise fulfilled Mum! I finished it!

Always grateful for your legacy. I miss you.

Printed in Great Britain
by Amazon

84930173R00132